rare and precious that we all treasure: a novel that makes you happy.'
– *PtitBlog*

'Filled with love and tenderness that takes unexpected but irresistible turns . . . *P.S. from Paris* makes us laugh, smile, feel; it touches us and opens our eyes to what's going on in the world . . . A lovely reunion with some beloved characters.' – *Le Monde de NoA*

'Thank you, Mr. Levy, for this wonderful and tender moment . . . How delightful to finish a book with butterflies in your stomach!' – *Plaisir de Lire*

'As soon as you pick up a new Marc Levy, you know you're in for an all-nighter . . . but what a joy! A breath of fresh air . . . A true gem.' – Christele Daquin, buyer, Espace Culturel Leclerc

'A fresh, funny, and bubbly comedy.' – *Cecibondelire*

'Marc Levy takes us by the hand to lead us lovingly toward humor, without ever taking himself seriously.' – *Idboox*

'How pleasing to see this new Marc Levy going back to his roots. Thank you for this moment of joy.' – *Les Aventures Livresques de Nane*

'I had never read Marc Levy . . . I am truly delighted to have discovered this author and think I shall be equally tempted to read his future and previous works.' – *Mille et Une Pages*

'*P.S. from Paris* is an amusing, unpredictable, and irresistible love story.' – *Le Blog de Moon*

'385 pages of pure joy.' – *Manon se Livre*

# PRAISE FOR *P.S. FROM PARIS*

'A charming and bubbly story . . . Touching, funny, original, and surprising.' – *Le Parisien*

'With *P.S. from Paris* . . . chef Marc Levy offers us a delectable recipe . . . spiced with a dash of humor.' – RTL Radio Network (France)

'Extraordinary, hilarious . . . delightful!' – RCJ Radio Network (France)

'You'll devour the latest Marc Levy in a single bite . . . Unpredictable . . . To all his fans and critics, beware: the most popular author in France is back. And with a brilliant novel. In fact, by far his best. On top of being lovely, the story is also very clever. There is even suspense. The characters from *If Only It Were True* are also back. They've kept us up all night and would agree that "that's what counts."' – *Femme Actuelle*

'Marc Levy marks his great return to comedy, with moving characters, humor, and finesse.' – TF1 TV (France)

'Levy introduces a delightful mix of secondary characters and describes the film and publishing worlds with a derisive and self-deprecating eye. No, Marc Levy isn't Hemingway, and has never pretended to be, but he definitely knows how to tell a good story and bring a bit of happiness to his millions of readers.' – *Le Figaro Littéraire*

'A beautiful, uplifting love story with plenty of twists and turns . . . A passionate novel.' – France Inter Radio

'A delectable comedy you'll read in one sitting.' – *Version Femina*

'Magnificent . . . a beautiful, feel-good story.' – *Le Journal Inattendu*, RTL

'Autobiographical and funny. Marc Levy's best.' – *VSD* magazine

'Once you dive into this book, it's difficult to put it down.' – *La Dépêche*

'It feels great to rediscover Marc Levy in *P.S. from Paris* . . . a beautiful novel.' – Wendy Bouchard, EUROPE 1

'Marc Levy . . . makes a remarkable return to romantic comedy with his new novel, *P.S. from Paris* . . . Paul, the charming architect from *If Only It Were True*, comes to the fore in a brilliant manner.' – *Le Journal de Montréal*

'*P.S. from Paris* is a pleasure to read: emotion, tenderness, a few tears, but mostly a lot of laughter, with sharp dialogue that hits home.' – Web TV Culture

'Marc Levy is back with a comedy in the spirit of *If Only It Were True* . . . and it is frankly uplifting. As lighthearted as it is moving, he takes us once more on a wonderful excursion.' – *Au Boudoir Ecarlate*

'Marc Levy successfully embraces the challenge of surprising and seducing us . . . by means of subtle, ironic, and witty dialogue . . . Paris is a sumptuous backdrop for this comedy of mistaken identities . . . Marc Levy returns to his roots with intelligence and humor. A wonderful comedy . . . A bubble of tenderness and delicacy in the dark times we have seen recently.' – *Blue Moon*

'In the vein of his finest novels that make us laugh and smile as well as cry. It brings back memories, reminds us of someone, and at times makes us long to hold our friends in our arms. It offers something

# P.S.
## FROM
## PARIS

# ALSO BY MARC LEVY

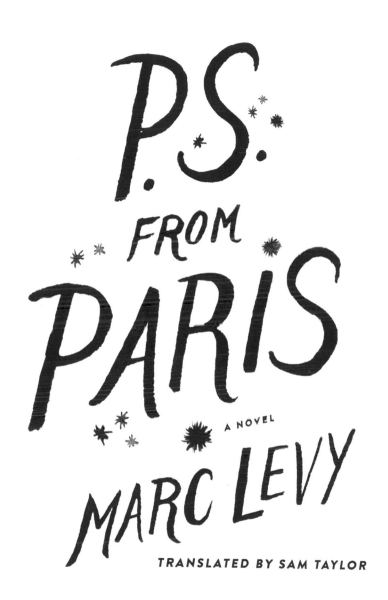

# P.S. FROM PARIS

A NOVEL

## MARC LEVY

TRANSLATED BY SAM TAYLOR

amazon crossing

Text copyright © Marc Levy/Versilio, 2015
Translated from French by Sam Taylor.
Translation copyright © Susanna Lea Associates, 2017.
All rights reserved.

Published by Amazon Crossing, Seattle

www.apub.com

Amazon, the Amazon logo and Amazon Crossing are trademarks of Amazon.com, Inc., or its affiliates.

ISBN-13: 9781611099812
ISBN-10: 1611099811

Cover design by Kimberly Glyder

Printed in the United States of America

*For my father*
*For my children*
*For my wife*

*One day, I'm going to live in theory,*
*because in theory everything goes perfectly . . .*

# 1

The rain washed down over the rooftops and façades, the cars and buses, the pavements and pedestrians. It seemed like rain had been falling on London ever since the start of spring. Mia had just come out of a meeting with her agent. She had been nervously awaiting his reaction to a preview of her latest film – in the industry of box-office hits, Creston's honest, at times biting, opinion never failed. 'It's crap,' he'd admitted, 'but it'll be a hit, if only because you and your husband are the co-stars.'

When she'd first fallen for David, he had been the star and she the novice. Now she couldn't get what Creston had said out of her mind: this time, the pupil had upstaged the master.

*In real life, he's the one who steals the show,* she thought with a wan smile.

She took a taxi to Oxford Street to clear her mind. Whenever she felt down, which had happened on more than one occasion in recent weeks, she would go for a stroll along the busy shopping street. With her long blonde hair tucked under a hat, she normally managed to pass through the crowds unnoticed.

Browsing the aisles of a department store, she tried calling David, but it went straight to voicemail.

What could her husband be doing at this time of the afternoon? Where had he been for the last two days? Two days and two nights without hearing a peep from him except for a single message on her voicemail. A brief message explaining that he was going to the country to recharge his batteries, and she shouldn't worry. But that was exactly what she was doing. Shooting the movie together hadn't exactly rekindled the sparks between them.

*'I think he's cheating on me.'*

*'Well, what couple isn't cheating these days, when you think about it?'* her agent had replied, checking his email.

*'Creston. I'm serious.'*

*He looked up.*

*'Cheating. How so?' he asked. 'That's to say: just on occasion, or all the time?'*

*'What difference does it make?'*

*'And you've never cheated on him?'*

*'No. Well, once. Just a kiss. My co-star was a good kisser, and I needed someone to kiss me. But that was to make the scene more lifelike, so that doesn't really qualify as cheating, now, does it?'*

*'They say it's the thought that counts. Which film was that?' Creston asked, raising an eyebrow.*

*Mia looked out through the window, and her agent sighed.*

*'All right, let's suppose he is cheating on you. What difference does it make, if you don't love each other any more?'*

*'He doesn't love me any more. I still love him.'*

Back home, Mia resolved to pull herself together. It was unthinkable for David to come home and find her upset. She had to remain dignified, in control. She mustn't let him think for one second that she had been moping around in his absence.

Then a friend called and begged Mia to go with her to the opening of a new restaurant, and so Mia decided to get all dolled-up. Two could play at the jealousy game. And besides, it was almost certainly better to be out on the town, surrounded by strangers, than to stay at home brooding.

The restaurant was huge, the music too loud, the room packed. Impossible to have a conversation or move a muscle without bumping into someone. *Who could possibly enjoy this kind of party?* she thought as she prepared to dive into the sea of people.

Dozens of camera flashes exploded as soon as she walked in. So that was why her friend had asked her to come. The hope of appearing in the society pages of a magazine. Fifteen minutes of fame. *For God's sake, David, how can you let me hang around on my own in a place like this? I'll make you pay for this! You'll see, Mr I-Need-to-Recharge-My-Batteries!*

Her phone rang: *Unknown Caller.* It had to be him, at this time of night. But how would she be able to hear him in the middle of all this noise? *If I could suddenly disappear, now would be the time,* she thought.

She scanned the horizon. She was halfway between the entrance and the kitchen. The crowd was sweeping her inwards, but she decided to push back against the tide. Answering the phone, she yelled, 'Don't hang up!' *Lovely, just lovely. So much for acting cool and casual . . .*

She elbowed her way out, past a creature perched on high heels with a besuited ape chatting her up, treading on the toes of the tall skeleton of a woman wriggling like an eel, skirting the pretty-boy eyeing her like prey. Only ten steps to the door . . .

'David! Stay on the line!' *Oh, tone it down, you silly fool! You sound pathetic.*

She shot a pleading look at the bouncer, in the hope that he would help her escape.

Marc Levy

And then, finally, fresh air bathed her skin in the relative calm of the street. She walked away from the mob of people waiting to enter that hell-hole.

'David?'

'Where are you?'

*Really? You have the nerve to ask me that?* 'Just out at a little party . . .'

'Enjoying yourself, baby?'

*Hypocrite!* 'Yes, everyone's having a merry old time here . . .' *Oh my God, woman, where do you come up with this crap?*

'What about you?' *You dickhead!* 'Where are you?' *And where the hell have you been for the last two days?*

'On my way home. Will you be back soon?'

'I'm in a taxi . . .' *Find a cab! Quick, a cab!*

'Oh, I thought you were at a party?'

'I was on my way out when you called.'

'All right, so you'll probably make it home before I do. Don't even bother waiting up, if you're tired, 'cause I'm actually stuck in an enormous traffic jam. Can you believe that? At this time of night? In London? Just unbelievable!'

*Ha! You're the one who's unbelievable! The nerve, telling me not to wait up, when you've already had me waiting for two whole days!*

'I'll leave a light on in the room.'

'Wonderful. See you in a bit. Love you . . .'

Shimmering pavement, couples sharing umbrellas . . .

*. . . and me, stuck on my own like an idiot. Screw the film, I don't care. Tomorrow, I'm doing it, I'm starting a new life, I swear! No, not tomorrow. Tonight!*

# 2

*Paris, two days later.*

'Why is it always the last key you try that opens the door?' Mia fumed, picking through the keys.

'Because life is messed up by design, my dearest friend. Which is also why we're stuck outside my apartment in the dark,' replied Daisy, using her phone to shine some light on the keyhole.

'I'm never going to fall in love with the idea of someone again. Next time, reality is all I'll settle for. Give me the present and only the present.'

'And give me a less uncertain future while you're at it,' sighed Daisy. 'Until then, why don't you just hand me my keys and take a turn shining the light, before my battery dies.'

The last key in the bunch was indeed the right one. Entering the apartment, Daisy flicked on the light switch. Nothing happened.

'Great. So no light in the entire building . . .'

'There's no light in my entire life,' Mia said.

'That's maybe overdoing it *just* a bit.'

'I needed to get away, Daisy, I don't know how to live a lie. I can't,' Mia continued, in a tone of voice that was just begging for compassion. But Daisy had known her too long to fall for that little trick.

'Enough of that crap. You're a talented actress, which basically makes you a professional liar . . . I know I have candles somewhere, just have to find them before my iPhone battery—'

Right on cue, the screen of her phone flickered to black.

'Just smile through the tears, like all the other A-listers? Is that it? What if I just told them all to go fuck themselves?' Mia whispered.

'Mia. Has it crossed your mind to maybe . . . start helping me out a bit?'

'I would, but it's pitch black in here.'

'Hallelujah! She noticed.'

Daisy groped her way forwards. Trying to negotiate the table, she bumped into a chair and let out a groan before finally reaching the worktop at the far end of the room. Still feeling her way around, she found the stove, picked up a box of matches from the shelf and lit one of the gas rings.

A bluish halo illuminated the spot where she stood.

Mia plopped right down at the table.

Daisy rummaged through the drawers one by one. Scented candles were strictly prohibited in her apartment. Her passion for gastronomy was high-maintenance, to say the least, and she was adamant that nothing should disturb the smell of a dish. Where some restaurant owners might put a sign on the door declaring 'No Credit Cards Accepted', she would have gladly posted: 'Customers Wearing Too Much Perfume Will Be Promptly Escorted from the Premises'.

At last she found the unscented candles and lit them. The bright flames chased the darkness from the room.

Daisy loved her kitchen, especially that it took up her whole apartment. It served as the living room, since it was bigger than the two small bedrooms and connecting bathroom put together. Her worktop held terra-cotta pots filled with thyme, bay leaves, rosemary, dill, oregano, bergamot and Espelette peppers. This kitchen was Daisy's laboratory, where she found exhilaration and release. It was here that she developed recipes for the clientele of her small restaurant perched on the slopes of Montmartre, just around the corner from her apartment.

Daisy hadn't gone to any fancy culinary school; her profession was inspired by her family and her native Provence. As a child, she would spend hours watching her mother, learning to mimic her techniques, while Daisy's friends played in the shade of the pine and olive trees.

'Are you hungry?' she asked Mia.

'Yes. Maybe. I'm not sure.'

Daisy opened the refrigerator and took out a plate of chanterelle mushrooms and a bunch of flat-leaf parsley, then tore a bulb of garlic from the string that hung to her right.

'Do you have to add garlic?' Mia asked.

'Why, are you planning on kissing somebody tonight?' Daisy retorted as she chopped the parsley. 'How about you tell me what's going on while I get dinner ready.'

Mia took a deep breath.

'Nothing. Nothing's going on.'

'Just as I'm closing up my bistro, you pop up out of nowhere with an overnight bag and a look on your face like the world just broke into a million pieces. And since then, you haven't stopped belly-aching once. I take it you didn't show up just because you missed me.'

'My world really *is* broken in a million pieces . . .'

Daisy abruptly stopped what she was doing.

'Enough's enough, Mia! I want to hear everything, but tone down the whining and moaning. Save it for the camera.'

'You'd make quite the director, you know,' Mia said.

'Quit stalling and talk to me.'

And as Daisy sliced the mushrooms, Mia spilled the beans.

7

They both jumped when the electricity came back on. Daisy dimmed the lights, then opened the electric shutters, revealing the view over Paris from her apartment.

Mia walked towards the window.

'Do you have any cigarettes?'

'On the coffee table. I don't even know where they came from.'

'You must be seeing a lot of men if you can't even keep track of who leaves what!'

'If you want to smoke, go out on the terrace.'

'Are you coming?'

'I have to know what happened next. So I guess I don't have a choice.'


'So you left the light on in your room,' Daisy confirmed as she poured more wine.

'Right, but turned off the light in the walk-in wardrobe. I planted a stool there so he'd bang into it.'

'Wow. I forgot you have a walk-in wardrobe.' Daisy snorted. 'Anyway. What happened next?'

'I pretended to be asleep. He got undressed in the bathroom and took a nice, long shower, then hopped into bed and turned off the light. I was waiting for him to whisper something, to give me a kiss. But maybe his 'batteries' hadn't fully recharged, 'cause all he did was fall fast asleep.'

'You want my opinion? Don't answer, I'm going to give it to you anyway. You married a bastard. The real question, and a simple one, is to figure out whether the good outweighs the bad. No, forget that. The real question is why you're in love with him in the first place if he makes you so miserable. Unless you're in love with him *because* he makes you so miserable . . .'

'He made me very happy . . . at the beginning.'

'I sure hope so! If all relationships started badly, Prince Charming would disappear from every fairy tale ever written and romantic comedies would be filed under horror. Don't look at me that way, Mia. If you want to find out if he's cheating, you need to ask *him*, not me. And put that out – you won't find love at the end of a cigarette.'

Tears streamed down Mia's cheeks.

Daisy sat next to her friend and put her arms around her.

'Go ahead – let it out, if it makes you feel better. A broken heart hurts like hell, I know, but it's better than being so empty you've got nothing to cry about.'

Mia had sworn to remain dignified under any circumstances, but with Daisy it was different. They had been friends for so long, they were like sisters.

'What are you talking about, empty?' she asked, wiping away her tears.

'Wow. Is that your way of finally asking me how I am?'

'Don't tell me you're alone too. Oh, Daisy, I'm afraid we're never going to find happiness.'

'Seems to me you came pretty close, these past few years. You're famous, a well-respected actress, you make more for one film than I could in a lifetime . . . and you're married. I mean, take one look at the news, the terrible things happening in the world, you'll see we can't really complain.'

'Why, what happened?'

'I don't have a clue, but if there'd been any *good* news, people would be out on the streets celebrating. What did you think of my chanterelles?'

'I think they work better than anti-depressants.'

'Music to my ears. Anyway, bedtime now. Tomorrow, I'll call your chump of a husband, tell him you know everything and that he betrayed the most wonderful woman I know, and now you're leaving him – not for somebody else, but just to be rid of him. He'll be the one in tears by the time I'm done with him.'

'You're not really going to do that, are you?'

'No, I'm not. You are.'

'I couldn't even if I wanted to.'

'Why, because you actually *want* to waste more time wallowing in a crappy melodrama?'

'No, because that big-budget film we're co-starring in opens in one month, remember? Not only do I have to do the press junket, I have to play a part off-screen too: the happiest woman in all of England. If people find out the truth about me and David, the sparks go out on-screen as well. The producers, my agent . . . they'd never forgive me. And while I'm not going to sit around in denial about his cheating, I don't need to add public humiliation on top of it all.'

'You ask me, only a heartless bitch could pull off a role like that.'

'Why do you think I ran off to Paris?'

'I see. For how long?'

'As long as you can stand me.'

# 3

At Porte de la Chapelle, the Saab convertible cut diagonally across three lanes, ignoring the flashing headlights of other cars, and left the ring road to join the A1 highway towards Roissy–Charles de Gaulle.

*'Why do I always have to go and get him at the airport? Friends for thirty years, but Arthur's never picked me up at the airport. I'm too nice. That's my problem. He and Lauren wouldn't even be together if it weren't for me. Is it too much to ask, just to show a tiny bit of gratitude? Apparently, it is!'* Paul Barton muttered, stealing a peek at himself in the rearview mirror. *'I mean, sure, they made me Joe's godfather, but who else were they gonna ask? George Pilguez?* Ha! *Good luck with that.*

*'You know, if the guy behind me flashes me one more time, I'm pumping the brakes! I've got to stop talking to myself. Then again, who else am I supposed to talk to? The characters from my novels? God – I sound like an old man. At least they can talk to their kids or grandkids. I'd better get around to that, having kids. Before I get old and senile.'*

He looked at himself in the rearview mirror again.

The Saab pulled up at an automatic toll booth, and Paul grabbed the ticket from the machine. 'Thank you,' he said out of habit, closing the window.

According to the arrivals board, flight AF83 was on time. Paul fidgeted and paced back and forth impatiently.

The first passengers began to enter the baggage-reclaim area, but only a few. Those in first class, probably.

Following the publication of his first novel, Paul had decided to put his career in architecture on hold. He had discovered an unimaginable freedom in writing. It was completely unpremeditated; he simply enjoyed the process of filling page after page – nearly three hundred of them by the time he typed *THE END*. Every evening, he found himself in the grip of his story. He stopped going out almost entirely and took to eating dinner in front of his computer.

At night, Paul became part of an imaginary world where he felt happy, in the company of characters who had become his friends. When he was writing, anything was possible.

It had all begun when that first novel was merely a finished stack of papers left on his desk.

Paul's life then changed dramatically a few weeks later, when Arthur and Lauren had invited themselves over to his house for dinner. As the evening stretched on, Lauren received a call from one of the hospital administrators. She asked Paul if she could take it in his office so he and Arthur could continue their conversation in the living room.

While taking the call, Lauren spotted the manuscript and began reading it. She was so captivated that she lost track of her conversation.

After the call with Professor Kraus ended, Lauren went on read
ing. A good hour went by before Paul poked his head inside the office
to check that everything was all right and found her there, smiling to
herself.

'Oh, sorry, am I disturbing you?' he called out, making her jump.

'You do know this is brilliant, right?'

'It didn't cross your mind to ask permission before you started
reading?'

'Can I take it home to finish it?'

'Don't answer my question with another question.'

'You started it! So can I take it home?'

'Do you really like it?' Paul asked, the doubt leaking through in
his voice.

'Yes, I really do!' Lauren replied, gathering up the pages.

Then she took the manuscript and went back into the living room,
passing straight by Paul without another word.

'I don't recall actually saying yes!' he protested as he caught up
with her.

And then, under his breath, he told her not to mention it to Arthur.

'Yes? Yes to what?' Arthur cut in, getting up from his seat.

'I can't even remember,' Lauren told him. 'Let's go. Are you ready?'

And before Paul had time to react, Arthur and Lauren, already
standing outside on the porch, thanked him for a lovely evening and
were gone.

Other passengers appeared, in greater numbers this time. At least thirty,
but still not the ones he had come to meet.

*'What are they doing, vacuuming the plane? God, just thinking about
these two brings back so many memories. Makes me think of what I really
miss from back home. The house in Carmel . . . I used to love going there*

*for the weekend, hanging out with them, watching the sunset on the beach.
It's been almost seven years since I moved to Paris . . . Skype is better than
nothing, but it's not the same as in-person visits. Actually, I should really
talk to Lauren about my recurring migraines – that's her field. No, she'll
want me to get them checked out. They're just migraines. It's ridiculous – not
every headache means a brain tumour. And if it was a tumour, I guess I'd
find out anyway, sooner or later. Are they ever going to get off that plane?'*

That fateful night, Green Street had been deserted. After parking the
Ford Focus, Arthur had opened the door for Lauren and together they
had climbed the stairs to the top floor of the small Victorian house where
they lived. It was unusual for a couple to have shared the same apartment
before ever having met each other, but that was a whole other story.

Arthur had to finish some sketches for a major client. He apologised to Lauren and kissed her before sitting down at his architect's
table. Lauren wasted no time getting into bed and picking up where
she had left off in Paul's novel.

Several times, Arthur thought he heard laughter coming from the
other side of the wall. Each time, he glanced at his watch, then picked
up his pencil again. Later that night, hearing sobs this time, he stood
up, quietly opened the bedroom door, and found his wife lying in bed
reading something.

'What is that?' he asked, concerned.

'Nothing,' she replied, closing the manuscript.

She grabbed a tissue from the bedside table and sat up straight.

'Aren't you going to tell me why you're so sad?'

'I'm not sad.'

'Did you get some bad news about a patient?'

'No, good news, actually. Very good news.'

'Good news is why you're crying?'

'Why don't you come to bed?'

'Not until you tell me why you're still up.'

'I don't think I'm allowed to tell you.'

Arthur stood squarely in front of Lauren, determined to extract a confession.

'It's Paul,' she blurted out finally.

'What, is he sick?'

'No, he's written a . . .'

'Written a what?'

'I really should ask his permission . . .'

'There are no secrets between Paul and me.'

'Apparently, there are. Don't worry about it. Come to bed, it's late.'

The next evening, Paul was at the agency when he received a call from Lauren.

'I have to talk to you. My shift ends in half an hour. Meet me at the coffee shop across from the hospital.'

Perplexed, Paul put on his jacket and left his office. He bumped into Arthur outside the lift.

'Where are you headed?'

'To pick up my wife from work.'

'Can I ride over there with you?'

'Are you sick or something, Paul?'

'Let's go, I'll explain later.'

When Lauren appeared in the hospital car park, Paul rushed over and cornered her. Arthur stood watching for a moment before deciding to join them.

'I'll catch up with you at home,' she told him. 'Paul and I need to talk.'

And, leaving Arthur on his own, they entered the coffee shop.

'Did you finish it?' Paul asked after dismissing the waitress.

'Yes, last night.'

'And you liked it?'

'A lot. I noticed quite a few things in there about me, actually.'

'Yeah, I know. I should have maybe . . . asked your permission about that.'

'Wouldn't have hurt, I have to be honest.'

'Anyway, nobody but you will ever read it, so . . .'

'Well, that's what I wanted to talk to you about. You have to send this to a publisher – I'm sure it would get published.'

Paul wouldn't consider it. First of all, he didn't believe for a minute that his novel might interest a publisher. And even if it did, he wasn't sure he liked the idea of a stranger reading what he had written.

Lauren used every argument possible, but Paul wouldn't budge. On her way out, Lauren asked if she could share their secret with Arthur. Paul pretended not to have heard her.

Back home, she handed the manuscript to Arthur.

'Here,' she said. 'We'll talk after you've read it.'

Then it was Lauren's turn to listen to Arthur laughing repeatedly, to wait during the ensuing silence for the emotion that overcame him on reading certain passages. Several hours later, he joined her in the living room.

'Well . . . ?'

'Well, the story is basically inspired by you and me, but I really like it.'

'I told him he should send it to a publisher, but he won't do it.'

'I can understand that.'

Getting Paul's story published became an obsession for the young doctor. Whenever she saw him or talked to him on the phone, she would ask him the same question: had he sent off the manuscript yet? Each time, Paul said no and urged her to stop asking him about it.

Then one Sunday, late in the afternoon, Paul's phone rang. It wasn't Lauren but an editor from one of the New York-based publishing houses.

'Ha ha, very funny, Arthur,' Paul said, irritated.

Surprised, the caller said that he had just finished reading a novel that he'd enjoyed immensely, and that he wished to meet the author.

They continued talking at cross-purposes for a while, Paul making more and more jokes. Going from amused to exasperated, the editor suggested Paul pay him a visit at his office in San Francisco the following day; that way he'd see it wasn't a joke.

Suddenly, doubt crept into Paul's mind.

'Just how did you get hold of my manuscript?'

'A friend of yours sent it to me.'

And, after the editor gave Paul the address for their meeting, the call ended. Paul paced up and down his apartment until he could stand it no longer, then jumped into his Saab and drove across the city to San Francisco Memorial Hospital.

In A&E, he asked to see Lauren immediately. The nurse pointed out that he didn't look especially sick. Paul glared at her and growled that not all emergencies were the medical kind. If she didn't page Lauren in two seconds, he was going to make a scene. The nurse started motioning for the security guard. Disaster was narrowly averted when Lauren spotted Paul and came over.

'What are you doing here?'

'Do you have a friend who's a publisher?'

'No,' she replied, shifting her gaze.

'Does Arthur?'

'Not at all,' she muttered.

'Is this another one of your pranks?'

'No. Not this time.'

'Just what did you do, Lauren?'

'I didn't really *do* anything. The decision is still up to you.'

'Elaborate. Please.'

'One of my colleagues has a friend who is an editor at a publishing house. I gave him the manuscript, just to get an outside opinion.'

'You had no right to do that.'

'I seem to recall you once doing something for me that I hadn't asked you to, and today I'm grateful for it. All I did was give fate . . . a little nudge. Like I said, it's still totally up to you, the decision is all yours.'

'What decision?'

'Whether you want to share what you've written with other people. Your story might bring a little happiness to people's lives. And these days, that's a tall order. Anyway, I have to get back to work now . . .'

She turned towards the doors of the A&E department.

'Of course, don't thank me, whatever you do,' she added.

'Thank you for what?'

'Go to that meeting, Paul. Don't be stubborn. And, in case you're wondering, I still haven't said a thing to Arthur.'


Paul went to meet the editor who was interested in his novel, and gave in to his offer. Each time he heard the word *novel*, he had a hard time making the connection with the story that had filled his nights at a time in his life when he wasn't very happy.

The novel was published six months later. The day after it was released in bookshops, Paul found himself sharing the lift at work with two architect colleagues, both of whom were holding a copy of his book. They congratulated him, and Paul, in a state of shock, waited until they got out before pressing the ground-floor button. He went to the coffee shop where he had breakfast every morning. The barista asked him to sign the copy she had bought. Paul's hand trembled as he held the pen. He paid his bill, went back home, and began to re-read his novel.

With every page, he sank a little deeper into his chair, wishing he could melt into it and never have to come out again. He had put a part of himself into the book, part of his childhood, his dreams, his hopes and failures. Without realising it, without ever imagining that, one day, strangers would read it. Or, even worse, people he rubbed shoulders with, people he worked with. Paul, whose loud voice and friendly manner disguised an almost pathological shyness, sat there wide eyed and helpless, yearning only to become invisible, like the character in his book was. Paul went into hibernation – and was only forced to come out when Arthur knocked on his door and drove him out of his hideaway. Unlike Paul, Arthur was delighted by the book's reception, and he brought good news.

The originality of the story had captured the media's attention. Maureen, the assistant at the architecture agency, had lovingly prepared a scrapbook of press clippings for him. Most of their clients had already read the book and called to offer their congratulations.

A film producer had tried to reach him at the agency and – Arthur kept the best for last – City Lights Bookstore, where he was a regular customer, had told him that the novel was selling like hot cakes. For the moment, his success was confined to the Bay Area, but at this rate, the bookseller was certain, it would soon spread across the whole country.

On the terrace of the restaurant where he had dragged Paul, Arthur told his friend he needed a shave, and to pay more attention to his appearance generally, to return his editor's calls (the poor man had already left twenty messages at the office) and, above all, to embrace the luck that had fallen into his lap instead of moping around as if somebody had died.

Paul remained silent for quite some time, then took a deep breath and thought that fainting in public would only make things worse. The final straw came when a woman, recognising his face, interrupted their lunch to ask if his novel was autobiographical.

In a solemn tone, Paul told his friend that, having given it a great deal of thought over the past week, he was going to hand over the reins of the agency to Arthur. It was Paul's turn to take a sabbatical.

'To do what?' Arthur asked, a little shaken up.

*To disappear,* Paul thought. In order to spare himself a lecture, he came up with an airtight pretext: to write a second novel, or at least try. How could Arthur object to that?

'If that's really what you want. I mean, you did the same for me when I was having a tough time and ran off to Paris. So . . . where exactly are you headed?'

Paul hadn't given the question a moment's thought, and seized on his friend's comment:

'Paris. You went on so much about it. The City of Light, all the wonders, bistros, bridges, the hustle and bustle of the arrondissements, the women . . . Who knows, with a bit of luck, maybe I can track down that gorgeous florist I heard so much about.'

'Maybe,' Arthur replied tersely. 'But not everything was as magical as I made it out to be.'

'That's because you were a mess, back then. I just need a change of scenery . . . to shake things up, get the creative juices flowing.'

'If that's really why you're going, then we'll be happy for you. And when are you leaving?'

'Let's have a dinner party at your place tonight. We can invite Pilguez and his wife, so the whole gang will be there to say goodbye. Then tomorrow, I'm off to France!'

Paul's plan clearly saddened Arthur. Paul knew his old friend had thought about protesting, or trying to insist it would be better for the agency if he waited a few months. If the roles had been reversed, of course, Paul would have done everything in his power to help, knowing that work would sort itself out.

After saying goodbye, Paul went home in a state of absolute dread. What on earth had come over him? Moving to Paris! On his own!

Pacing his apartment, he began trying to come up with arguments in favour of this crazy, improbable escape. Arthur had done it, so why not him? The second argument, even more convincing than the first, concerned the charms of Parisian women. And the third was that, ultimately, he *could* actually try writing another novel . . . which he wouldn't publish . . . or would only publish abroad. That way, he would be able to return to San Francisco once things had settled down. When all was said and done, there really was only one resounding argument: writer . . . American . . . *single* . . . in Paris!

And in Paris, where he had been living now for the past seven years, Paul had written five other novels. Growing wary of affairs with Parisian women, whose mood swings he found incomprehensible, he had chosen celibacy. Or maybe, more aptly put: celibacy had chosen him.

His five novels had not been as successful as he had hoped they would be. Not in Europe, anyway, or the United States. For some reason, however, they were very popular in Asia, and especially in Korea.

For the past few years, Paul had been romantically involved with his Korean translator. Twice a year, Kyong would come and visit him for one week, never any longer. She loved silence, and Paul was terrified of it. He sometimes imagined he had taken up writing precisely in order to fill the silence, the way ink filled a blank page. He and Kyong spent fourteen and a half days together every year, including trips to and from the airport.

When Kyong was there, he would spend hours looking at her without being able to tell if she was truly beautiful or only seemed so in his eyes. She liked when Paul looked at her with a gaze full of desire, and he was far more in love with her than he liked to admit. The only problem was that, when they were together, he could never find the right words, though words were supposedly his area of expertise – and hers too.

Although they didn't see each other very often, they had their habits. Whenever she was in Paris, she liked to go to the cinema on Rue Apollinaire, as if the venue were more important than the film; she liked to walk across Pont des Arts, and to eat ice cream at Berthillon, even in the middle of winter. She seemed to like all those things more than his writing, the very thing that had brought them together.

Kyong remained on Paul's mind when she wasn't there, becoming perhaps even more present. Why did he miss her so much?

As soon as he finished writing a manuscript, she would begin her first one-week visit. Showing none of the exhaustion that would overcome any normal person who had just spent twelve hours travelling, she always looked fresh as a daisy. After a frugal lunch, consisting invariably of egg with mayonnaise, a slice of bread and a glass of shandy (which perhaps was a miracle cure for jet lag – he really should test that out himself one day), which she would, also invariably, want to savour at the same café, on the corner of Rue de Bretagne and Rue Charlot, they would go up to Paul's apartment. Kyong would take a shower, then sit at Paul's desk to read the new manuscript. Paul would sit at the foot of the bed and watch her. This was inarguably a complete waste of time, as her face remained impassive while she read. It seemed to him that the question of whether or not she would leap into his arms depended on her assessment of the novel. As if her offer of 'friendship and maybe more' translated to 'more if I like your chapters'. For this reason, rather than expecting explicit feedback from the translator who was responsible for a substantial part of his income (since Paul lived off his Korean royalties), Paul sat tight until the moment when she would give herself to him.

He liked writing and living abroad. He liked Kyong's biannual visits. Were it not for the fact that the price of this existence was a certain solitude throughout the rest of the year, he would have found his new life almost perfect.

The glass doors opened and Paul gave a sigh of relief.

Arthur was pushing a luggage cart while Lauren waved.

# 4

Mia opened her eyes and stretched. It took her a few moments to get her bearings, geographically and emotionally. She climbed out of bed, opened the bedroom door and went to look for Daisy. Yet the apartment was empty.

Breakfast awaited her on the kitchen island, accompanied by a note in an old earthenware dish.

> *Seemed like you needed the sleep. Meet me at the restaurant when you're ready.*

Mia turned on the kettle and walked over to the window. By daylight, the view was even more stunning, as artists and locals filled the streets below on their way to the market, and she spotted the dome of Sacré-Cœur above the rooftops in the distance. She wondered what to do with her day, and the days to come. She looked at the oven clock and tried to imagine what David might be doing now; whether he was alone or making the most of her absence. Had she been right to leave, in hopes that he would miss her? Wouldn't it have been better to stay and try to recapture what was lost?

Mia didn't know what she wanted, but she knew what she didn't want any more. The waiting, the silence, the suspicion. She wanted to rediscover her appetite for life and to stop waking up with her stomach in knots.

The sky was grey, but at least it wasn't raining. That was a good start. She decided not to go and meet Daisy; instead, she would wander around Montmartre, poke about the shops, maybe even get her picture drawn by one of the many caricaturists. Totally kitschy, of course, but that was just what she felt like doing. In France, fewer people would recognise her. She was going to make the most of this freedom.

Mia rummaged through her travel bag, found an outfit, and then paused to give in to the temptation of exploring her best friend's apartment. She ran her gaze over the white-painted bookcase, its shelves groaning under the weight of books. She pilfered a cigarette from the pack that someone had left on the coffee table, looking for any clue that might reveal the identity of its owner. Was it a man? A friend? A lover? Odd that Daisy hadn't said anything. The mere thought that Daisy was sharing her life with someone rekindled Mia's desire to call David, to go back in time to before that film with the supporting actress who had caught his eye. That affair probably wasn't the first, but actually standing by helplessly as it unfolded in front of her had been a cruel experience, to say the least. Out on the terrace, she lit her cigarette and watched it burn between her fingers.

She went back into the apartment and sat at Daisy's desk. The screen of her laptop was locked.

Mia texted her friend:

What's your password? I need to check my email.

Can't you do that on your phone?

Not when I'm abroad . . .

Ha! Cheapskate.

Is that the password?

You're kidding, right?

Well, then what is it?

I'm working. Chives.

????

That's my password.

Imworkingchives?

Just 'chives', dummy!

Not much of a password.

Nope. And don't even think of snooping
through my files.

I wouldn't dream of it.

Mia put down her phone and typed in the password. She logged in to her account and found a message from Creston asking her where she was and why she wasn't answering her phone. A fashion magazine had requested a photo shoot at her home, and her agent needed her consent as soon as possible.

She began to reply, pausing for a moment to collect her thoughts:

Dear Creston,

I've gone away for a while, and I'm
relying on your discretion. Please
don't tell anyone - and I mean anyone.
In order to keep up this façade with
David, I need to be alone, without taking orders from a director, a photographer, you, or any of your assistants.
So: I will not be posing for a fashion
magazine, because I don't feel like it.
I made a list of resolutions last night
on the Eurostar, and the first was to
stop being a pushover. I need to prove
to myself that I'm capable of that, at
least for a few days. I'm going out for
a walk now, though I'll be in touch
soon. And don't worry, you can count
on my absolute discretion.

All the best,

Mia

She read it through, then hit 'Send'.

A tab at the top of the screen caught her eye, and she clicked on it.
Her eyes widened as she found herself staring at a dating site.

She had agreed not to go through Daisy's files, but this was different . . . Besides, Daisy would never know.

She checked out the profiles of the men selected by her friend,
burst out laughing at some of the messages she read, and spotted two
bios that struck her as quite interesting. When a ray of sunlight glinted

off the screen, she decided it was time to leave this virtual world and go outside into the real one. She turned off the laptop and borrowed a light jacket from the coat-rack in the hallway.

After leaving the building, she walked up the street towards Place du Tertre, stopped outside a gallery, then continued on her way. A tourist couple stared at her. She saw the woman point and heard her say to her husband: 'I'm sure it's her! Go and ask!'

Mia speeded up and went into the first café she came across. The couple waited outside the window. Mia stood close to the counter and ordered a bottle of Vittel, eyes glued to the mirror above the bar that reflected the street. She waited for the rude couple to get bored, then paid and left.

She reached Place du Tertre and was watching the caricaturists at work when a young man approached her with a friendly smile. Mia found him attractive in his jacket and jeans . . .

'You're Melissa Barlow, aren't you?' he asked in perfect English. 'I've seen all your films.' Melissa Barlow was Mia Grinberg's stage name. 'Are you here on a shoot or just visiting?'

Mia smiled at him.

'I'm not here at all. I'm in London. You *thought* you saw me, but turns out it wasn't really me. Just a woman who looks like me.'

'Sorry?' he replied warily.

'No, if anyone should be apologising, it's me. I realise that what I just said couldn't possibly make any sense to you. So *I'm* sorry. I hope I haven't disappointed you.'

'How could Melissa Barlow disappoint me when she's back in England?' The young man nodded respectfully, started to walk away, then turned around.

'If you're ever lucky enough to bump into her in London – it is a small world, after all – would you tell her that I think she's a wonderful actress?'

'I certainly will. I know that would make her very happy. Very happy indeed.'

Mia watched him disappear into the distance. 'Goodbye,' she whispered.

She fished her sunglasses out of her handbag and walked a bit farther until she spotted a hair salon. It struck her that Creston would give her a severe talking-to, and this idea alone made her even more determined to put her plan into action. She pushed open the door, sat down in one of the chairs, and emerged one hour later as a short-haired brunette.

To test out her scheme, she sat on the steps of Sacré-Cœur and waited. When a tour bus with a United Kingdom licence plate stopped in the square, Mia walked up to it as the passengers were getting off and asked the tour guide for the time. Sixty people, and not one of them recognised her! She blessed the hairdresser who had given her a new identity. Now she was just a simple British tourist visiting Paris.

Paul circled the block twice before finally double-parking. He turned to his two passengers with a big smile.

'I hope you two aren't feeling too out of whack . . .'

'What, from your driving?' Arthur replied.

'Have you ever told him about that night when I spent two hours curled up under an operating table because of him?' Paul asked Lauren.

'Yes, she has. Only twenty times or so,' Arthur answered. 'Why?'

'No reason. Here are the keys. Top floor. Bring up your bags while I find a place to park.'

Lauren and Arthur were busy unpacking their bags in their room as Paul came in.

'It's a shame you couldn't bring Joe with you,' he said with a sigh.

'It's a long trip for a kid his age,' Lauren explained. 'He's staying with his godmother, which I think he's pretty happy about.'

'Right, but he would have been even happier if he were staying with his godfather.'

'The two of us were kind of hoping for a romantic getaway,' Arthur pointed out.

'Romantic getaways come and go. You have time for that. I, on the other hand, very rarely get to see my godson.'

'Move back to San Francisco – you'll see him every day!'

'Do you two feel like having something to eat? Where did I put that cake?' Paul muttered, rifling through his kitchen cupboards.

Lauren and Arthur exchanged a glance, which he caught.

Smiling at their silent humour, he made coffee and then outlined the schedule he'd drawn up.

As it was sunny, the first day would be spent sight-seeing: Eiffel Tower, Arc de Triomphe, Île de la Cité, Sacré-Cœur. And if they ran out of time, they could continue their tour the next day.

'Right . . . and the "romantic" part of the getaway?' Arthur reminded him.

'Oh . . . yeah,' said Paul, a little embarrassed.

Lauren needed a rest before such a marathon, suggesting the two friends eat lunch without her to catch up.

Paul offered to take Arthur to a nearby café with a sun-drenched terrace.

Arthur put on a clean shirt and followed him out the door.

Sitting at a table, the two men looked at each other for a moment without speaking. As if both were waiting to see who would speak first . . .

'So, you're happy here?' Arthur finally asked.

'Yeah. Well, I think so.'

'You think so.'

'Who could ever be sure that they're really happy?'

'Nice Zen koan, or whatever that was, but don't dodge the question.'

'What do you want me to say?'

Arthur shrugged. 'Just tell me the truth.'

'I love my job, even if I still sometimes feel like a fraud with only six novels. Apparently, lots of writers feel that way.'

'So you do see other writers.'

'There's a writing club not far from here. I go one night a week. We chat, talk about writer's block, and then end the evening in a bar. It's funny – listening to myself describe it, it does sound kind of dull.'

'I won't argue with that.' Arthur offered up a smile.

'So what about on your end? Is the company booming?'

'We're talking about you, Paul.'

'I write. That's all there is to say, really. I go to a few book fairs. Sometimes I do book signings in shops. Last year I went to Germany and Italy, where my books are doing okay. I work out at the gym twice a week, which I hate, but I really don't have much of a choice, given what I eat. Apart from that, what else can I tell you? Ah, yes. I write. Which I'm pretty sure I already mentioned.'

'Sounds like a real barrel of laughs,' Arthur said.

'Well, I guess I'm happiest at night . . . being with my characters and all . . .'

'Are you seeing anybody?'

'Yes and no. She's not here very often – hardly ever, I guess, but she's on my mind constantly. You know what that's like.'

'Who is she?'

'My Korean translator. Not too shabby, eh?' Paul said, trying a bit too hard to sound jovial. 'Yep, I'm huge in Korea. It's too hard to visit, though. I still haven't recovered from the flight over here.'

'That was seven years ago,' Arthur exclaimed.

'Feels like yesterday. Eleven hours of turbulence. It was a nightmare.'

31

'Well, you will have to come back one day, you know.'

'Not necessarily. I've got my resident card now. Though I guess I could take a boat back . . .'

'And this translator?'

'Kyong is wonderful, even if I don't really know her all that well. Long-distance relationships can be a bit tricky.'

'You . . . do seem kind of alone here, Paul.'

*'Alone doesn't have to mean lonely. Weren't you the one who said that once?'* he mumbled, before asserting, 'Now enough about me! Show me some pictures of Joe. He must have gotten so big by now . . .'

A beautiful woman sat down at the table next to theirs. Paul didn't even give her a second glance, which clearly worried Arthur, judging by his expression.

'Don't give me that look,' Paul protested. 'I've had more "action" here than you could imagine. Plus, there's Kyong. It's different with her. I feel like I can be myself – no façades, no pretending. I don't feel forced to be charming. She got to know me through my books, which is ironic, because I don't really think she likes them much.'

'Well, no one's forcing her to translate them.'

'Maybe it's an act to get under my skin, or help me improve as a writer. I don't know.'

'But between visits, you're on your own?'

'At the risk of sounding like I spend my whole life paraphrasing you, didn't you also say it was "possible to love someone, even when you're alone"?'

'My situation was kind of unique, though, don't you think?'

'So is mine.'

'Listen, you're a writer, why don't you write a list of the things that make you happy?'

'I *am* happy, for Christ's sake!'

'Right. You seem to be positively bursting with joy.'

'Shit, Arthur, don't start picking me apart. You don't know a thing about my life.'

'We've known each other since high school. I don't need a study guide to figure out what's going on with you. You remember what my mother used to say?'

'She said a lot of things. Actually, speaking of which, I'd like to use the house in Carmel as the setting for my next novel. It's been ages since I was there.'

'Well, whose fault is that?'

'Want to know what I really do miss?' Paul grinned. 'Those walks we used to take. Out to Ghirardelli, or Fort Point, all those nights just hanging out, or fighting in the office, all the elaborate plans for the future without ever getting anywhere . . . just you and me.'

'I bumped into Onega the other day.'

'Did she ask about me?'

'She did. I told her you were living in Paris.'

'Is she still married?'

'She wasn't wearing a ring.'

'She never should have dumped me. You know, believe it or not,' Paul added with a smile, 'she was always jealous . . . of you and me.'

Mia watched the caricaturists at work on Place du Tertre. There was one she particularly liked the look of, a handsome guy dressed in cotton slacks, a white shirt and a tweed jacket. She sat on the folding chair in front of him and asked him to be as faithful as possible.

'"The only love that's faithful is *amour propre*", according to Guitry,' said the caricaturist in a husky voice.

'Guitry was right.'

'Had some bad luck, eh?'

'Why would you say that?'

'Because you're alone and you've just had your hair done. You know what they say: "New look, new life."'

Mia stared at him, taken aback.

'Do you always speak in quotations?'

'I've been drawing portraits for twenty-five years. I've learned to read quite a few things in people's faces. Yours is very pretty, but it looks like it could do with some cheering up. My pencil can take care of that if you keep still.'

Mia sat up straight.

'Are you on holiday in Paris?' the caricaturist asked, sharpening his charcoal.

'Yes and no. I'm spending a few days with a friend. She has a restaurant near here.'

'I bet I know it. Montmartre is like a little village, you know.'

'La Clamada.'

'Ah, the lovely lady from Provence! She's a brave one, your friend. Her food is creative but reasonably priced. And unlike some, she hasn't sold out to the tourists. I eat lunch at her place now and then – it has real character.'

Mia looked at the caricaturist's hands and noticed his wedding ring. David, never far from her thoughts, returned to haunt her.

'Have you ever been attracted to a woman? I mean, other than your wife.'

'Maybe, but only briefly. Only for the time it takes to look at someone else – and to remember how much I loved her.'

'You're not together with your wife any more?'

'Oh, we're still together.'

'So why the past tense?'

'Stop talking now. I'm drawing your mouth.'

Mia let the artist concentrate. When the man was done, he invited her to come and view the final product on his easel. Mia smiled as she saw a face she didn't recognise.

'Do I really look like that?'

'Today, yes,' said the caricaturist. 'I hope you will soon be smiling like you are in the picture.'

He took his phone from his pocket, snapped a picture of Mia, and compared it to the drawing.

'It's very good,' Mia said. 'Could you draw a portrait from just a photo?'

'I might be able to, as long as it's a clear one.'

'I'll bring you one of Daisy. I'm sure she would love to see herself as a work of art, and I think you have the talent to do her justice.'

The caricaturist bent over to rummage around in one of the portfolios propped up against his easel. He took out a stiff sheet of paper and handed it to Mia.

'Your friend is positively ravishing,' he said. 'She walks past here every morning. Go ahead, take it. It's a gift.'

On the finely textured paper was a gorgeous drawing of Daisy – not a caricature, but a real portrait, capturing her expression with skill and sensitivity.

'In that case, let me leave you mine in exchange,' she said, before waving goodbye to the caricaturist.

Paul had given them a whistle-stop tour of Paris, much to Lauren's delight. With the kind of nerve that he alone was capable of, he had cut the line that stretched out at the foot of the Eiffel Tower, saving at least an hour. At the top, a spell of vertigo kept Paul a safe distance away from the edge, gripping the guard-rails with shaking hands, while Lauren and Arthur admired the view. After taking the lift back down again with his eyes clenched shut, he'd regained his dignity and led his friends to the Tuileries Garden.

Seeing children riding on the merry-go-round, Lauren was seized by the need to hear her son's voice, so she called Nathalia, Joe's godmother.

She invited Arthur to join her on the bench where she was sitting. Paul took the opportunity to go and buy candy-floss from one of the fairground stalls. Lauren watched him in the distance as Arthur chatted with Joe.

Without taking her eyes off Paul, Lauren took the phone from her husband, heaped words of love upon her little boy, promised to bring him a gift from Paris, and was almost disappointed to realise that he didn't seem to miss her all that much. He was having a great time with his godmother.

She blew kisses into the phone and kept it pressed to her ear as Paul came back towards them, struggling manfully to carry three sticks of candy-floss in one hand.

'How do you think he's doing, for real?' she whispered to Arthur.

'Was that to me or to Joe?' Arthur asked.

'Joe hung up already.'

'Then why are you pretending to still be on the phone?'

'So Paul keeps his distance.'

'Well . . . I think he's happy,' Arthur replied.

'I think you're a pretty terrible liar.'

'And that's a bad thing?'

'No. Just an observation. Have you noticed that Paul mutters incessantly?'

'He's very lonely. He just doesn't want to admit it.'

'Isn't he seeing anybody?'

'Paul claims to have his own long-distance romance. She lives in Korea. He's even thinking of giving it a shot with her over there. Apparently, his books have a huge following in her neck of the woods.'

'In Korea?'

'Yup. To be honest, the whole thing sounds a bit far-fetched.'

'Why? What if he really is in love with her?'

'I get the impression she might not love him as much as he loves her. And the guy is terrified of flying! If he manages to get there, he may never come back. Can you imagine him living alone in *Korea*? Paris is far enough from San Francisco as it is.'

'You can't stop him. I mean, if that's what he wants . . .'

'I can try to talk him out of it, though.'

'We are talking about the same Paul here, aren't we?'

Paul, who was tired of waiting by now, walked resolutely towards them.

'Can I talk to my godson, by any chance?'

'Ah, you just missed him,' replied Lauren, blushing slightly.

She put her phone away and gave Paul a big smile.

'What have you two been conspiring about?'

'Nothing,' replied Arthur.

'Don't worry, I won't be hanging around all the time during your stay. As much as I want to enjoy your company, I promise to leave the two of you in peace very soon.'

'But we want to enjoy your company too. Why else do you think we came to Paris?'

Paul looked thoughtful. What Lauren had said made sense.

'I still think you were plotting something. So what were you talking about?'

'A place I'd like to take both of you tonight,' Arthur said. 'A restaurant I used to go to all the time when I lived in Paris. But you have to let us go back and get some rest first. I think we've had enough playing tourist for one day.'

Paul accepted the invitation, and the three friends walked along Rue de Castiglione until they reached Rue de Rivoli.

'There's a cab-stand not far from here,' said Paul, stepping out on to the pedestrian crossing.

The lights turned green, and Arthur and Lauren didn't have time to follow him. They stood separated by the flow of traffic. A bus went by and Lauren noticed the advertisement on its side:

*You might meet the woman of your dreams on this bus . . . unless she takes the métro . . .* proclaimed an Internet dating site.

Lauren elbowed Arthur and the two of them stared at the passing bus.

'You can't be serious,' whispered Arthur, turning to her.

'I don't think you need to whisper, he's all the way over there.'

'There's no way he would ever go along with that kind of thing!'

'Who says he has to know?' she replied with a wry smile. 'Sometimes fate needs a little nudge . . . Doesn't that sound a bit familiar?'

And she crossed the road without waiting for Arthur.

Mia put on the pair of tortoise-shell glasses she'd bought from an antique dealer that afternoon. The thick lenses blurred her vision. She pushed open the door of the restaurant.

Even with her poorer eyesight, she could tell the place was packed. Through a slot window in the back wall, Mia could just make out Daisy hard at work in the kitchen, as could all of the patrons from their individual tables. Her sous-chef moved from one spot to the next like he didn't know which way to turn. Daisy cleared some plates and disappeared. A door opened and she reappeared, walking briskly towards a table of four. She served them and went off again just as quickly, brushing past Mia without paying her any attention. Just before she went into the kitchen, she took three steps backwards.

'I'm so sorry,' she said, 'we're fully booked tonight.'

Mia, whose glasses were making her cross-eyed, did not give up.

'Can't you fit me somewhere? I can wait,' she said, disguising her voice.

Daisy scanned the room, looking put out.

'The people over there have already asked for the bill, but they won't stop chatting away . . . Are you alone? I could give you a spot at the bar,' she suggested.

Mia agreed and went to sit down on a stool.

In a few minutes, Daisy returned. She popped behind the bar, set a place for Mia, and then turned around to grab a wine-glass from the rack. She produced a menu and announced that there were no more scallops. The restaurant used only ingredients bought that day, and they had sold out.

'What a shame. I came all the way from London to taste your scallops.'

Daisy peered at her doubtfully, then jumped.

'Oh my God!' she shouted. 'It's a good thing I wasn't carry-ing dishes – I would have dropped everything. You are absolutely insane!'

'You didn't recognise me?'

'I didn't really get a good look at you. But what the hell came over you?'

'What, you don't like it?'

'I don't have time to come to a verdict – my waitress left me in the lurch, tonight of all nights. Look, if you're hungry, I'll fix you some-thing, but if not . . .'

'What if I help out? You look like you could use all the help you can get.'

'Melissa Barlow, waitress? Somehow, I just don't see it.'

'Keep your voice down! Melissa as waitress, maybe not. But how about Mia?'

Daisy looked her up and down.

'You think you're capable of holding a plate without spilling it?'

'I had to play a waitress once, and I'll have you know I trained for the role.'

Daisy hesitated. She heard her assistant ringing the bell. The customers were getting restless. They were going to need reinforce-ments.

'Fine. Take off those ridiculous glasses and follow me.'

Daisy led Mia into the kitchen, handed her an apron, and pointed to six plates waiting under heat-lamps.

'Take those to table eight.'

'Table eight?'

'To the right of the entrance. Table with the loud guy. Be nice to him, though – he's a regular.'

'A regular,' Mia repeated, picking up the plates. 'Got it.'

'Keep it to four at a time till you get the hang of it, please.'

'Whatever you say, boss,' Mia replied, balancing the plates on her arms.

Her mission accomplished, she came back straightaway, ready for the next round.

Freed of waitressing duties, Daisy took control of her kitchen again. As soon as each meal was ready, the bell rang and Mia rushed over. When she wasn't serving, she was clearing tables, picking up bills and coming back for more instructions. Daisy watched her, amused.

Around eleven o'clock, the restaurant started to empty.

'One euro and fifty cents. That's the whopping tip your "regular" left me.'

'I didn't say he was generous.' Daisy smiled.

'Then he just sat there . . . like he was waiting for a "thank you"!'

'You did thank him, didn't you?'

'You've got to be joking!'

'Maybe it's your brand-new look. What in the world possessed you to do something so strange?'

'Are you saying you don't like it? It's quite handy for remaining incognito.'

'It just doesn't look like . . . you. Give me some time to get used to it.'

'It must have been a long time since you watched any of my films. Believe me, I've looked worse.'

'Don't hold it against me. I'm too busy with the restaurant to go to the movies. Do you mind serving these desserts? I want to close asap so we can get home and crash.'

Mia played her role to perfection until the end of the evening. Daisy was impressed: she would never have believed her friend capable of such a feat.

At midnight, the last customers left the restaurant. Daisy and her chef cleaned up the kitchen while Mia tidied the dining room.

When Daisy had finally locked up, they walked back to her apartment through the sloping streets of Montmartre.

'Is it really like that every night?' Mia asked.

'Six days a week. It's exhausting, but I wouldn't change a thing. The restaurant is like home to me, even if it's hard to make ends meet.'

'Really? It was packed in there!'

'We had a good night tonight.'

'What do you do on Sundays?'

'Sleep.'

'And what about your love life?' Mia wondered again about the cigarettes left behind.

'Let's see, love life . . . I must've misplaced that somewhere between the kitchen and the meat freezer.'

'You mean you haven't met anybody since you opened the restaurant?'

'I've been out with a few men, but none that have been able to deal with my hours. You share your life with a man who has the same job as you. How many other men would put up with you being away shooting films, things like that?'

'Share my life? Can't say we share all that much these days.'

Their footsteps echoed in the empty streets.

'You think we'll end up alone?' said Daisy.

'Maybe you. Not me.'

'Thanks a lot! Then what's with all the moping? What's stopping you from enjoying yourself a little?'

'I'm still married, at least for now. What's stopping *you*? These men you've been out with, did you meet them at your restaurant?'

'Definitely not. I never mix work and play,' Daisy replied. 'Except once. The guy used to come to the restaurant a lot – maybe too much. In the end, I realised that he wasn't just there for the food.'

'What was he like?' Mia asked, intrigued.

'He was . . . not bad. Not bad at all, in fact.'

They reached the door of Daisy's building. Daisy punched in the code and flicked on the light before climbing the stairs.

'How "not bad"?'

'Charming.'

'Go on . . .'

'What do you want to know?'

'Everything! How he won you over, what it was like the first time, how long the romance lasted, how it ended . . . Everything.'

'If you really want me to tell you all that, let's wait till we're inside.'

Entering the apartment, Daisy collapsed on to the sofa.

'I'm beat. Could you make some tea? That's the only thing you English people know how to do in a kitchen.'

Mia gave her the finger and slipped behind the kitchen island. She filled the kettle and waited for Daisy to keep her word and tell the story.

'We met one night in early July, last year. The restaurant was almost empty, and I was about to turn off the ovens. And that's when he walked in. I hesitated at first, but what could I do? I let my chef and server go home. I could manage one last customer on my own. As I handed him the menu, he took my hand and asked me to choose for him. And, like a dummy, I fell for it and found the whole thing charming.'

'Why like a dummy?'

'I sat across from him while he ate. I even nibbled at a few things from his plate. He had a great sense of humour, was very upbeat. He wanted to help me clean up. I thought it was a funny idea, so I let him. After we'd closed the restaurant, he invited me to come for a drink. I said yes. We sat outside at a café. By the time we finished talking, we seemed to have solved all of humanity's problems and the world was a beautiful place. He was passionate about food, and he wasn't bluffing – he knew what he was talking about. I have to admit, it was like a miracle. He walked me home, didn't even ask to come up . . . just a goodnight kiss and that was all. The perfect man had just fallen out of the sky. After that, we saw each other constantly. He'd come to see me at the end of a shift and help me close up. We spent every Sunday together . . . until the end of summer. And then, just like that, he announced it was over.'

'But why?'

'Because his wife and kids had come back from their summer holidays. Please don't say anything – I'm not going to discuss it. I'm just going to take a bath and then I'm going to bed.' And Daisy closed her bedroom door. Mia was taken aback – not only by her friend's story, but also by Daisy's dignity. If only she could see things that clearly herself . . .

Coming out of Chez L'Ami Louis, Lauren stopped to admire the old façades on Rue du Vertbois.

'Paris is working its charms on you, huh?' Paul asked.

'Sure. That, or the gargantuan feast we just ate,' she replied.

They took a taxi home, where Paul said goodnight to his friends and shut himself up in his office to write.

Lauren got into bed and began tapping away on her Mac. Arthur came out of the bathroom ten minutes later and climbed between the sheets.

'You're checking your email at this time of night?' he asked, surprised.

She placed the laptop on his knees. When Arthur realised what she was up to, she laughed out loud at his dumbfounded look.

He had to re-read the first lines of what Lauren had written:

*Novelist, single, hedonist, often works nights, loves humor, life and serendipity . . .*

'I think you drank too much wine tonight.'

As he closed the screen, he accidentally clicked the 'Confirm Registration' button.

'He'd never forgive you, even for just messing around with something like this.'

'Me? You'd better start thinking of your own apologies – and fast – 'cause I think you just hit the wrong button, sweetheart . . .'

Arthur hurriedly reopened the laptop, mortified at his blunder.

'Relax! We're the only ones who have access to his account, and even you admit his life needs a bit of a shake-up.'

'I'm telling you – this is a hell of a risk,' Arthur replied.

'And what about the risks he took for us? Remember that?' she said, turning off the light.

Arthur lay in the dark with his eyes open for a long while. Hundreds of memories came flooding back to him – mad escapades and dirty tricks. Paul had even risked jail for him. Arthur owed his present happiness to his friend's courage.

Paris reminded him of sad times, years of great solitude. Now Paul was going through something similar, and Arthur knew how heavy it could be to bear that weight. But there had to be better ways of helping him than a dating site.

'Go to sleep,' Lauren whispered to him. 'We'll see if anything interesting happens.'

Arthur snuggled against his wife and shut his eyes.

Mia tossed and turned, unable to fall asleep, the joyless events of the last few weeks going around and around in her head. Today had been by far the happiest day she could think of in a long time, even if she still missed David.

She got dressed and crept out of the apartment.

Outside, the dark streets were wet with drizzle. She walked up the hill until she reached Place du Tertre. The caricaturist was putting away his easel. He looked up as she sat down on a bench.

'Tough night?' he asked, coming to sit next to her.

'Insomnia,' she said.

'I know the feeling. I can never fall asleep before two in the morning.'

'What about your wife? Does she wait up for you every night?'

'Whatever time of day, all I can do is hope she's waiting,' he replied in his gravelly voice.

'What does that mean?'

'Did you give your friend the portrait?'

'I haven't had a chance yet. I'll give it to her tomorrow.'

'Can I ask you a favour? Don't tell her it's from me. I like eating lunch at her place, and I don't know – somehow I'd feel embarrassed if she knew.'

'Why?'

'Well, it's a bit intrusive to draw someone's portrait without asking.'

'And yet you did it anyway.'

'I enjoy watching her pass my easel . . . so I wanted to capture the woman who puts a smile on my face every morning without fail.'

'Could I put my head on your shoulder? Without complicating things?'

'Sure. My shoulder never complicates things.'

Together, they gazed in silence at the thinly veiled moon that shone in the sky over Paris.

At two o'clock in the morning, the caricaturist cleared his throat.

'I wasn't sleeping,' said Mia.

'Neither was I.'

Mia stood up.

'Perhaps it's time to say goodbye,' she suggested.

'Goodnight, then,' the caricaturist said as he got to his feet.

They left Place du Tertre and went their separate ways.

# 5

Daisy liked to walk through the quiet streets just as the sun came bursting over the horizon. The concrete smelled of cool morning. She stopped at Place du Tertre, stared at an empty bench, and shook her head before continuing on her way.

Mia woke up one hour later. She made herself a cup of tea and sat down opposite the bay window.

She lifted the cup to her lips, then caught sight of her friend's computer and crossed over to the desk.

First sip. She checked her inbox, skimming through everything that reminded her of professional obligations.

Second sip. Not finding what she'd hoped for, she closed the laptop.

Third sip. She turned to look down at the street below and thought of her moonlit jaunt the night before.

Fourth sip. She opened the laptop again and went straight to the dating website.

Fifth sip. Mia carefully read the instructions for creating a profile.

Sixth sip. She put down her cup and got to work.

# CREATING A PROFILE

Are you looking for a relationship? Definitely, No Way, Let's See What Happens.
*Let's see.*

Your marital status: Never Married, Separated, Divorced, Widowed, Married.
*Separated.*

Do you have children?
*No.*

Your personality: Considerate, Adventurous, Calm, Easy-going, Funny, Demanding, Proud, Generous, Reserved, Sensitive, Outgoing, Spontaneous, Shy, Reliable, Other.
*All of the above.*

Please make a single selection.
*Easy-going.*

Your eye colour.
*Right. I'd be perfect for you, if only my eyes were a different colour. Does 'blind' count as a colour?*

Your physique: Normal, Athletic, Skinny, A Few Pounds Overweight, Plus Size, Stocky.
*It's like the entry form for a cattle fair! Normal.*

Your height.
*In centimetres? No clue. Let's say 175. Any more and I sound like a giraffe.*

Your nationality.

*British. Bad idea: we turned off the French with that whole Waterloo thing. American? Not much better, as far as the French are concerned. Danish? Makes me think of pastries. Mexican? I don't speak Spanish. Irish? My mother would kill me if she found out. Icelandic? Nah, they'll expect me to recite Björk all day long. Latvian? Sounds good, but I'd never have time to learn the language. Then again, it would be fun to invent an accent and speak a made-up language, given that the likelihood of meeting a real Latvian in Paris is pretty slim. Thai? Let's not go there. New Zealander? I have always been good with accents!*

Your ethnic origin.

*Didn't we learn anything from World War II? What is it with questions like this?*

Your vision and values: Religion.

*Right, because religion is the only way to define your vision and values? Agnostic – that'll show them!*

Your views on marriage.

*Blurred.*

Do you want children?

*I would rather meet a man who wanted to have children with me than a man who just wanted to have children.*

Your level of education.

*Oh, crap! A lie for a lie, let's say PhD . . . No, I'll just end up with a bunch of boring nerds. Okay, a First seems like the ticket . . .*

Your profession.

*Actress, but that would be playing with fire. Insurance agent? No. Travel agent? Not that either. Nurse? Even worse. Soldier? Definitely not. Physical therapist? Nah, they'll just want massages all the time. Musician? But I can't sing. Restaurant owner? Hmm, like Daisy . . . Good idea.*

Describe your job.
*I cook . . .*
*A bit over the top considering I can't even make an omelette, but to hell with it!*

Your sports: Swimming, Hiking, Jogging, Pool and Darts . . .
*Hm. Is darts really a sport?*

. . . Yoga, Martial Arts, Golf, Sailing, Bowling, Football, Boxing . . .
*I wonder how many women put 'boxing'.*

Do you smoke?
*Occasionally.*
*Best to be honest or else I could end up with an anti-smoking fanatic.*

Your pets.
*My soon-to-be ex-husband.*

Your interests: Music, Sports, Cooking, Shopping . . .
*Shopping? Great choice, that just oozes intelligence! It would go perfectly with 'boxing', up there. Dancing? Nah, they'd expect me to squeeze myself into a tutu – let's not risk disappointment. Writing? Sure, writing is good. Reading too. Cinema? No. No. No! Absolutely not. The last thing I need is a film buff. Museums and exhibitions? Depends. Animals? Negative, I don't want to spend my weekends visiting zoos. Video games, fishing and hunting? Yuck. Creative leisure pursuits? Am I supposed to know what that means?*

Going out: Cinema.
*Yes. But we'll have to just say no.*

Eating out.
*Yes.*

Evenings with friends.
*I'm all set with that for now.*

Family.
*Kept to an absolute minimum, thank you very much.*

Bars/Pubs.
*That's a yes.*

Nightclubs.
*That's a no.*

Sporting events.
*Double no.*

Your taste in music and films.
*I feel like I'm getting the third degree here! Enough with the interrogation.*

# WHAT YOU'RE LOOKING FOR IN A MAN

Height and physique: Normal, Athletic, Skinny, A Few Pounds Overweight.
*I couldn't care less!*

His marital status: Never Married, Widowed, Single.

*All three.*

He has children.
*That's his business.*

He wants children.
*We have time.*

His personality.
*Finally! I thought you'd never ask . . .*
Considerate, Adventurous, Calm, Easy-going, Funny, Generous, Reserved, Sensitive, Outgoing, Spontaneous, Reliable.
*All of the above!*

# DESCRIBE YOURSELF

Mia's fingers hovered above the keyboard, unable to type a single word. She went back to the home page, entered Daisy's email for the username and *chives* once again for the password, and read her profile.

*Young woman, loves life and laughter, but with challenging working hours. Restaurant chef, passionate about her job . . .*

She copied and pasted her friend's profile, then clicked the button to confirm her registration.

Daisy opened the door to the apartment. Mia slammed the laptop shut and jumped to her feet.

'What exactly are you up to?'

'Nothing. Just checking my email. Where were you? It's early, isn't it?'

'It's nine o'clock and I'm back from the market. Get dressed – I need a hand at the restaurant.'

Mia understood from her tone of voice that the matter was not up for debate.

After they finished unloading the crates from the van, Daisy got her friend to help her take inventory. She listed her purchases in a notebook while Mia, following orders, distributed the food.

'You don't think you're exploiting me here just a teensy bit?' she said, rubbing her lower back.

'Oh, you poor thing. I do this myself every day, so it's nice to have a bit of help for once. Did you go out again last night?'

'Couldn't sleep.'

'Come wait tables here with me again tonight – that'll tackle your insomnia, believe me.'

Mia went into the cold room, carrying a box of aubergines. Daisy called her back.

'Wait! We keep vegetables at room temperature, otherwise they lose their flavour.'

'I've just about had enough of this!' Mia said, turning around.

'But the fish does go in the refrigerator.'

'Ugh.' Mia turned around again. 'I wonder if Cate Blanchett ever has to pack fish into restaurant fridges,' she shouted from the walk-in.

'Let's talk about it after you've won an Oscar.'

Mia emerged with a slab of butter, grabbed a baguette from the bread-basket, and sat down at the bar. Daisy brought the rest of the food through and finished putting it away.

'I accidentally stumbled upon something funny while I was checking my email,' said Mia, her mouth full.

'And what was that?'

'A dating site.'

'Accidentally, you said?'

'Cross my heart, hope to die!' said Mia.

'I told you not to go through my stuff.'

'Tell me this. Have you actually met men that way?'

'What are you, my mother? Don't look so shocked. It's not like it's a porn site, you know.'

'I know, but still . . .'

'Still what? On the bus or the métro, or even walking down the street, people spend more time staring at their phones than looking at what's going on around them. The only way you can get anyone's attention these days is online.'

'You haven't answered my question,' said Mia. 'Does it actually work?'

'I'm not an actress, I don't have an agent, I don't have any fans, I don't do red-carpet events, and there aren't any pictures of me on magazine covers. Given that I spend most of my life inside a kitchen, I don't fit the profile of a desirable woman. So yes, I joined a dating site, and yes, I have met men that way.'

'Any nice ones?'

'Nice ones are rare, but you can't blame the Internet for that.'

'How do you do it?'

'Do what?'

'The first date, for example. How does it work?'

'Same as if you'd met in a café, except that you know a bit more about him.'

'Well, you know what he chooses to tell you, anyway.'

'Once you learn to read between the lines of a profile, you can usually tell the difference.'

'And how do you learn to read between the lines?'

'And why do you care?'

Mia thought about this.

'For a role,' she said evasively.

'For a role,' Daisy muttered. 'Of course.'

She sighed and sat down next to Mia.

'The username often tells you quite a bit about a guy's personality. "Mum, I'd like you to meet Teddybear21, who is much kinder and gentler than Maximus_the_Menace, your own personal favourite." How about

Misterbig – subtle, eh? ElBello? Maybe just a bit vain . . . Or how about this: I once received a message from a guy who went by the name of Gazpacho2000. Can you imagine getting hot and heavy with a Gazpacho?'

Mia burst out laughing.

'Then there's what they write about themselves. You wouldn't believe some of the things they say, not to mention the spelling errors. Honestly, it's pathetic at times.'

'Wow. That bad?'

'My chef won't be here for another hour. Why don't we head home and you can see for yourself?'

Back at the apartment, Daisy logged on to the dating site and gave Mia a demonstration.

'Here. Have a look at this.'

*Hi, are you beautiful and fun? If the answer's yes, I'm the man for you. Not only am I loads of fun, but I'm also charming and passionate . . .*

'Sorry, no match, Hervé51, since I'm ugly and boring . . . Seriously, though, where do they come up with this crap? And look,' she went on, 'here it shows the guys who have visited your profile.'

A new window opened, and Daisy scrolled through the roster of potential suitors.

'This one describes himself as calm, and I believe him – it looks like he smoked a bong before taking the picture! And it was taken in an Internet café, of all places . . . how reassuring. And look at this one: *I'm looking for someone to pose for me . . .* Please, say no more.'

She moved on down the list.

'That one looks okay,' said Mia. '*Never married, adventurous, executive, likes music, going to restaurants.*'

'Not so fast, check this bit out,' said Daisy, pointing out another line: '*I'll bet you a bag of Kinders that you read my profile all the way to the bottom.* You can take your chocolates and shove them, Dandy26.'

'And what are those over there?' Mia asked.

'The profiles automatically selected by the site. Based on what you enter about yourself, they have compatibility algorithms that suggest matches for you. It's the digital equivalent of a matchmaker, with a dash of chance.'

'Let's try it!'

Other profiles appeared, some of them provoking huge gales of laughter. Mia paused on one of them.

'Hang on, that one looks interesting. Look!'

Mia bent over the screen.

'Hmm . . . ,' Daisy said.

'What's wrong with him?'

'Novelist?'

'So? That's not a bad thing.'

'I'd like to see what he's published first. Any guy who claims he's a writer and is still working on typing the first page of his novel is the type of guy who takes a dozen acting classes and suddenly he's Kevin Spacey, or who fiddles around with three chords on a guitar and now he's John Lennon. They're just looking for a sucker to bail them out while they marinate in the juices of their artistic careers. And believe me, there are lots of those guys around.'

'I think you're being extremely harsh. And cynical. Also, for your information, *I* took acting classes myself.'

'Maybe, but I've been out with a few of those losers. Although I must admit your writer here does look like a nice guy from the picture, with those three huge sticks of candy-floss . . . He must have three kids.'

'Either that or one giant sweet tooth!'

'Well, I guess I'll let you get back to preparing for "your role". I have to go set up the lunch shift.'

'Wait a second. That little envelope icon and the speech balloon under the photo . . . what are those?'

'The envelope contains any messages he sends you. And that speech balloon, if it's green, means you can connect to chat with him. But don't start messing with that, and certainly not from my computer. There are also certain . . . codes and customs you should know about.'

'Like what?'

'If he asks you to meet him at a café in the *early* evening, it means he's hoping to get laid first, then eat dinner afterwards. If he mentions "restaurant", that might be better, but you have to find out where he lives. If it's less than five hundred yards from the place he's chosen, that tells you a lot about his intentions. If he doesn't order a starter, he's a cheapskate. If he orders *for* you, he's a super-cheapskate. If he just talks about himself for the first fifteen minutes, run for your life. If he mentions his ex within the first half-hour, he's not over her. If he starts digging around with questions about your past, he's the jealous type. If he asks you about your short-term plans, he's trying to gauge if you'll sleep with him that night. If he keeps checking his mobile, he's got several prospects going at once. If he tells you how unhappy he is, he's looking for a mother, not a lover. If he goes on and on about the wine he chose and how great it is, he's a show-off. If he tries splitting the bill, chivalry is dead and so are his chances of a second date. And if he says he's forgotten his credit card, your Romeo might just be a con artist.'

'And us? Are there rules for what we're supposed to say or not say?'

'*Us?*'

'You, us, whatever. I'm asking: what is *one* expected to do?'

'Mia, I have to work. "We" can talk about this later.'

Daisy stood up and walked away.

'And don't do anything silly on my computer! I mean it. This whole thing is not a game.'

'That never even crossed my mind.'

'My God, are you a bad liar!'

The apartment door banged shut.

# 6

First thing in the morning, he got a call from his editor, who said he had important news. He refused to say more on the phone, however, and demanded to see Paul as soon as possible.

Gaetano Cristoneli had never before suggested meeting Paul for breakfast, and he had certainly never arranged anything before 10 a.m.

An erudite man totally in love with his job, he had – despite being Italian – devoted himself to French literature. At the end of his adolescence, insofar as it ever came to an end, while he was on holiday in Menton, he found a copy of Romain Gary's *La Promesse de l'Aube* on a bookshelf in the house his mother was renting. Reading that book changed the course of his life. Gaetano had a strife-ridden relationship with his mother, and that novel was like a lifeline. When he turned the final page, everything became clear to him – except for his vision, which blurred with tears at the book's denouement. Gaetano would go on to devote his life to literature and would never live anywhere but France. Years later, in a strange twist of fate, Romain Gary's ashes were scattered in the very place where Gaetano had first fallen in love with literature. He saw this as an unquestionable sign that he had made the right choice.

He'd started out as an intern at a publishing house in Paris, where he lived a life of luxury, having been taken under the wing of a rich woman ten years his senior, who made him her lover. Numerous conquests followed, all of them equally wealthy, although the age difference narrowed over the years. Women liked Gaetano, partly due to his erudition, but perhaps also because he bore an uncanny resemblance to Marcello Mastroianni, which, one must admit, is quite a considerable asset in a young man's sexual life. Thus, he could be described as an original and learned man, and it certainly took a lot of originality and talent to be an Italian editor publishing an American author in France.

Despite being able to read French just as astutely as he read his native language, and despite the keen ability to spot a single typo in a five-hundred-page manuscript, Gaetano struggled terribly when it came to actually speaking French, mixing up and bungling his words, sometimes to the point of inventing entirely new ones. According to his analyst, this was because his brain worked faster than his mouth, a diagnosis that Gaetano wore like a badge of honour from God himself.

At nine thirty in the morning, Gaetano Cristoncli was sitting in the Deux Magots, waiting for Paul with a plate of croissants.

'What's up? Nothing serious, I hope,' Paul said, sitting opposite his editor.

The waiter brought over the coffee that Gaetano had ordered for Paul.

'My dear friend,' said Gaetano, opening his arms wide, 'this morning at dawn I received an absolutely extraordinary telephone call.'

Gaetano added so many o's to the word *extraordinary* that Paul had time to gulp down his entire espresso before the editor had even finished his sentence.

'Perhaps you would like another one?' the editor asked, somewhat taken aback. 'In Italy, you know, coffee is usually savoured in two or sometimes three mouthfuls, even when it's *ristretto*. The best part is at the bottom of the cup, but I digress. Let us return to what concerns you, my dear Paolo.'

'Paul.'

'Yes, yes. So, this morning we received a craaaaaaaaaaaazy phone call.'

'I'm very happy to hear that.'

'We have sold, or, rather, *they* have sold three hundred thousand copies of your latest novel . . . on the tribulations of an American living in Paris. It's quite ree-maaar-kable!'

'Three hundred thousand? In France?'

'Ah, no. Here, we have sold seven hundred and fifty copies, but that too is, of course, in its own way, completely spectaculous.'

'So where? Italy?'

'Given our figures, the Italians don't want to publish you at the moment. But don't worry, my idiot countrymen will change their minds in the end.'

'Do I have to keep guessing? Germany?'

Gaetano said nothing.

'Spain?'

'The Spanish market is feeling the full brunt of the financial crisis, I am afraid.'

'Fine, I give up. Where was it?'

'Korea. You know – capital city of Seoul? Just below China? Your success over there just keeps on growing, my friend. Can you believe it? Three hundred thousand copies – that's absolutely extonishing! We are going to have jacket bands printed here to tell readers – and booksellers, of course.'

'Why, do you really think that would make a difference?'

'Maybe yes, maybe no, but it can't do any harm.'

'Couldn't you have told me this on the phone?'

'Right you are, yes. But there is something else that is completely marvelful, and for this I had to see you in person.'

'I won the Korean Prix de Flore?'

'No! Imagine the Café de Flore opening a branch in Korea, where they start handing out French wine and literary prizes? Very original!'

'A good review in the Korean *Elle?*'

'It is possible, but I don't read Korean, so unfortunately, I could not say.'

'All right, Gaetano, so tell me: what is this other marvelful news?'

'You are invited to the Seoul Book Fair.'

'In Korea.'

'Well, yes. This is where one would expect to find Seoul, yes?'

'A thirteen-hour flight away.'

'No, no, don't exaggerate. It's eleven, maybe twelve – at the very most!'

'Lovely invitation, but you'll have to apologise and say I can't attend.'

'And why not? Tell me why,' Gaetano demanded, waving his arms around again.

Paul wondered what frightened him most: the flight, or the idea of meeting Kyong on her home territory. They had never seen each other anywhere but in Paris, where they had their points of reference. What would he do in a country where he didn't speak the language, understood none of the customs? How would she react when faced with his total ignorance?

Another reason was that the plan of one day going to live there with her was, in his mind, a sort of pipe dream. The possibility of which was precisely what he wanted to avoid, at least for now.

Forcing his dreams into a head-on collision with reality risked their very survival.

'Kyong is like . . . the ocean in my life. And I'm like a guy with a fear of swimming. Ludicrous, isn't it?'

'No, not at all. That is a very pretty sentence, even though I have no clue what you're talking about. It could be the first line of your next novel. Immediately, the reader wants to know what happens next.'

'I'm not sure I came up with it. I might have read it somewhere.'

'Oh, in that case . . . let us return to our dear Korean friends. I have bought you a premium economy ticket: more leg space and a special seat that tilts back.'

'Don't even mention tilts. The tilts and turns are exactly what I hate about flying.'

'Like everybody. All the same, it is the only way of getting there.'

'Then I won't go.'

'My dear author – and you should know how dear you are to me, with the advances I pay you – we cannot live solely on your European royalties. If you want me to publish your next masterpiece, you must help me out a bit, do your share.'

'And that means going to Korea?'

'That means meeting the readers who actually read you. You will be welcomed there like a star. It will be fantasmic!'

'"Fantasmic" doesn't exist. Nor does "marvelful", for that matter.'

'Well, now they do, yes?'

'I can only see one way of doing this,' Paul said, sighing. 'And that's if I take a sleeping pill in the business lounge, and you lug me on to the plane and get me to my seat in a wheelchair, and don't wake me up until we land in Seoul.'

'I don't think a premium economy ticket lets you into the business lounge. And besides, I cannot come with you.'

'You're sending me over there *all by myself?*'

'I'm afraid I am very busy during those dates.'

'Wait, when is this supposed to happen?'

'You leave in three weeks. So you have plenty of time to prepare.'

'No. No way. Impossible,' Paul replied, shaking his head.

Although the neighbouring tables were empty, Gaetano leaned towards his author, his tone turning urgent.

'Your future is in Korea. If you cement your success there, we'll be able to get the whole of Asia interested in your work. Think about this:

Japan, China . . . if we play this right, we might even be able to convince your American publisher to ride the wave with us. Once you have really cracked the American market, you will be a huge hit in France and the critics will adore you.'

'But I already cracked the American market!'

'With your first novel, yes. But ever since then . . .'

'It's absurd. I live here in France! Why should I have to be successful all the way over in Asia and the US before people in Caen or Noirmoutier start reading my books?'

'Between you and me, I could not say, I haven't a single clue. But that's how it is. No prophet is accepted in his own country, et cetera. Especially a foreigner.'

Paul's face sank down into his hands. He thought about Kyong, smiling as he arrived at the airport, saw himself gliding towards her with the casual ease of an experienced traveller. He imagined her apartment, her bedroom, her bed, and remembered the way she always looked as she undressed and the smell of her skin, and he dreamt of tender moments they had shared. And then, suddenly, Kyong morphed into a flight attendant, coldly announcing that there would be turbulence for the entire flight. His eyes popped open and he shuddered at the thought.

'Are you all right?' his editor asked.

'Yeah,' Paul mumbled. 'Let me think about it, okay? I'll let you know as soon as possible.'

'Here is your ticket,' said Gaetano, handing him an envelope. 'And who knows, you might find fantastic material for a new novel while you're out there! You'll meet hundreds of readers, they'll tell you how much they love your books. It will be an even more amazifying experience than the publication of your first novel.'

'My French editor is Italian, I'm an American writer living in Paris, and most of my readers are in Korea. Why is my life so damn complicated?'

'It's you, my dear friend. Take it from me. Catch this plane and stop acting like a spoiled child. I have other authors who would kill to be in your shoes.'

Gaetano paid the bill and left Paul alone at the table.

Arthur and Lauren met him outside the church on Place Saint-Germain-des-Prés, half an hour after he had called them.

'So what's the emergency?' Arthur asked.

'I don't even know where to start. Feels like somebody with a cruel sense of humour is meddling with my . . . destiny,' Paul replied, looking dead serious.

Lauren snorted out a laugh from behind his back, and Paul turned to face her. She tried to cover it up quickly with a concerned look.

'What's so funny?'

'Nothing. I have allergies. Pollen. Go on, cruel sense of humour . . . ?'

'Maybe cruel is an understatement. Call it *twisted*,' Paul went on, sighing.

Lauren snorted once more, even louder.

'Please inform your wife that she is starting to get on my nerves,' Paul grumbled, turning back to Arthur.

He walked to a bench and sat down. Arthur and Lauren followed suit, sitting on either side of him.

'Is it really that bad?' Lauren asked.

'Well . . . not in itself, I suppose.'

And he told them about the conversation with his editor.

'You don't have to go if you don't want to,' Arthur advised him, giving Lauren a look that Paul could not interpret.

'Well, I don't want to. Not at all.'

'So that's it, then,' Arthur said.

'No, that's not it!' Lauren exclaimed.

'What?' the two men chorused.

'Tell me: what, exactly, is your idea of happiness? A trip to the laundromat? Plopping down in front of the TV with a plate of cheese and a glass of wine? Is that how you picture the life of a great writer?' Lauren fumed. 'How can you give this up without even trying? It's like you enjoy disappointing yourself. Or maybe it's just easier that way. Unless something more important happens between now and then, you are getting on that plane, mister! Finally, you'll be forced to find out how you really feel about that woman, and how she feels about you. And if you come back alone, at least you won't have to worry about getting over a relationship, because you'll know it was never really a relationship to begin with.'

'And you'll be there to console me, just waiting at my laundromat with a sandwich, right?' Paul smirked.

'You want the truth, Paul?' Lauren said. 'Arthur is even more scared than you are about you going over there, because the distance between the two of you already bothers him more than anything. He misses you, we both miss you. But because he's your friend, he's going to tell you that you ought to go. If there's even a tiny chance the trip might end with you finding true happiness, you have to take that chance.'

Paul turned to Arthur, who – clearly with great reluctance – nodded his head in agreement.

'Three hundred thousand copies sold . . . of one single novel . . . I guess that really is something, isn't it?' Paul whistled, eyeing two pigeons nearby. '*Amazifying!* As my editor would say.'

She was sitting on a bench, eyes glued to the screen of her phone. David had called half an hour ago. Mia had not picked up.

The caricaturist left his chair and went to sit down next to her.

'The important thing is to make a decision,' he said.

'Make what decision?'

'One that will enable you to live in the present instead of constantly wondering what the future will be like.'

'Look, I know you're trying to be nice, and it's really very kind of you, but it's just not the right time. I need to think.'

'If I were to tell you that in one hour your heart was going to stop beating, what would you do?'

'And here I thought you were a caricaturist, not a psychic.'

'Answer the question!' the caricaturist ordered in an authoritarian tone that terrified Mia.

'I'd call David and tell him he's a bastard, that he ruined everything, that there's no way we can go back to the way it was before, that I don't ever want to see him again, even if I do still love him, and that I need him to know these things, even if it's with my dying breath.'

'There you go,' said the caricaturist in a softer voice. 'That wasn't so hard, was it? Call him, tell him exactly what you just told me . . . except for the last point. Because I'm not actually a psychic.'

And with these words, the caricaturist returned to his easel. Mia ran after him.

'But what if he's changed? What if he somehow went back to being the man I knew when we first met?'

'Are you going to keep running away from him or suffering in silence? For how long?'

'I don't know.'

'You like putting on a performance, don't you?'

'What is that supposed to mean?'

'You know exactly what that means. And keep your voice down – you'll scare away my customers.'

'There's nobody else here!' Mia yelled.

The caricaturist looked around. It was true: the square was fairly empty. He signalled Mia to come closer.

'That guy does not deserve you,' he whispered.

'How would you know? Maybe I'm impossible to live with!'

'Why do girls always fall madly in love with men who only make them suffer, while they barely bat an eye at the ones who would move mountains for them?'

'Ah, I see . . . Because you're James Stewart from *It's a Wonderful Life*, huh?'

'No, because my wife was just like you when I first met her. Madly in love with some handsome bastard who kept breaking her heart. And it took her two years before she woke up and moved on, two whole years we lost. And I get enraged just thinking about it. Because we could have spent that time together.'

'Enraged about two years? What difference does two years make now that you're together for life?'

'You really want to know? Go and ask her. Walk down Rue Lepic to the bottom of the hill, until you hit Montmartre Cemetery, and you can ask her yourself.'

'What?'

'A beautiful day, just like today, and a truck comes out of nowhere and cuts in front of our motorcycle.'

'I'm so sorry,' Mia whispered, lowering her eyes.

'Why? You weren't driving the truck.'

Mia nodded, took a step backwards, and began to walk towards her bench.

'Miss!'

'Yes?' she said, turning around.

'Every day counts.'

She walked down a narrow passage with stone steps, sat on a step halfway down, and dialled David's number. Straight to voicemail.

'I'm calling to say it's over, David. I never want to see you again, because . . .' *I love you so much . . . Shit, this was so much easier on the bench, the words just seemed to flow . . . A pause this long is ridiculous. It's too late to stop, just keep going*... 'Because you make me unhappy. You ruined everything, and I need you to know these things, even if it's with my dying—' Mia cut herself off. *Why do I still love you so much*...?

She hung up, wondering if it was possible to delete a message remotely. Then Mia took a deep breath and called him back.

'One day soon, I will meet a James Stewart...' *Ugh, that makes no sense at all... did I really say that out loud?* 'A man who would move mountains for me. I won't let my feelings for you get in the way. So I'm going to delete them, just like you'll probably delete this message...' *Oh, stop it, this is pathetic.* 'Don't call me back...' *Unless you call in the next five minutes to tell me you've changed and that you're coming straightaway on the next train...* *No! Please, please don't call me back...* 'I'll see you at the premiere and the junket, and we'll play our roles. The show must go on, after all...' *Yes, that's better, professional and determined. Now stop there, not another word, it's perfect.* 'Well, I'm going to hang up now...' *Great. Utterly pointless, just dragging it out.* 'Goodbye, David. Um... this is Mia, by the way.'


She waited ten minutes. Then, with a sigh, she slipped her phone into her raincoat pocket.

The restaurant was only a few streets away. As she made her way there, despite her heavy heart, her footsteps became lighter.


'You again? If I can ever actually afford a trip to London, don't expect me to waste my time hanging around on one of your film sets,' Daisy said as Mia entered the restaurant. 'What are you doing here? You should be out exploring the city!'

'Don't you need a waitress at lunchtime?'

Without waiting for a reply, Mia went into the kitchen. Daisy followed her, removing the apron that Mia was attempting to tie around her waist.

'Something you want to talk about?'

'Not now.'

Daisy went back to her ovens and passed plates to Mia. There was no point giving her instructions: only one table was occupied.

After lunch, Paul left Arthur and Lauren to wander around Paris. He was doing a reading in a bookshop in the ninth arrondissement that evening and had refused to tell them which one, for fear they would turn up and surprise him. He gave them a copy of his apartment keys and said he'd see them the next day.

Arthur showed Lauren around the neighbourhood where he had lived, pointing out the window of his former studio flat along the way. They stopped for coffee in the bistro where he'd spent many an hour thinking about her before life had brought them back together again. Then they strolled along the banks of the river before heading back to Paul's apartment.

Lauren was so exhausted, she fell asleep without eating. Arthur watched her for a moment, then borrowed her laptop. After checking his email, he thought for a long time about the conversation between Paul and Lauren in the little square at Saint-Germain-des-Prés.

The happiness of his childhood friend was more important than anything else. Arthur would make any kind of sacrifice for his sake, including seeing him go to the other side of the world. But surely this Kyong wasn't the only person capable of making Paul happy. Maybe it was worth giving fate 'a little nudge'. He remembered the story of an old man who went into a church one day to reprimand God for never having helped him win the lottery – not once, not even a single little prize, and he was about to celebrate his ninety-seventh birthday. And then, from within a celestial ray of light, God's voice boomed down to him: 'Try buying a ticket first.'

# 7

Daisy had no idea what time she had fallen asleep, but she knew it would be a long day. She tried to remember what was left in the walk-in at the restaurant so she could work out whether or not she needed to go to the market, and decided that, given the way she was feeling, she absolutely had to get a little more sleep. At 10 a.m., she opened one eye, swore out loud as she leapt out of bed, swore again as she washed her face, and again as she got dressed. She was still swearing as she left her apartment, and as she hopped up the street while pulling on her shoes. The night before, Mia had talked non-stop. She had gone over her entire relationship with David, from the day they'd first met to the phone call she had made ending it definitively.

Mia awoke to this flood of obscenities and did not dare show her face until the storm had passed.

She hung around the apartment, switched on the computer, decided not to check her email, but checked it anyway and found another message from Creston – a very short, simple message, begging her to get in touch.

For fun – and purely for fun – she logged on to the dating site. She didn't see anything interesting and was about to log off when she decided to check out that strange little folder of profiles chosen by mathematics rather than chance. Only one candidate appeared, and Mia couldn't help finding him attractive; she felt almost certain she knew his face. Had she seen him around the neighbourhood? He wasn't going by any vulgar or supposedly funny username. She was surprised to see that the small envelope beneath his picture was flashing. The message he had sent her was nothing like any of those she'd looked at with Daisy. It was actually simple and polite. It even made her smile.

> I was an architect living in San Fran-
> cisco when I got the crazy idea to write
> a novel, which went on to be published.
> I'm American - but hey, nobody's per-
> fect - and I now live in Paris. I still
> write. I've never joined one of these
> dating sites before, so I don't know
> what I'm supposed to say or not say.
> You're a chef, which is an interest-
> ing job, and means we have something
> in common: we both spend our days and
> nights working to bring a bit of hap-
> piness to others. What drives anyone
> to do this kind of work, I can't really
> say, but I admit I love the challenge.
>
> I have no idea how I mustered the courage
> to write you, or if I'll ever receive a
> reply. Why do my characters have so much
> more courage than I do? Why do they dare
> to do so much and we so little? So here

```
goes nothing: tonight, I will be eating
dinner at 8pm at Uma, a restaurant on
Rue du 29 Juillet. The chef there has a
dish I've heard wonderful things about,
a baked sea bream infused with exotic
herbs. And anyway, I love that street
- every time I go, it seems to be warm
and sunny. If this culinary experience
sounds tempting, please come as my guest
- no strings attached, of course.

Best wishes,

Paul
```

Mia quickly closed the message as if it had burned her eyes. And yet she continued to stare at the screen. She tried to stop herself from reading it again, but soon gave in to the temptation. She wound up printing it out and folding it in four. If her mother ever found out she'd even thought about going on a blind date – worse, with someone off the Internet – she would crucify her, and Creston would help sharpen the nails.

*Why do my characters have so much more courage than I do?*

How many roles had she played, dreaming of the freedom they offered her? How many times had David reminded her that her fans were not in love with her but with her character? Why not take a brave step like Paul had?

Her fingers rested on the keyboard.

```
Dear Paul,

I really enjoyed your message. I'm new
to this kind of website too. In fact,
```

I think I would have made fun of my
friends if any of them had told me
they'd agreed to dine with a stranger
because of a message on a dating site!
But what you said is so true. Is it the
freedom of characters in fiction that
we find so inspiring, or the way that
freedom transforms them? Why do they
dare to do so much and we so little?
(Apologies for the repetition - I'm not
much of a writer!)

Since I'm unlikely to bump into these
characters in reality, I would be happy
to talk to someone who breathed life
into them. It must be wonderful to
have your characters accomplish anything you want them to. Is it really
that simple? You must be very busy, so
I suppose we can save this detail for
when we're face to face.

See you tonight - no strings attached!

Mia

P.S. I'm British, and far from perfect
myself.

'Unbelievable. Just unbelievable!' Lauren exclaimed.

She waited for the waiter to leave their table, drank her lemonade in a single gulp, and wiped her mouth with the back of her hand.

'My message wasn't all that bad, huh?'

'It was good enough to get her to write back. Arthur, I know you'd do anything to stop Paul from going to Korea, but you've really got to stay out of it.'

'I seem to recall this whole thing was your idea, remember?'

'But that was before he met with his editor . . .'

'I don't mind if he goes to the book fair, I just want to make sure he comes back.'

'And what about the other reason for the trip?'

'All the more reason for a little nudge!' Arthur smiled.

'And how do you plan to convince him to turn up at this restaurant?'

'That's where I need you.'

'You always need me.'

'I'm going to invent a dinner date with an important client and invite Paul along as back-up.'

'You two haven't worked together as architects for seven years. How much help could he be?'

'As a translator, maybe?'

'You speak French as well as he does, if not better.'

'He knows Paris better than I do.'

'And what's the project all about?'

'Good question. I need to come up with something convincing.'

'Tell him it's for a restaurant,' Lauren said.

'That wouldn't be big enough for the agency, not so far from home.'

'A very big restaurant?'

'Ah. What about a beloved American restaurant considering a location in Paris?'

'Is that credible?'

'It's perfect! I'll say Alioto's has decided to open a restaurant here. That's his favourite place back in San Francisco.'

'So what role do I play in this little yarn?'

'If I ask him myself, he might think something's up, or just flat-out refuse, but if you're the one who insists, he'll say yes. He'd do it for you.'

'This is a really dirty trick, Arthur.'

'Maybe, but it's for his own good. He'll be grateful.'

'Oh, I seriously doubt that, once he realises you've taken him for a ride. And from that moment on, the evening will be a disaster. What are we supposed to talk about during the meal?'

'What are "we" supposed to talk about? Nothing. We won't be there!'

'So you're planning to send him to dine alone with a stranger who accepted an invitation on a dating website, when he thinks he's there to be talking architecture with a client?' Lauren burst out laughing. 'I would love to be a fly on the wall for that meal.'

'Same here, but let's not push our luck.'

'It'll never work. They'll figure out what's happened before the first course.'

'Maybe. But imagine: what if there's a chance it does work, even just a tiny one? How many times have you attempted something impossible in the operating room, when everyone else was telling you to throw in the towel?'

'Don't try to win me over by stroking my ego. Honestly, I can't figure out if this plan of yours is totally evil or totally hilarious.'

'Probably a little bit of both. Unless it works . . .'

Lauren asked the waiter for the bill.

'Where are we headed?' Arthur asked.

'To pack our bags and find a hotel. I'm afraid Paul's going to kick us out tomorrow morning.'

'Good idea. Let's bust out of Paris tonight. I'll take you to Normandy.'

◆ ◆ ◆

Paul thought it rather high-handed of Arthur to book the table under Paul's own name, and he was further irritated at being the first to arrive. The waitress showed him to a table for four, with only two places set. He pointed this out to her, but she slipped away without replying.

Mia arrived almost on time. She greeted Paul and sat down across from him.

'I thought writers were quite old,' she said with a smile.

'As long as they don't die young, they all inevitably end up that way.'

'That was a Holly Golightly line.'

'Ah. *Breakfast at Tiffany's.*'

'One of my favourite films.'

'Truman Capote,' said Paul. 'A great man, one I hate with a passion.'

'Really? Why is that?'

'That much talent in one person? It's enough to drive you nuts with jealousy. Couldn't he have shared a little bit with the rest of us?'

'I guess so.'

'I apologise. It's unusual, showing up this late . . .'

'Five minutes isn't late for a woman,' Mia replied.

'No, I wasn't talking about you; I would never say something like that. I mean them. I don't know what they're up to. They really should be here by now.'

'Um . . . Okay . . . If you say so . . .'

'Sorry, I haven't introduced myself. My name is Paul, and you must be . . .'

'Mia, of course.'

'I'd rather wait for them to get here before we really get started, but that doesn't mean we have to sit in silence. You have an accent – are you British?'

'Well, yes. I did mention that in my P.S., didn't I?'

'No, he didn't say a word about that! I'm American, but let's continue speaking in the language of Molière. The French hate it when people speak English in their country.'

'All right, French it is.'

'I'm sorry, I didn't mean to frighten you off by what I said. The French love foreign restaurants. And it's an excellent idea to open one here in Paris.'

'What I cook is more Provençal, actually,' said Mia, putting herself in Daisy's shoes.

'Okay. So you're not planning on staying faithful to the original?'

'You have no idea how fond I am of staying faithful. But what if it's possible to be faithful and original at the same time?'

'Right. Sure. Why not?' replied Paul, puzzled.

'So what do you write about?'

'Novels, but that doesn't stop me from continuing with the day job.'

'Architecture, is that right?'

'Bingo. If not, why else would I be here?' Paul asked, prompting a confused look on Mia's face. 'What did he tell you exactly?'

Mia found herself muttering under her breath. *Referring to himself in the third person! My God, I sure know how to pick them . . .'*

'Did you say something? I didn't quite catch that,' Paul said.

'Oh, nothing, sorry. Bad habit – talking to myself.'

Paul gave her a big grin.

'Can I let you in on a secret?'

'Fire away.'

'I do that too. I mean, at least that's what they tell me. You know, this is really too much. I'll be sure to give them a hard time about being so late. I'm just – totally dumbfounded.'

'I know the feeling,' Mia said.

'It's completely unprofessional. Let me just reiterate that this is not like them at all.'

Mia muttered once more, *'And now he's completely gone off the deep end . . . God, what am I doing here?'*

*'She's rambling under her breath. This is awful. I'm going to kill Arthur and chop him up into tiny pieces. Give people an inch, they take a mile. Where the hell are they, damn it?'*

'You were just muttering there, yourself,' said Mia.

'I . . . don't think I was. You were, for sure.'

'Maybe this isn't such a great idea. Like I said, it's my first time, and it's . . . well, it's even more awkward than I expected.'

'You're telling me this is your first time in Paris? Your French is impressive – where did you learn it?'

'What? No, that's not what I meant. This is not my first time in Paris at all. My best friend is French – we've known each other since we were kids. She came to stay with my family to learn English, and then I went to Provence to spend my holidays with her family.'

'Ah, so that's why the food at your restaurant is Provençal?'

'Exactly.'

A silence descended. It only lasted a few minutes, but to them it seemed an eternity. The waitress came back with the menus.

'If they don't show up soon, we should just order without them,' Paul exclaimed. 'It would serve them right.'

'I think I may have lost my appetite,' Mia said, putting the menu back on the table.

'That's a shame, they make some amazing food here. I've read some really great reviews about this place.'

'Right. "Baked sea bream infused with exotic herbs", like you told me in your message.'

'Message? What message?' Paul asked, wide-eyed. 'When did I send you a message?'

'Are you on some sort of medication?'

'No. Why, are you?'

'Oh my God. Okay. I get it,' Mia sighed. 'You're trying to make me laugh, to get me to unwind. But you can stop, because it's really not working. In fact, your whole – *thing* – kind of has me a little frightened. I mean, fair play, fine. Now I get it, and you can just stop.'

'I wasn't pulling any kind of prank . . . And what did I do to freak you out?'

'*All right, confirmed, the guy is completely, stark raving mad. Just don't upset him. Worse comes to worst, I order just a starter, and I'm out in under fifteen minutes.* You're right, let's not wait any longer for them – it's their fault for not being on time.'

'Exactly! Let's order, and then you can tell me about your project.'

'What project?'

'Your restaurant!'

'Not much more to tell you – southern French cuisine. Niçois, to be precise.'

'I love Nice! I was invited there for the book fair last June. The heat was kind of unbearable, but the people were really friendly. Well, the few who lined up to get their books signed.'

'How many novels have you written?'

'Six. The first one included, of course.'

'Why wouldn't it be included?'

'No reason . . . Well, actually, it's because I didn't really know I was writing it while I was writing it.'

'*This guy is really driving me up the wall. What on earth is wrong with him?*' Her muttering was beginning to get louder. 'Um, what is it you thought you were doing – building a sand-castle?'

'*Either she is a complete and utter moron or she's sitting there thinking that's what I am.* No, what I mean is that I couldn't conceive of it being published at the time. I hadn't even thought of sending it to a publisher.'

'But it was published?'

'Yes. Lauren sent it on my behalf – without asking my permission, actually – but hey, I guess I can't hold that against her. It wasn't easy at first, but it's thanks to what she did that I ended up moving out here.'

'Can I ask you a weird question?'

'You can. I mean, I can't guarantee I'll answer.'

'Do you live far from here?'

'In the third arrondissement.'

'Which is more than five hundred yards from where we are.'

'We're actually in the first, so yeah, it's pretty far. Why?'

'No reason.'

'And what about you?'

'I live in Montmartre.'

'That's a beautiful area. Let's order, shall we?'

Paul called over the waitress.

'So. Sea bream?' Paul suggested, looking at Mia.

'Does that take long to cook?' she asked the waitress, who shook her head and departed.

Paul leaned towards Mia, his lips quirked in a grin.

'I don't want to stick my nose in where it's not wanted, but if you're going to open a seafood restaurant, it might be helpful to know how long it takes to cook sea bream. Just a thought,' he said, chuckling.

This time, the silence stretched on and on. Paul looked at Mia and Mia looked at Paul.

'So, you like San Francisco?' Paul asked. 'Did you use to live there?'

'No, but I've been there several times for work. And it is a beautiful city – I love the quality of the light out there.'

'Now I get it! You trained as a chef at Alioto's and that's why you've decided to bring their concept over here.'

'Who in the world is Alioto?'

*I'm going to kill him. I'm going to kill them both,'* Paul muttered – this time, unfortunately, loud enough for Mia to hear him. 'This is on him, a hundred per cent. I mean, the least he could do is provide accurate intel.'

'So, this double murder – you meant that figuratively, I hope?'

*My God, how thick is this woman? What the hell am I doing here? Seriously, why am I here when I could be at home?* 'Yes, I can assure you beyond the shadow of a doubt that I have no intention of murdering anyone, but you have to admit the situation is a little off! I must come across as an incompetent chump who doesn't even know the ins and outs of the project he's working on . . .'

'Okay. So I'm a "project", then?'

'Are you doing this deliberately? I don't mean you personally, but whatever it is that's brought us both here.'

'Well,' said Mia in a firm tone, hands flat on the table, 'I think we've covered the essentials, and as I'm not really so hungry any more . . .' *Nope, not hungry. Absolutely starving.* 'I'll let you enjoy the sea bream without me.'

'I completely understand how that sounded,' said Paul, blushing. 'That was a clumsy thing to say. Please accept my apology. In my defence, it's been a long time since I've done this kind of thing. I think I must have lost my touch. I told him I wouldn't be any good at it – I should have just flat-out turned him down. And, of course, he never should have left me on my own like this. That was really unfair of him. Both of them.'

'Are you being haunted by ghosts or do the people you keep mentioning actually exist?'

*'She's completely nuts! I'm stuck at a restaurant with a crazy person. There's no way this project even exists.'*

'You're muttering again.'

'"They" refers to my former business partner, Arthur, and his wife, Lauren. You were in contact with them to help design your new restaurant . . . ?'

'I don't think so,' she replied warily.

'Well, obviously not any more. But before this disastrous meeting of ours, that was what you were planning, right?'

'I'm afraid I haven't the faintest idea what you're talking about.'

'Now I'm confused. Then why are you here?'

'You know, for a while there I wasn't a hundred per cent sure. But I am now. You're completely mad. Daisy warned me – I should have listened.'

'Well, that's charming! I don't see how Daisy could have told you I'm mad, because I don't even know a Daisy. Well, one Daisy, to be fair, but that was an ambulance, not a person. Scratch that – long story. Who is your Daisy?'

Mia looked around for the waitress so she could leave. This nutcase wouldn't dare follow her out on to the street with the restaurant staff looking on. Once she got rid of him, she would go back to Montmartre and delete her profile from that damn website, and everything would go back to normal. After that, she would eat dinner at La Clamada, because she was starving to death.

'Why do you think I'm mad?' Paul asked.

'Listen, this is not working out. I was messing around, playing games, and I regret it.'

Paul gave a long sigh of relief.

'Of course! I should have known. You've been pulling my leg this whole time. The three of you probably planned it out together. Great, you got me. Bravo!' He applauded her. 'All right, where are they hiding? You can tell them to come out. I admit defeat. And I gotta admit, it was a good one!'

Grinning, Paul scanned the restaurant for Arthur and Lauren. Mia kept looking towards the kitchen.

'Are you . . . really a writer?' she asked, her face tight with dismay.

'Of course I am,' he said, turning to face her again.

'Well, that must be it. Characters take hold of the author and end up becoming an actual part of his life. That's not necessarily a bad thing – I suppose there's even a kind of poetry to a gentle madness like that.

And your message was charming. But now, if you don't mind, I'm going to leave you with "them" and go home.'

*Message?* 'Remind me again what I said in this "message".'

Mia took the sheet of paper from her pocket, unfolded it, and handed it to Paul.

'These are your words, correct?'

Paul read the text attentively and looked up at Mia, confused.

'It's true I have a lot in common with this guy – I could have even written the same thing, more or less, to be honest – but the jig is up, quit messing around.'

'I am not messing around. A picture of you was on the profile!'

'What profile?'

'The profile you posted on the dating site, with *your* picture.'

'I've never been on a dating site in my life, and I have no idea what you're talking about. The only plausible explanation is that we're *both* supposed to be meeting someone else.'

'Look around. I don't see your doppelganger anywhere.'

'Maybe we both got the wrong address?' Paul said, then instantly realised the absurdity of what he was suggesting.

'Unless . . . the man I had arranged a date with started this charade of mistaken identity . . . after a sudden change of heart when he saw what I looked like in person.'

'Impossible. He'd have to be blind.'

'Thank you for that, at least. I read so much honesty in your note. It's a shame you're not the same way in person.'

Mia stood up. Paul did the same, and took her hand.

'Hold on, wait. Please sit down. There's got to be a logical explanation for all this, unless . . . No, there's no way. They wouldn't dream of pulling such a dirty trick.'

'Your invisible friends, you mean?'

'You don't know the half of it. This is not the first time I've been left holding the bag for Lauren, and had to face the consequences.'

'Whatever you say. Now, I'm leaving. Promise you won't . . . follow me?'

'Why on earth would I follow you?'

Mia shrugged. She was about to leave the table when the waitress appeared. The sea bream looked and smelled divine and Mia's stomach began growling so loudly that the waitress smiled as she placed the dish in the middle of the table.

'Sounds like I arrived just in time!' she said. 'Bon appétit.'

Paul sliced fillets from the fish and put two on Mia's plate. He had received a message on his phone, and he paused to read it.

'Okay. This time, I really am apologising to you – wholeheartedly and in all seriousness,' he said, placing his phone on the table.

'Apology accepted. But as soon as we're done eating, I'm off.'

'Don't you want to know what I'm apologising for?'

'Not particularly, but I imagine I'm about to find out . . .'

'I admit, I actually thought you were the nutcase. Now I have proof that you're not.'

'What a relief. Unfortunately, I can't really say the same about you . . .'

Paul handed his phone to Mia.

```
Paul,

We wanted to give fate a little nudge
and, as you'll have guessed by now, we
played a hell of a trick on you. I hope
you managed to have a nice evening, all
the same. I must admit that we've spent
our night in a dizzying mix of guilt
and hysterical laughter. Your revenge
will have to wait, because we left for
Honfleur this afternoon. In fact, I'm
```

writing from the restaurant where we're
having dinner. The fish is excellent,
the town is picture-postcard gorgeous,
and Lauren totally fell in love with
it. Plus, the inn we're staying at
tonight seems absolutely perfect. We'll
be back in a couple of days, maybe
more, depending on how long it takes
for you to forgive us. I'm sure you're
furious for the time being, but in a
few years we'll be laughing over this
together, and who knows? If this Mia
becomes the love of your life, you'll
be eternally grateful to us!

In light of all the pranks you've
played on me... we're even now. Well,
almost...

Love,

Arthur and Lauren

Mia put the phone down on the table and drained her glass of wine
in one go. Paul found this quite surprising, but he was getting used to
the feeling.

'Well,' she said, 'good news is: at least I'm not eating dinner with
a lunatic.'

'What's the bad news?' Paul asked.

'Your friends have a very twisted sense of humour, particularly for
the victims of their jokes. This whole thing has been downright humiliating for me.'

'I beg to differ. If anyone looks like an ass right now, it's me!'

'At least you didn't actually join a dating site, though. I feel pathetic.'

'I have thought about it occasionally,' Paul admitted. 'I promise that's the truth – I'm not just saying that to be polite. I could have totally joined one.'

'But you didn't.'

'It's the thought that counts, right?'

Paul filled Mia's glass and suggested a toast.

'And what exactly are we drinking to?'

'To a dinner that neither of us can ever tell a living soul about. That in itself makes it completely unique. I have a proposal for you – no strings attached.'

'If it's dessert, count me in. This fish is not exactly filling.'

'Dessert. Absolutely!'

'But what did you have in mind?'

'Could you show me the message I was supposed to have written? I just want to re-read part of it.'

Mia gave it to him.

'There, that's the line. Let's prove we're braver than fictional char-acters. At least let's have enough courage not to leave this table both feeling completely humiliated. Let's erase everything that's happened up until now, every word we've said. It's easy – think of it like hit-ting a key on the computer and we go back and delete the text. Let's rewrite the scene together, starting from the moment when you walked in.'

Mia smiled at these words.

'Well, I know one thing for sure – you certainly are a writer.'

'See? That's a great opening sentence for a chapter. We could follow with your Truman Capote quote.'

'I thought writers were quite old,' she repeated.

'As long as they don't die young, they all inevitably end up that way. So did you like the message I wrote?'

'There were things that appealed to me – enough to make me show up tonight.'

'It took me hours to write.'

'I'm sure it took me just as long to reply.'

'I would love the chance to "re-read" that reply. So, you have a restaurant serving Provençal cuisine? Pretty original for a Brit.'

'All my summers growing up were spent in Provence. Funny how childhood memories can be so formative in terms of taste, figuring out what you want. What about you? Where did you grow up?'

'San Francisco.'

'So how does an American writer end up Parisian?'

'It's a long story. But I don't like going on and on about myself – boring subject.'

'I suppose I'm not really crazy about myself as the subject either.'

'Careful. We run the risk of getting writer's block.'

'What about a description of this place? That could certainly fill a few pages.'

'You only need two or three details to set the scene. More than that and you can lose the reader's interest.'

'I thought there was no formula for good writing.'

'I was speaking as a reader, not a writer. Do you like long descriptions?'

'No, you're right, they can be rather tedious. So what do we write now? What do the two protagonists do next?'

'Order a dessert?'

'Just one?'

'Good point. Two. It's their first date, remember. We need to maintain a certain distance between them.'

'As co-writer, I might point out the fact that Madame's glass is empty, and she'd love it if her date would pour her another.'

'Excellent idea! Although he really should have taken care of that before she had to ask.'

'Except she might have thought he was trying to get her drunk.'

'Ah. I forgot she's British.'

'Aside from that, what are your biggest turn-offs with women?'

'If you don't mind me saying so, what if she rephrased the question in a positive light? For example: what do you like most in a woman?'

'Oh, no, not so fast – that's not the same thing at all. And if the question had been put that way, it could seem like she's trying to hit on him.'

'That's debatable, but fine. Anyway, biggest turn-off is lying. But to put it in a positive light, my answer would have been "honesty".'

Mia looked at him for a long time, then said: 'I'm not going to sleep with you.'

'I beg your pardon?'

'Just a bit of honesty.'

'Thanks, I think. That might have been more brutal than honest. And what do you look for in a man?'

'Sincerity.'

'I sincerely had no intention of trying to sleep with you.'

'You don't find me attractive?'

'I think you're beautiful. So should I infer that you don't find *me* attractive?'

'I didn't say that. You're definitely awkward, which you've admitted – and that's quite a rare thing, and maybe even a little touching. I didn't come on this date hoping for a new start, I just wanted to close a door on the past.'

'What brought me here is my fear of flying.'

'Sorry, I don't see the connection.'

'Consider it an ellipsis – a sort of mystery that will come to light in a later chapter.'

'Oh, so we're going to have another chapter, are we?'

'Why not? If we both already know we're not going to sleep with each other, there's nothing to keep us from trying to become friends.'

'That's original. Don't people normally make that kind of declaration – "Let's be friends" – when they're breaking up?'

'Exactly. Which makes this an incredibly unique idea.' Paul laughed.

'Cut "incredibly".'

'Why?'

'Adverbs lack a certain elegance. I'm more keen on adjectives – though never more than one in a sentence.'

'All right, so let me start again . . . Since I'm not your type of guy, do you think I could be your type in terms of a friend?'

'As long as your real name isn't Gazpacho2000.'

'Don't tell me that's the screen name they gave me!'

'No, not to worry,' said Mia, laughing. 'I'm just winding you up. That's something friends do, isn't it?'

'I suppose so,' Paul replied.

'If I were going to read one of your books, which one would you recommend?'

'I'd recommend one by another author.'

'Oh, come on, answer my question.'

'Choose one where the flap copy makes you want to meet the characters.'

'I would think to start with the first one.'

'No way, definitely not that one.'

'Why not?'

'Because it's the first. Would you want the people who come to your restaurant to judge you based on the first dish you ever cooked?'

'Friends don't judge friends. They just gradually learn to understand them better.'

The waitress brought them two desserts.

'One lucuma-and-kalamansi éclair, and one fig tart with *fromage blanc* ice cream,' she announced. 'Compliments of the chef.'

And she slipped away as quickly as she had arrived.

'What do you reckon lucuma and kalamansi are?'

'Clearly not part of your Provençal repertoire. One is a Peruvian fruit,' Paul explained. 'The other is a citrus fruit, like a cross between a tangerine and a kumquat.'

'Impressive!'

'Truth is, I read it earlier, before you showed up. They explain it in the menu.'

Mia rolled her eyes.

'You should have been an actress,' said Paul.

'What makes you say that?'

'Your face is just . . . so expressive when you speak.'

'Do you like cinema?'

'I do. But I never go. It's awful – I haven't seen one movie since I moved to Paris. But I write at night, and going to the movies alone just isn't much fun.'

'I like going to the cinema on my own, blending in with the audience, looking around the theatre . . .'

'Have you been single for a long time?'

'Since yesterday.'

'Wow. That is recent. So you weren't even single when you joined the dating site?'

'I thought that part of our reworked scene had been cut out. Yesterday made it official. In reality, I've been single for a few months. What about you?'

'Well . . . strictly speaking, I'm not. The woman I'm involved with lives on the other side of the world. But to be honest, I don't really know what we have any more. So, to be fair, I guess I've been single since the last time she visited, six months ago.'

'Don't you ever visit her?'

'I have a fear of flying.'

'Don't people say that love gives you wings?'

'Yes, cheesy as that may be. No offence. The wings don't seem to be working.'

'What does she do?'

'She's a translator. In fact, she's my translator, although I doubt that we're exclusive in that sense. What about your other half – what does he do?'

'He's a chef, like me. Well . . . more of a sous-chef, really.'

'Did you use to work together?'

'At times. Terrible idea.'

'How so?'

'He ended up sleeping with the dish-washer.'

'Ouch! That's tactless, at best.'

'Have you always been faithful to your translator?'

The waitress brought them the bill. Paul reached for it automatically, preventing any of the usual awkwardness.

'Let's split it,' Mia protested, 'since we're just friends.'

'You had enough to put up with during this meal. Don't hold it against me – I'm clumsy and old-fashioned.'


Paul accompanied Mia to the taxi rank.

'I hope your night wasn't too bad, all things considered.'

'Can I ask you a question?' Mia said.

'You just did.'

'Do you think a man and a woman really can be just friends without any grey zones? No ambiguity?'

'Yeah. Sure. Imagine one of them just came out of a relationship, and the other is in love with someone else, for example. It's nice to be able to bare your soul to a stranger without any fear of being judged.'

She lowered her eyes and added: 'I have to admit . . . I could really do with a friend at the moment.'

'Here's an idea,' said Paul. 'A few days from now, if we feel like seeing each other again, as friends, we'll get in touch. But only if we feel like it. No obligation.'

'Okay,' agreed Mia as she got into a taxi. 'Can't I drop you off somewhere?'

'I have my car just around the corner. I'm sorry – I should have offered to drive you, but it's too late now.'

'Well, see you soon, then. Maybe . . .' Mia smiled, closing the cab door. 'Rue Poulbot, in Montmartre,' she told the driver.

Paul watched the taxi move away, before walking back up Rue du 29 Juillet. The night was clear, his spirits were high, and his car was impounded.

*'All right, so the evening ended better than it began, but you'd better stick to your resolutions. As soon as you get back to Daisy's apartment, delete your profile – no more dates with strangers. I hope you learned your lesson.'*

'I've been driving a cab for twenty years, mademoiselle,' said the driver. 'I don't need directions, so you can stop mumbling.'

*'Even if he wasn't insane, he might very well have been. What would you have done in that case? And, my goodness, what if someone had recognised you in that restaurant? Okay, calm down, stay calm. No one could have recognised you . . . Better not tell anyone what happened tonight, ever, not even Daisy . . . in fact, especially not Daisy, because she'd kill you. Never tell anyone. It'll be your little secret. Maybe tell your grandchildren when you're old. But really old!'*

*'Why can I never find a taxi in this city?'* grumbled Paul as he walked along Rue de Rivoli. *'What a night! I really thought she was nuts. Arthur*

*and Lauren must have laughed their asses off tonight. You think we're even? Ha! You don't know me half as well as you think you do. Think I need your help finding a date? I date who I want, when I want! Who do you think I am? And she was kind of crazy, wasn't she? Maybe that's a little unfair – I'm just annoyed, it's not her fault. Anyway, she'll never call me and I'll never call her. It would be too embarrassing, after what happened tonight. And my car! The wheels were barely even touching the crosswalk. This sucks. The cops in this city are a total pain in the ass . . .* Taxi!' Paul yelled, waving his arms.

The taxi dropped her at the corner on Rue Poulbot, and she entered the apartment building.

'*I don't even have his number, and he doesn't have mine,*' she muttered as she walked up the staircase, searching blindly through her handbag for her keys. '*I mean, talk about a recipe for disaster, if he were to have my—*' Her hand grazed over an unfamiliar object in her bag. She took it out: 'Oh shit, I've got his phone!'

Inside the apartment, she found Daisy sitting at the kitchen table, a pen in her hand.

'You're home already?' Mia asked.

'It's half past midnight,' Daisy replied, staring at a notebook. 'That was quite a long film you went to see.'

'Yes . . . well, not exactly. I actually missed the eight o'clock show-ing, so I went to the later one.'

'Was it any good, at least?'

'It got off to a very strange start, but got better as it went.'

'What was it about?'

'A dinner party where the guests didn't know each other.'

'Sounds very Swedish.'

'What are you doing?'

'Accounting. You look weird,' Daisy said, glancing up at her friend.

Avoiding eye contact, Mia yawned and disappeared into her bedroom.

When he got home, Paul sat down at his desk and turned on his computer, ready to start work. Stuck to the screen was a Post-it note in Arthur's handwriting with the username and password for Paul's profile on the dating site.

# 8

After breakfast, Paul realised that he'd lost his mobile phone. He went through his jacket pockets, lifted up the various piles of paper covering his desk, scanned the shelves of his bookcase, checked that it wasn't in the bathroom and tried to recall the last time he'd used it. He remembered giving it to Mia so she could read Arthur's message. Now he was sure that he must have left it behind on the table. Furious with himself, he called the restaurant, but it went straight to voicemail. The place wasn't open yet

If the waitress had found it, she might have taken it with her. After all, he had left a generous tip. So he dialled his own number. You never know . . . could get lucky . . .

Mia was eating breakfast with Daisy when suddenly they heard Gloria Gaynor belting out 'I Will Survive' from somewhere near the window.

Both women looked up in surprise.

'Sounds like it's coming from the sofa,' said Daisy indifferently.

'You have a musical sofa?'

'Actually, I think it might be your handbag doing its morning exercises.'

Mia's eyes widened and she rushed over to the source of the music. She was rummaging around inside the bag when the tune suddenly cut out.

'Did Gloria get tired?' Daisy asked sarcastically from the kitchen.

The song erupted again, even louder this time.

'Nope,' she went on, 'she was just saving herself for the encore. That Gloria sure knows how to work an audience!'

This time, Mia got to the phone in time and answered.

'Yes,' she whispered. 'No, it's not the waitress . . . Yes, it is, live and in person. I didn't expect you to call so soon . . . I know, of course, I'm just kidding . . . Sure, I can do that . . . Where? I have no idea where that . . . In front of the Opera, one o'clock . . . Right, got it, see you later . . . Yup, bye . . . You're welcome . . . Bye.'

Mia put the phone back in her bag and returned to the table. Daisy poured her some more tea and eyed her knowingly.

'Sounds like the usher was Swedish too.'

'Sorry?'

'Tell me about this Gloria Gaynor.'

'It was just someone who forgot his phone at the cinema. I found it and he was calling so I could give it back to him.'

'You English are so civilised! You're going all the way to the Opera to give a stranger his phone back?'

'Why not? If it were my phone, I'd be relieved it was in the hands of someone decent.'

'What about this waitress?'

'What waitress?'

'Never mind. I'd rather be kept in the dark than treated like an idiot.'

'All right, all right . . . ,' Mia sighed, wondering how to get out of this tight spot. 'The film was a total bore, so I left, and so did the guy who'd been sitting next to me. We bumped into each other outside and ended up having a drink at a café. He left his phone by accident, I picked it up, and now I'm going to give it back to him. Now you know the whole story. Happy?'

'And what was he like, this guy from the cinema?'

'Not much to tell. I mean, he was okay. Pretty nice.'

'Okay *and* pretty nice!'

'Stop it, Daisy. We had a drink, that's all.'

'Just a little weird you neglected to mention any of this when you came home last night. You sure were a lot chattier the night before.'

'I was bored to death and felt like having a drink. You can imagine whatever you want. I'm going to give him his phone back and that'll be the end of it.'

'If you say so. Are you coming round to help out at the restaurant tonight?'

'Sure. Why wouldn't I?'

'I don't know. I just thought you might want to go to the cinema again . . .'

Mia stood up, put her plate in the dish-washer, and went off to take a shower without saying another word.

Paul was waiting on the pavement outside the opera house, which teemed with people. He recognised her face as she climbed the stairs out of the métro. She was wearing sunglasses and a headscarf, and carrying her handbag on her arm.

He waved to her. She smiled back shyly and moved towards him.

'Don't ask me how it happened, I have no idea,' she said by way of greeting.

'How what happened?' Paul replied.

'I don't have a clue. I suppose it must have slipped in.'

'Tell me you haven't started drinking this early in the day . . .'

'Hold on a second,' she went on, plunging her hand inside the bag.

She searched in vain, lifting one leg so she could rest the bag on her knee and continue her search, balanced somewhat precariously.

'Are you a flamingo?'

With a look of reproach, she produced the telephone with a flourish.

'I'm not a thief. I have no clue how it ended up in my bag.'

'The thought never even crossed my mind.'

'So we're agreed that this time doesn't count?'

'What do you mean, doesn't count?'

'You didn't call me because you wanted to see me, and I didn't come because I wanted to see you. Your phone is the sole reason for this encounter.'

'Okay, fine. It doesn't count. Can I have it back now?'

She handed him the phone.

'Why the Opera?'

Paul turned to look at the ornate building behind him.

'My next novel is set here. Have you ever been inside?'

'Have you?'

'Dozens of times, even when it was closed to the public.'

'Show-off!'

'Not at all. I just know the director.'

'So tell me: what exactly happens inside this opera house?'

'Opera, of course, but in my story, the main character is an opera singer who loses her voice, then ends up lingering at the opera house, sort of haunting the place.'

'Oh.'

'What do you mean, "oh"?'

'Nothing.'

'You're not going to leave me with just "oh" and "nothing", are you?'

'What do you want me to say?'

'I don't have a clue. But you'd better think of something.'

'How about we admire the façade together for a minute?'

'Writing is a fragile thing – unimaginably fragile. Your "oh" is enough to give me three solid days of writer's block.'

'Really? Is my "oh" truly that powerful? Let me assure you that it was a perfectly harmless "oh".'

'A book's description is anything but harmless. It can absolutely make or break a book. It can even decide its fate in a lot of ways.'

'Wait. Are you saying that what you just told me is the actual synopsis of the story?'

'Oh, fantastic! Now we've bumped it up to at least a week of writer's block.'

'I should probably simply stop talking.'

'Too late. Damage has already been done.'

'Oh, you're pulling my leg!'

'No, I'm serious. People think writing is an easy job, and in some ways it is. Flexible hours, no boss, no real structure . . . but working without any structure is a bit like sailing a boat in the middle of the ocean. All it takes is an unexpected wave and you're dead in the water. Try asking an actor if someone coughing in the middle of a play can make them forget their lines. Maybe that's tough for you to imagine . . .'

'Right, it probably is,' Mia replied abruptly. 'I am truly sorry. I really didn't intend for my "oh" to upset you so badly.'

'No, it's not your fault. I'm just in a bit of a funk. I didn't manage to get a single word down last night, and I was up really late.'

'Because of our dinner?'

'That's not what I meant.'

Mia looked attentively at Paul.

'It's too crowded here,' she announced.

And, as Paul seemed confused, she took him by the hand and led him towards the steps of the opera house.

'Sit down,' she ordered, then sat two steps above him. 'Tell me what happens to your main character. The girl?'

'Are you really interested?'

'I wouldn't ask if I wasn't.'

'No one can figure out what's wrong with her. She's not sick. She spends all she has on a bunch of treatments that don't do a thing, and ends up living like a recluse inside her apartment. Because the opera was her life, and because she is now too poor to even go as a spectator, she gets a job as an usher. The same people who used to pay a fortune to hear her sing are now slapping a stingy little tip in her hand when she shows them to their seats. Then, one day at the opera, a music critic catches sight of her and is sure that he recognises her.'

'Nice role. Seems promising. So what happens next?'

'I don't know. I haven't written it yet.'

'Does it have a happy ending?'

'How should I know?'

'Oh, come on – tell me it has a happy ending.'

'Will you give it a rest with your "oh"s? I haven't figured out the ending yet.'

'Don't you think we have enough tragedy in real life? People suffer more than enough misfortune, deceit, cowardice and cruelty. Why would you want to add to all that by putting stories out there with unhappy endings?'

'Novels should reflect reality to some extent, otherwise they risk being sentimental.'

'Who cares? All the people who don't like happy endings can go and wallow in their own pessimism, as far as I'm concerned.'

'That's one way of looking at it.'

'Well, it's all a question of common sense and courage. What is the point of acting or writing or painting or sculpting, of taking any of those risks, if not to make people happy? Why write tear-jerkers just because they get you better reviews? You know what you have to do to win an Oscar these days? Play a character who's lost an arm, or a leg, or a mother, or a father, or preferably all of the above. Make it miserable and squalid and base, so people will cry their eyes out and call you a genius, but if you inspire people or make them laugh? You're not even under consideration when awards season rolls around. I'm sick of this cultural hegemony of depression. Your novel needs a happy ending. Full stop!'

'Okay, then,' Paul replied tentatively. A little taken aback by the emotion on her face and in her tone, he had absolutely no desire to upset her any further.

'So she'll get her voice back, won't she?'

'We'll see.'

'She'd better. Otherwise, I'm not buying it.'

'You don't have to. I'll give you a copy.'

'I won't read it.'

'All right, I'll see what I can do.'

'I'm counting on you. Now, let's have a coffee and you can tell me what this critic does after he recognises her. Is he a nice guy or a bastard?' Without giving Paul time to answer, she went on with the same impassioned tone, 'I know what would be great: if he was a bastard to begin with and then he became a nice guy because of her – and she got her voice back because of him. Isn't that a nice idea?'

Paul took a pen from his pocket and handed it to Mia.

'Here's an idea. You write my novel while we stroll to the café, and then I can cook a bouillabaisse.'

'Are you going to be grumpy?'

'No. Why?'

'Because I have no desire to go for coffee with someone who's grumpy.'

'Then I won't be.'

'All right. But it still doesn't count.'

'I bet they have a great time, the people who work for you in your kitchen.'

'May I take that as a compliment or are you being sarcastic?'

'Watch out!' he yelled, yanking her back by the arm as she took a step out into the road. 'You're going to get run over! This is Paris, not London, you know – they drive on the other side here.'


They sat down at an outside table at Café de la Paix.

'I'm actually feeling a bit peckish,' Mia said.

Paul handed her the menu.

'Is your restaurant closed for lunch?'

'No.'

'Who's minding the store?'

'My business partner,' said Mia, averting her gaze.

'It must come in handy, having a business partner. That would be a bit tricky in my line of work.'

'Your translator's a sort of partner, isn't she?'

'She can't really write my novels for me while I go out to lunch, though. So what made you leave England for a new life in France?'

'I only had to hop across the Channel, not cross an ocean. Why did you come, with your fear of flying?'

'I asked you first.'

'Let's call it . . . a desire to be elsewhere. To change my life.'

'Because of your ex-boyfriend? Although I assume you didn't just get here the day before yesterday.'

'I'd rather not go into it. How about telling me why you left San Francisco?'

'After we order. I'm pretty hungry myself.'

When the waiter had left them, Paul recounted the episode that had followed the publication of his first novel, and how difficult he had found his first brush with fame.

'So becoming a celebrity sort of did you in?' Mia asked, amused.

'Well, let's not overdo it. A writer will never be as famous as a rock star or movie star. But I wasn't playing a role – I really did pour my guts into that book, metaphorically speaking. And I'm almost pathologically shy. When I was in high school, I used to shower with my underwear on. How's that for shy?'

'Fame doesn't last, though,' Mia pointed out. 'Your picture is on the front page of the newspaper one day, and the next they use that same paper to wrap fish and chips.'

'Do you serve fish and chips at your restaurant?'

'It's back in fashion, believe it or not,' she replied with a smile. 'Thanks, by the way – now I'm craving some!'

'You homesick?'

'More like . . . lovesick.'

'Wow. He hurt you that badly, huh?'

'I think the worst part was that I didn't see it coming – and everyone else did.'

'You know what they say: love is blind.'

'In my case, the cliché turned out to be true. But tell me – what's really holding you back from going to live with your translator? Writers can work anywhere, right?'

'I'm not sure she wants me to. If she did, I'd imagine she'd have told me.'

'Not necessarily. Are you in touch very often?'

'We Skype every weekend, and exchange emails occasionally. I've only ever seen one tiny little corner of her apartment – the part that's visible in the background on the computer. The rest of it I can only imagine.'

'When I was twenty years old, I fell in love with this guy in New York. I think the distance intensified my feelings for him. The impossibility of seeing him, of touching him . . . everything played out in my imagination. One day, I scraped together all the money I could and flew over there. I had one of the best weeks of my life. I came back exhilarated and full of hope, and decided to find a way of going back there permanently.'

'And did you?'

'No. As soon as I told him my plans, everything changed. He started sounding distant whenever we spoke, and our relationship tapered off in the run-up to winter. It took me a long time to get over him, but I never regretted the experience.'

'Maybe that's why I'm staying here . . . to spare myself from having to get over her.'

'So your fear of flying isn't really all that's holding you back.'

'Well, we all need a good excuse for keeping our heads buried in the sand. So what's yours?'

Mia pushed away her plate, drank her water in one gulp, and set the glass back down on the table.

'At the moment, I'd say the only excuse we need to think up is one to justify our next encounter,' she said, smiling as she dodged his last question.

'You really think we need one?'

'Yes, unless you want to be the first one who "feels like" calling the other.'

'No, no, no, that'd be way too easy. There's no law saying that men have to make the first move, especially not when you're just friends. In fact, in the spirit of equal treatment, I think women should have to do it.'

'I couldn't agree with you less.'

'Of course not, because it doesn't work in your favour.'

They fell silent for a few moments, watching the passers-by.

'Would you like a private tour of the Opera? When it's closed to the public?' Paul asked.

'Is it true there's an underground lake?'

'And beehives on the roof . . .'

'I think I would like that very much.'

'Good. I'll set it up and call you with the details.'

'I'll have to give you my number first.'

Paul picked up his pen and opened his notebook.

'Go ahead.'

'You have to ask for it first. Just because we're only friends doesn't mean these things don't matter.'

'May I please have your phone number?' Paul sighed.

Mia grabbed the pen and began scribbling in his notebook. Paul looked at her in surprise.

'You kept your English number.'

'I did,' she admitted, blushing slightly.

'You have to agree that you are complicated.'

'Me in particular, or women in general?'

'Women in general,' Paul muttered.

'Just imagine how dull men's lives would be if we weren't. Oh, and this one's on me. No ifs, ands or buts.'

'I'm not sure the waiter's going to go for that. I come here for lunch every day, and he has been given strict orders. Besides, I'm not sure they take British credit cards . . .'

Mia was obliged to accept.

'See you soon, then,' she said, shaking his hand.

'You got it. See you soon,' Paul replied.

He watched her disappear down the steps of the métro.

# 9

Arthur was waiting for Paul on the landing.

'Guess what? It seems I may have lost your spare keys,' he said.

'It just gets better and better,' Paul replied, opening the door. 'How was Honfleur?'

'Gorgeous, charming.'

Paul entered the apartment without another word.

'Are you really still mad at me? It was only a joke.'

'Where's your wife?'

'She's visiting a colleague who's interning at the American Hospital.'

'Do you have anything planned for tonight?' Paul asked as he started making coffee.

'You're going to leave me in suspense – is that your sweet, sweet revenge?'

'Grow up, will you? I'm not going to waste my breath.'

'That bad, huh?'

'You mean during the half-hour when this lovely woman thought she was having dinner with a psycho? Or afterwards, when I realised just how god-awfully ridiculous you made me look?'

'She seemed nice. You might have had a good time together.'

Paul thrust a cup of coffee into Arthur's hands.

'Tell me how she could have a good time when the best friend of the guy she was out with had mocked her in a way no man should be allowed to mock a woman.'

'You like her!' Arthur gasped. 'You do! If you're defending her honour, you must like this woman!'

He clapped his hands, walked over to Paul's desk, and sat down in his chair.

'Make yourself at home, why don't you?'

'I know you're plotting your revenge. But for now, put vengeance on the back burner. Tell me what happened.'

'Nothing to tell. The whole farce lasted about ten minutes. I mean, how long did you think it would take for two reasonably intelligent people to realise that they were the victims of a nasty trick? I apologised on your behalf. I explained to her that my best friend was a nice guy, but a total jackass, and we went our separate ways. I don't even remember her name.'

'And that's all?'

'Yes, that's all!'

'So, it actually wasn't that bad.'

'No, not that bad. But you got one thing right: I will get you back for this.'

Coming out of the métro, Mia headed towards a bookshop. She wandered around the displays and, not finding what she was looking for, asked one of the staff. The man typed something into his computer and then made his way to the back to search a shelf.

'I think I have one in stock,' he told her, standing on his tiptoes. 'Yes, here it is. This is the only one of his books we have.'

'Could you order the others?'

'Yes, of course. But I could recommend some other authors if you're an avid reader.'

'Why? Is this author not for avid readers?'

'Well, I guess I could recommend more . . . *literary* works, shall we say.'

'Have you actually read any of his novels?'

'Unfortunately, I don't have time to read everything.' The bookseller shrugged.

'So how can you judge his writing?'

The man looked her up and down and went back behind the counter.

'Would you like me to order the others?' he asked, ringing up her purchase.

'No,' replied Mia. 'I think I'll start with this one and then order the others from a less . . . *literary* bookshop.'

'I didn't mean to be disparaging. He's an American author. Often books can lose a lot in translation.'

'I work in translation,' said Mia, hands on her hips.

For a few seconds, the bookseller was speechless.

'Well, after a faux pas of that magnitude, I think I'm going to have to offer you a discount!'

Mia walked down the street, leafing through the novel. She turned it over to read the back cover and smiled when she saw Paul's photograph. This was the first time she had held a book written by someone she knew, even if she could hardly claim to know him very well. She thought back to the conversation she'd had with the bookseller and wondered why her reaction had been so testy. It really wasn't like her, but she was glad to have expressed her feelings on the matter. Something inside her was changing, and she liked the new inner voice telling her to be more assertive. She hailed a taxi and asked the driver to drop her off on Rue de Rivoli, outside the English bookshop.

She came out again a few minutes later with the original American edition of Paul's first novel. She began reading it on the way to Montmartre, continued as she walked up Rue Lepic, and then sat on a bench in Place du Tertre to read some more.

The caricaturist was sitting behind his easel. He threw a smile her way, but she didn't even notice.

It was late afternoon when she arrived at the restaurant to find Daisy hard at work in the kitchen. Handing over the reins to Robert, her sous-chef, she took Mia aside.

'I know you don't have the right CV for this type of work, but my waitress is gone for good and it'll take me at least a few days to find a replacement. You did really well the other night. I know it's a lot to ask, but—'

'Yes,' Mia said before Daisy could finish her sentence.

'You're in?'

'Like I said: yes.'

'What would Cate Blanchett think?'

'Leave her out of this. Anyway, if I were her, I'd invest in a restaurant. You have money problems, I don't. We could spruce up the decor, and you could hire a reliable waitress and pay her enough that she'd stay for good—'

'My restaurant doesn't need sprucing up,' Daisy interrupted. 'Right now, all I need is a hand.'

'You don't have to give me an answer now. Think about it.'

'How was the Opera?'

'I gave him his phone and left.'

'That's all?'

'Yup.'

'Is he gay?'

'I didn't think to ask.'

'You go all the way across Paris to give him his phone and all you get is a "thank you and goodbye"?'

Mia did not engage her further. She put on her apron and began to set tables.

◆ ◆ ◆

Paul had eaten dinner with Arthur and Lauren in a bistro on Rue de Bourgogne. The wine flowed freely, helping turn the joke they had played on him into a distant memory. The next day his friends were leaving to visit Provence, and he wanted to make the most of the remaining time with them.

'I think she was right,' Paul said as they walked across the Esplanade des Invalides.

'Who?' asked Lauren.

'My . . . editor.'

'I thought your editor was a man?' Arthur objected.

'Of course he is,' Paul replied.

'And what was he right about?' Lauren went on.

'I should go to Korea and set things straight once and for all. It's ridiculous, this fear of flying.'

'Or . . . you could ride this new wave of bravery and come back to San Francisco,' Arthur suggested.

'Let him be,' Lauren said. 'If he wants to go to Seoul, you should be encouraging him.'

Arthur took Paul by the shoulder, turning him to meet his gaze.

'If that's where you think you'll find happiness, fine. It'll only put you another few thousand miles away from us.'

'No offence, but you really suck at geography, Arthur. Or maybe you forgot if you fly west instead of east, we'd actually be closer? Breaking news – the world is round!'

Back at his apartment, Paul sat down, uninspired, in front of his computer. Around one in the morning, he wrote an email.

Kyong,

I should have come to see you a long
time ago. I think about you when I
wake up, all day, and late into the
night, but I never give voice to these
thoughts. I only have to close my eyes
to picture your face. You're here,
leaning over my desk, reading me and
translating me at the same time in your
thoughts, without ever saying a word.
You know I'm watching you, so you keep
your feelings concealed.

If only heartache were contagious, you
would love me as much as I love you.

When feelings are hard to pin down, we
hope that they will take shape as they
grow. Mine are now fully grown, but I
have been trying hard not to show it.
You and I can do anything with words.
We create beautiful stories. So why is
it so complicated to create our own
story together in real life?

I am coming to Seoul, not just for the
book fair, but for you. And if you
feel like it, we can spend some time

```
together. You can introduce me to your
city and your friends. Or I could sim-
ply sit down and write, and this time,
you would be the one watching me.

I'll be counting the days, with bated
breath... as my longing for you slows
time to a crawl.

Paul
```

As he finished writing the message, it occurred to him that Kyong had already woken up. When would she read the words he had sent her? This thought kept him awake long into the night.

Arthur sat with the laptop on his knees. He entered the address of the dating site, logged in with the username and password, and accessed the profile he had created, this time with the sole intent of deleting it. A little envelope was blinking under the image of his best friend's face. Arthur turned to Lauren, but she was asleep. He hesitated – two seconds, maybe less – then clicked on the envelope.

```
Dear Paul,

We talked about calling but we didn't
mention email, so this doesn't count.

My email address is at the bottom of
this message, because I'd rather avoid
this site from now on, in an attempt
```

to forget how humiliating that whole debacle was . . .

I wanted to thank you for our impromptu lunch, and to tell you not to worry about my 'oh'. I have been thinking more about your story and I really want to know what happens next - so I can only hope that you soon overcome your writer's block.

I'm excited about the idea of visiting the Opera, especially when it's closed to the public. Things that are out of reach are always more desirable.

A gruelling night tonight at the restaurant. Lots of people - too many, almost - but that's the price of success. It seems my cuisine is absolutely irresistible!

Goodnight, and see you soon...

Mia

◆ ◆ ◆

'Can I have my laptop back?' Daisy asked, poking her head into Mia's room.

'Sure. I just finished.'

'Who were you writing to? I heard you working those keys like crazy.'

'I have trouble writing on a French keyboard, with the letters in all the wrong places.'

'So who were you writing to?' Daisy pressed, sitting at the foot of the bed.

'Creston. I was just giving him an update.'

'Only good things, I assume?'

'Yes, I rather like my life in Paris. I even like my job at the restaurant.'

'There weren't many people there tonight. If it goes on, I'll be forced to close down.'

Mia shut the laptop and focused all her attention on Daisy.

'It's just a phase. People are strapped for cash right now, but the crisis won't last forever.'

'You can count me among those strapped for cash, and at this rate, my restaurant won't be around to see the end of the crisis.'

'Daisy, if you don't want me as a partner, at least let me lend you some money.'

'Thanks, but no thanks. I may be penniless, but I still have my dignity.'

Daisy lay down next to Mia. The pillow was oddly uncomfortable; she slid her hand beneath it and discovered a book. She turned it over to read the blurb.

'Why do I feel like I recognise this face?' she asked, looking at the photo of the author.

'He's a very well-known American novelist.'

'I never have time to read. But I'm sure I've seen this face before. Maybe he came to the restaurant.'

'Who knows?' Mia replied, turning bright red.

'Did you buy it today? What's it about?'

'I haven't started it yet.'

'You bought a book without even knowing what it's about?'

'It came recommended by the bookseller.'

'All right, well, I'll leave you to your reading. I'm off to bed.'

Daisy stood up and walked towards the door.

'Um, the book?' Mia said timidly.

It was still in Daisy's hand. She took another look at the photograph and tossed the book on the bed.

'See you tomorrow.'

She closed the door and then, almost immediately, opened it again.

'You're acting weird.'

'Weird how?'

'I don't know. Was it that stranger on the phone who gave you this book?'

'Well, if it was, wouldn't it be written in a dialect from northern-most Sweden?'

Daisy frowned at Mia before leaving the room.

'You're definitely being weird,' Mia heard her mutter from outside the door.

# 10

The alarm went off. Lauren stretched like a cat and then curled up against Arthur.

'Did you sleep okay?' she asked, kissing him.

'Never better.'

'What's put you in such a good mood?'

'There's something you have to see,' he said with a grin as he sat up.

He picked up the laptop from under the bed and opened it.

'For a date that only lasted ten minutes, this is one solid follow-up!'

Lauren rolled her eyes.

'So they hit it off, despite your tasteless joke – good for them. But don't jump the gun.'

'Just making observations from what I read, is all.'

'He's in love with his Korean translator, so I'm not sure this mysterious stranger would make any difference. Or if she even wants to.'

'In the meantime, I'm going to print this out and leave it right on his desk where he can see it.'

'Why would you do that?'

'Just to let him know I'm not stupid.'

Lauren read the letter again.

'She just wants to be friends.'

'And you know this because . . . ?'

'Because I'm a woman, and it's plain to see, written in black and white. *Emails don't count*. Translated into womanspeak: *I'm not trying to get you into bed*. And she talks about something that might be pretty important going on at this restaurant, but Paul doesn't seem to have anything to do with it.'

'And what about the whole "things that are out of reach are always more desirable" thing? Come on, you don't think she's flirting there, just a little bit?'

'I think your mind is playing tricks on you because you're so desperate for Paul to stay in Paris. If you want my opinion, this woman is fresh out of a relationship, on the rebound. She seems to be genuinely looking for a friend and that's that.'

'You should have gone into psychology instead of neurosurgery.'

'I won't dignify that with a response. But even assuming that there are mixed messages . . . if you want Paul to take the bait, the last thing you should do is bring it up.'

'You think?'

'How is it I sometimes feel like I know your best friend better than you do? Or at least the way his mind works.'

With that, Lauren went out to make breakfast.

In the living room, she could see Paul asleep on the sofa. As soon as she entered, he opened his eyes and yawned, then slowly got up.

'Didn't quite make it to your bed, huh?'

'I was working late. I only meant to take a break, but it seems I must have crashed.'

'Do you always work that late?'

'Yeah, pretty often.'

'You look awful. You have to stop burning the candle at both ends.'

'Is that my physician speaking?'

'No. It's your friend.'

While Lauren poured him a cup of coffee, Paul checked his email, even though he knew that Kyong almost never replied right away. Nonetheless, he retired to his bedroom with a stung look on his face.

Just at that moment, Arthur came in. Lauren waved him over.

'What?' he whispered.

'Maybe we should push back our departure a few days.'

'What's up with him?'

'Nothing's up, everything's down. He seems really bummed.'

'He was in good spirits just last night.'

'That was last night.'

'Hey! My spirits are fine!' Paul shouted from his room. 'And I can hear every word you're saying,' he added as he came through to join them. Arthur and Lauren remained silent for a moment.

'Why don't you come along with us, spend a few days in the South?' Arthur suggested.

'Because I'm writing a novel. I leave in three weeks and I want to have at least a hundred pages for Kyong. And, more importantly, I want her to *like* those pages. I want her to be proud of me.'

'You need to stop living in your books, man, and try living in the real world for a change. You need to go out and meet people – and I don't just mean other writers.'

'I meet plenty of people during book signings.'

'And I'm sure you have very meaningful exchanges with them, spanning "hello", "thank you" and deep thoughts like "goodbye",' Arthur said. 'Do you call them on the phone when you're feeling lonely?'

'No, I have you for that, even if the time difference is sometimes tricky. Please stop worrying about me. If I keep listening to you, I'm going to end up believing I have a problem – and I don't. I like my life, I like my work, I like spending the night diving into my stories, I like the way it feels. You know the feeling, Lauren. You like the way it feels to spend nights in the OR sometimes, don't you?'

'*I* don't like it, though,' Arthur sighed.

'But it's her life, and you don't try to stop her, because you love her just the way she is,' Paul replied. 'We're not so different. Enjoy your romantic getaway, and if my Korean trip cures me of my flying phobia, I'll come and see you in San Francisco in the fall. Now, there's a nice title for a novel: *Autumn in San Francisco*.'

'True. But only if you're the main character.'

Arthur and Lauren packed their suitcases. Paul accompanied them to the station, and when the train pulled away from the platform, in spite of everything he'd told them, he felt the heavy weight of solitude bearing down on his shoulders.

He stood a few moments in the place where he'd said goodbye to his friends. Then, hands in pockets, he turned on his heel.

When he picked up his car from the car park, he found a note stuck to the windscreen.

*If you move to Seoul, I will come and see you in the fall*
*— I promise.*
*Autumn in Seoul could also be a nice title.*
*I'm gonna miss you, man.*
*Arthur*

He read the note twice, then put it in his wallet.

After wondering how to brighten up his morning, he decided to go to the Opera. There was a favour he wanted to ask the director.

Mia was sitting on the bench in Place du Tertre, lost in Paul's words. The caricaturist was watching her. He must have seen her open her bag and take out a tissue, because he left his easel to go and sit next to her.

'Bad day?' he asked.

'No, good book.'

'A real – what do they call it – tear-jerker?'

'Actually, up to now it's been very funny. But the main character just got a letter from his mother after her death. I know it's ridiculous, but it really touched me.'

'There's nothing ridiculous about expressing your feelings. Did you lose your own mother?'

'Oh, no, she's very much alive. But I would love it if she wrote me something like this.'

'Maybe one day she will.'

'That'd be very surprising, given our relationship.'

'Do you have children?'

'No.'

'Then wait till you're a mother yourself. You'll view your childhood very differently, and your mother through completely new eyes.'

'I don't really see how I could.'

'There is no such thing as the perfect parent, just like there is no such thing as the perfect child. I should go, though – there's a tourist hanging around my stand. Oh, that reminds me – what did your friend think of her portrait?'

'I still haven't given it to her. I'm sorry, it slipped my mind. I'll do it tonight.'

'No hurry. It was just sitting in my portfolio.'

And the caricaturist returned to his easel.

Paul sneaked in through the artists' entrance. Stage-hands were busy moving parts of the set. He walked around them, climbed the stairs, and knocked on the director's door.

'I'm sorry. Do we have a meeting?'

'No, but it won't take long. I have a small favour to ask.'

'Another one?'

'Yeah, but this one's really small.'

Paul made his request and the director refused. He had made an exception for him before, but for him alone. Because the Opera was being used as the back-drop for Paul's novel, the director had wanted things to be described as they were rather than as one might imagine them. But the areas prohibited to the public had to remain prohibited.

'I understand,' said Paul, 'but the woman is my assistant.'

'Was she your assistant when you entered my office?'

'Of course. I didn't hire her in the last thirty seconds.'

'You said she was "a friend"!'

'She's my friend and my assistant. The two things aren't mutually exclusive.'

The director stared at the ceiling as he thought.

'No, I'm sorry. I can't allow it. And please don't insist.'

'Then don't blame me if I get anything wrong in my descriptions of your Opera.'

'All you need to do is devote more time to your research. Now I must ask you to leave. This is a busy time for the Opera.'

Paul left the office, but he was determined not to let the matter go. A promise was a promise, and he had defied far more powerful authorities in his lifetime. He stopped at the box office, bought two tickets for that evening's performance, and went off to mull over his plan.

Once outside on the steps, he started dialling Mia's number, then changed his mind and sent her a text instead:

```
Our tour of the Opera will take place tonight.
Bring a sweater and a raincoat, and whatever
you do, don't wear high heels (although I
haven't seen you wearing any up until this
point). You'll understand why when you get
there. I can't say another word – it's a
surprise.
```

8.30pm, on the fifth step.

Paul

P.S. Texts don't count.

Mia's phone vibrated. She read the message and smiled. Then, remembering the promise she'd made to Daisy, her smile quickly faded.

Gaetano Cristoneli was waiting for Paul at a table outside Le Bonaparte.

'You're late!'

'My office isn't just around the corner, like yours. I got stuck in traffic.'

'Really?' his editor said sceptically. 'What was this something urgent you mentioned on the phone? Do you have a problem?'

'Is this the latest thing, everyone thinking I have problems? Are you going to start in on this too?'

'What did you want to tell me?'

'I've decided I am going to the book fair in Seoul.'

'Fantasmic news! Not that you really had a choice.'

'There's always a choice. And I may still change my mind. Speaking of which, I have something personal to ask. If I decided to spend a year or two in Seoul, would you be able to provide me with a small advance? Just enough to get me on my feet over there. I can't ditch my apartment in Paris until I'm sure.'

'Sure about what?'

'Sure I want to stay there.'

'Why would you go and live in Korea? You don't even speak the language.'

'Good point. I hadn't thought about that. I guess I'll have to learn it.'

'You? You're going to learn Korean?'

'Nan niga naie palkarakeul parajmdoultaiga nomou djoa.'

'What is that gibberish?'

'It's Korean for "I like it when you suck my toes."'

'That's it. You've completely lost your mind!'

'I didn't come here for your thoughts on my mental well-being. I came for an advance on my royalties.'

'So, you are serious?'

'You were the one who said that success over there would give my numbers a boost in the US and thus in Europe. My understanding is, if I catch that plane, we make a fortune. Right? So, according to your own logic, a small advance shouldn't pose that much of a problem.'

'That was just in theory . . . Only time will tell whether or not I'm right.'

Cristoneli looked pensive, then finally added, 'Then again, if you were to tell the Korean media that you're moving to their country, the effect would be enormous. If your publisher over there had you on hand, they'd be more inclined to double their efforts at promoting your books.'

'Yadda yadda yadda,' muttered Paul. 'So we have an agreement?'

'On one condition! No matter what happens over there, I remain your primary editor. I don't want to hear anything about a new book contract signed between you and any Korean publisher – am I clear? I've driven your career forwards single-handedly up to now!'

'Granted, you haven't driven it very far.'

'What ingratitude! Do you want this advance or not?'

Paul stopped arguing. He scrawled the figure he hoped to extract from Cristoneli on a paper napkin. His editor rolled his eyes, crossed out the number, and cut it in half.

They shook hands on the deal – as good as a contract in the world of publishing.

'I'll give you the cheque when we're on our way to the airport. That way, I can make sure you actually catch your flight.'

Paul left Cristoneli to pay the bill.

Back at home after the lunch shift, Daisy found Mia lying on the sofa in a dressing gown, with a box of Kleenex at hand and a damp towel over her eyes.

'What's wrong?'

'Retinal migraine,' said Mia. 'Head feels like it's about to explode.'

'Want me to call a doctor?'

'There's no point. I've had one before. It usually lasts about ten hours and then goes away on its own.'

'And when did it start?'

'Mid-afternoon.'

Daisy looked at her watch, and then back at her friend.

'Well, there's no way you're working in this state. Let's forget the restaurant for tonight – you can help me out tomorrow instead.'

'No, no,' Mia protested, 'I'll manage,' whereupon she put her hands to her forehead and let out a small groan.

'Looking like that? You'll scare away the customers! Go and lie down in bed.'

'No, it'll be okay,' said Mia, still lying on the sofa, one arm trailing on the floor. 'I don't want to let you down!'

'Robert will have to make do in the kitchen while I wait tables. We've done it before. Now go to bed – that's an order.'

Picking up the box of Kleenex and holding the towel over her eyes, Mia got to her feet and groped her way towards her room.

She came out again just as soon as Daisy had left the apartment. She put her ear to the front door and listened to the sound of her friend's footsteps fading to silence. Then she ran to the bay window and watched as Daisy disappeared around the corner and out of sight.

She hurried to the bathroom and washed her face with cold water to remove the talcum powder from her cheeks and the eyeliner from under her eyes. If she'd learned anything useful in her profession, it was the art of make-up. Looking for a raincoat in Daisy's wardrobe, she was surprised that she didn't feel guilty at all. In fact, she was in a very good mood, and it had been too long since she'd felt that way. She had to make the most of it.

She decided to wear trainers, wondering, at the same time, why she would need to dress like that for a night at the opera. In England, people tended to overdress rather than underdress for such occasions.

Examining herself in the mirror, she thought she looked a little bit like Audrey Hepburn, which pleased her. She considered adding a pair of sunglasses to her outfit, but decided in the end to keep them in her handbag.

She half-opened the front door, checked that the coast was clear, and then hurried over towards the taxi that had been waiting for her on the opposite side of the street.


Paul was waiting on the fifth step of the Opera.

'You look like Inspector Clouseau,' he said to Mia as she approached him.

'What a gentleman you are! You told me to wear a raincoat and flat shoes.'

Paul looked her over.

'I take it back. You look lovely. Follow me.'

They joined the line of people entering the Opera. After passing through a series of lobbies, Mia stopped to admire the large ceremonial staircase. She insisted they go closer to the statue of Pythia.

'Exquisite!' she exclaimed.

'Yes, amazing,' Paul agreed, 'but we have to hurry now.'

'I feel ridiculous dressed like this, surrounded by so much beauty. I should have worn a dress.'

'No, trust me, you're better off. Come on!'

'I don't understand. I thought you were going to show me around when it was closed to the public. Are we here for a performance?'

'You'll see.'

Reaching the mezzanine, they walked through the orchestra gallery.

'What is tonight's performance?' Mia asked as they approached the entrance to the auditorium.

'No idea. Hello, gentlemen!' he said, walking past two statues.

'Who were you talking to?' Mia whispered.

'Bach and Haydn. I listen to them while I'm writing, so the least I can do is say hi, right?'

'Are you ever going to tell me where we're heading?' Mia said as Paul led them on.

'To our seats.'

The usher showed them to two folding seats. Paul offered the first to Mia and then sat on the one behind her.

The seat was hard and uncomfortable, and they could see only the right-hand side of the stage. It was a far cry from the film premieres Mia was used to attending, where she always had one of the best seats in the house.

*Funny, he doesn't strike me as a cheapskate,* she thought as the curtain lifted.

Ten minutes passed. Mia kept shifting in her seat, trying to find the least uncomfortable position. Paul tapped her on the shoulder.

'Sorry I keep fidgeting, but my bottom hurts in this chair,' she whispered.

Doing his best not to laugh, Paul leaned in close and whispered in her ear: 'Please extend my sincere apologies to your posterior. But now we have to go – follow me.'

He walked, bent double, towards the emergency exit, which was located just in front of them. Mia watched him, dumbfounded.

*Or maybe he really is mad . . .*

'Come on!' hissed Paul, still crouching in front of the door.

Mia obeyed, imitating his peculiar stance.

He softly pushed open the door and led her into a corridor.

'So has your back gone out, or are we supposed to keep walking around like this?'

Paul shushed her, grabbed her hand, and set off down the corridor.

The deeper they went into the labyrinthine building, the more she began to wonder what in the world was going on.

At the end of another passageway, they came to a spiral staircase. Paul suggested Mia go first in case she tripped, while also advising her not to do so.

'Where are we?' Mia breathed, beginning to get swept up in the game.

'We need to get across this walkway. But please be absolutely silent: we're going right over the stage. I'll go first this time.'

Paul crossed himself and, in response to Mia's surprised look, whispered that he suffered from vertigo.

When Paul reached the other side, he turned around and saw her, motionless in the middle of the walkway, staring at the auditorium below. He felt he was getting a glimpse of how she must have looked as a child; even her raincoat suddenly seemed too large. She was no longer the woman he had met on the steps of the Opera, but a little girl suspended in the air, wholly enchanted by the magical sight below.

He waited a few moments, then risked a small cough to catch her attention.

Mia gave a broad smile and walked over to join him.

'That was incredible,' she whispered.

'I know. But trust me, the best is yet to come.'

He took her hand again and led her towards a door that opened on to another staircase.

'Are we going to see the lake?'

'You Brits are very odd. Do you really think they'd put the lake on the top floor?'

Mia looked through the doorway. 'Those steps could have led down!'

'Well, they don't. We're headed up these steps. There is no lake – it's just a reservoir of water in a concrete tank. Otherwise, I'd have brought my snorkel and flippers.'

'In that case, what's the raincoat for?' Mia asked, annoyed.

'I told you: you'll see.'

As they were climbing an old wooden staircase, they heard a thunderous rolling sound. Mia froze with fear.

'Don't worry. It's just the stage machinery,' Paul reassured her.

When they reached the final landing, Paul pushed the panic bar on a metal door and ushered Mia through.

She found herself looking out at a walkway that spanned the rooftop of the Opera, offering an absolutely stunning view of Paris.

She swore out loud, then turned to Paul.

'Go ahead,' he told her. 'It's perfectly safe.'

'Aren't you coming?'

'Yeah, just give me a minute.'

'Why would you come all the way up here if you can't even take a look?'

'So you could. There isn't another view like this anywhere in the world. Keep going – I'll wait for you here. Take a good look. There aren't many people lucky enough to see the City of Light from this vantage point. One winter night, you'll be sitting by the fireside in an old English manor and you'll be able to tell all your little great-grandchildren about the night you saw Paris from the roof of the Opera. You'll be so old that you won't even remember my name, but you'll remember that you had a friend in Paris.'

Mia watched Paul as he clung to the door handle. Then she walked out over the rooftop. From where she stood, she could see the Madeleine church and the Eiffel Tower with its roaming searchlights. Mia looked up at the sky like a child who is convinced she can count every star in the heavens. Then she looked over at the skyscrapers in the Beaugrenelle district. How many people were eating, laughing or crying behind those windows, each looking as tiny as those stars twinkling in the vast firmament above? Turning around, she saw the Sacré-Cœur perched on the hill of Montmartre and spared a thought for Daisy. The whole of Paris lay stretched out before her. She had never seen anything so beautiful in her whole life.

'You can't miss this.'

'There's no way I can make it out there . . .'

She went back to where Paul was standing, took off her scarf, and tied it around his head, covering his eyes. Then, holding his hand, she guided him along the walkway. Paul walked as if he were on a tightrope, but he didn't resist.

'I know it's selfish,' she said, removing the blindfold, 'but how could I tell all my little great-grandchildren about this moment without having actually shared it with my Parisian friend?'

Paul and Mia sat on the ridge pole and admired the view together.

A fine rain began to fall. Mia took off her raincoat and spread it over their shoulders.

'Do you always think of everything?'

'I try. Now . . . can you please take me back?' he asked, softly pulling at her scarf.

Two security guards awaited them at the foot of the stairs. They escorted Paul and Mia to the director's office, where three police officers stood, arms folded.

'I know, I went against what you said,' Paul said to the director. 'But we didn't do any harm.'

'Sorry – do you know this man?' asked Officer Moulard, the highest-ranking police officer in the room.

'Not any more,' said the director. 'You can take him away.'

Officer Moulard nodded to his colleagues, who took out two pairs of handcuffs.

'I really don't think that's necessary,' Paul protested.

'I disagree,' said the director. 'These people strike me as the very definition of unruly.'

As Mia held out her wrists for the policeman, she glanced at her watch. Seeing how late it was, she suddenly felt nervous.

The detective took their statements. Paul acknowledged the charges against them, taking full responsibility himself while playing down the seriousness of their misdemeanour. He solemnly swore they would never do it again if they were allowed to go. Surely they weren't going to be kept overnight at the station?

The detective sighed.

'You are foreign nationals. Until I am able to contact your respective consulates and verify your identities, I couldn't possibly let you go.'

'I have a resident card,' Paul said. 'I left it at home, but I assure you I am a French resident.'

'And I'm supposed to just take you at your word on that?'

'They're going to kill me,' Mia muttered.

'Someone is threatening you, mademoiselle?' the detective asked her.

'No. Just a figure of speech.'

'Please exercise some caution with your vocabulary. This is a police station.'

'Who's going to kill you?' Paul asked, leaning towards Mia.

'What did I just say?' the inspector demanded.

'I heard you! This isn't school! Apparently, this situation has put my friend in an awkward professional position. You could show just a little flexibility.'

'You should have thought of that before breaking and entering into a public building.'

'There was no breaking and entering. All the doors were open, including the one leading to the roof.'

'And you think walking on the roof of the Palais Garnier is not a security breach? Would you find it normal if I did the same thing in your country?'

'If you really wanted to, detective, I wouldn't have any objections at all. I could even recommend a few spots with breath-taking views.'

'I've heard enough,' the policeman sighed. 'Lock these two clowns up. And deal with the comedian first.'

'Wait!' Paul begged. 'If a French citizen came here to testify to my identity, and brought you proof, would you consider letting us leave?'

'If your citizen makes it here within the next hour, I'd consider it. After that, my shift is over and you would have to wait until morning.'

'Could I use your phone?'

The detective handed Paul the phone from his desk.


'You can't be serious.'

'Perfectly serious.'

'At this hour of night?'

'You don't really get to choose what time this kind of thing happens.'

'May I know why?'

'Just listen to me, Cristoneli, because we're running short on time. If you don't go to your office, photocopy all my papers, and then come to the police station in the ninth arrondissement within the next hour, I'll sign my next book over to Mr Park.'

'Who is Mr Park?'

'I have no idea. But there must be someone with a name like that at my Korean publishers!' Paul yelled.

Cristoneli hung up on him.

'Is he coming?' Mia asked in a pleading voice.

'Anything's possible with him,' Paul replied dubiously, laying the phone back in its cradle.

'Well,' said the detective, getting to his feet, 'if this man you were yelling at is stupid enough to help you, you'll be sleeping at home tonight. If not, we have blankets here. France is a civilised country.'

Paul and Mia were escorted to the cells. Out of courtesy, they weren't put in with the two drunks who had been left to sober up.

The door banged shut behind them. Mia sat on the bench and held her head in her hands.

'My business partner will never forgive me.'

'Why? It's not like we ran over an old lady or something. Anyway, what are you so worried about? There's no way she'll find out we're here.'

'She's also my flatmate. When she gets back from the restaurant, she'll see I'm not there. And I won't be there tomorrow morning either.'

'You are allowed to sleep out at your age, aren't you? Seems like a pretty controlling business partner. Unless she's . . .'

'She's what?'

'Nothing, forget it.'

'I pretended to have a migraine so I wouldn't have to work tonight, even though she needed me.'

'Ah. That wasn't a very nice thing to do.'

'Thanks for twisting the knife.'

Paul sat next to her and said nothing.

Finally, he cleared his throat. 'I have an idea, just an idea. Maybe you could neglect to mention the arrest and the police station and the handcuffs and all that to your great-grandchildren . . .'

'Are you kidding me? That would be their favourite part. Imagine Granny spending a night in the nick!'

They heard the sound of a key in the lock. The door to their cell opened and a policeman ordered them out. He led them to the detective's office, where Cristoneli, after handing over a photocopy of Paul's residence permit, signed a cheque to pay his fine.

'Perfect,' said the detective. 'You can take him with you.'

Turning around, Cristoneli noticed Mia and stared accusingly at Paul.

'What is the meaning of this?' he exclaimed angrily, turning back to the inspector. 'I should be able to take them both for that price!'

'Mademoiselle does not have her papers.'

'Mademoiselle is my niece!' Cristoneli said. 'On that, I give you my word.'

'You're Italian and your niece is English? That's quite the international family you've got there!'

'I am a naturalised Frenchman, detective,' Cristoneli replied. 'And yes, my family has been a mix of nationalities for three generations. You can call us immigrants, or the future of the continent, depending on how open-minded you are.'

'Okay, okay, just get the hell out of here, all of you! And you, mademoiselle, I want to see you again tomorrow afternoon, with your passport. Is that understood?'

Mia nodded.

Outside the police station, Mia thanked Cristoneli, who bowed respectfully.

'The pleasure was all mine, mademoiselle. It's strange, but have I met you before? Your face is very familiar.'

133

'I doubt it,' Mia replied, blushing. 'Maybe you know somebody who looks like me?'

'Probably. Although . . . I could have sworn that I—'

'Pathetic!' Paul groaned, cutting him off.

'What's the matter with you?' Cristoneli asked, turning to face him.

'Is this how you try to seduce women, using stale old clichés like that? "Have I met you before?"' he repeated mockingly. 'Pitiful!'

'You are the one who is pitiful, my friend. I was being completely sincere. I do feel quite sure I have seen mademoiselle somewhere before.'

'Look, we're in a rush: mademoiselle's carriage is about to turn into a pumpkin, so let's just skip the pleasantries, shall we?'

'And that is all the thanks I get, I suppose?' Cristoneli grumbled.

'It goes without saying that we're eternally grateful. Goodnight!'

'It also should go without saying that the fine will be deducted from your advance.'


'You two are like a grumpy old married couple,' Mia said, amused, as Cristoneli got back in his sports car.

'Well, he's certainly got the "old" part covered. Come on, let's get a move on. What time does your business partner get back from the restaurant?'

'Usually between eleven thirty and midnight.'

'So, worst-case scenario: twenty minutes. Best case: fifty. Let's do this!'

And he led Mia in a mad dash to his car.

After opening the door and telling her to buckle up, he drove off at top speed.

'Where do you live?'

'Rue Poulbot, in Montmartre.'

The Saab sped through the streets of Paris, veering into bus lanes and zigzagging between taxis, incurring a volley of abuse from a motorcyclist at Place de Clichy and a group of pedestrians at an intersection on Rue Caulaincourt, and swinging on to Rue Joseph-de-Maistre with tyres squealing.

'Don't you think we've had enough brushes with the law tonight? You might want to slow down,' Mia suggested.

'And what if we get there after your business partner does?'

'Good point. Keep going.'

The car accelerated, zipping up Rue Lepic. On Rue Norvins, Mia shrank back in her seat.

'Is the restaurant around here?'

'We just passed it,' she whispered.

At last, they turned on to Rue Poulbot. Mia pointed out her building. Paul slammed on the brakes.

'Hurry up!' he urged her. 'We'll say goodbye another time.'

They exchanged a look, and Mia rushed towards the front door. Paul waited to check that she'd got in, staring at the windows of the building, then smiled as the lights on the top floor came on briefly and then went out again. He was about to drive away when he saw a woman walking up the street and entering the building. He honked his horn three times before setting off again.

Daisy came into the apartment, completely exhausted. The living room was dark. She turned on the lights and collapsed on to the sofa. Her gaze wandered to the coffee table, where she spotted a book. She picked it up and examined the author's photo again.

After getting up, she knocked gently at Mia's door and opened it a crack.

Mia pretended to wake up.

'How are you feeling?'

'Better. I should be fine again tomorrow.'

'I'm so glad to hear that!'

'I hope it wasn't too tough at the restaurant tonight.'

'It was pretty crowded, believe it or not, despite the rain.'

'Did it rain a lot?'

'Incessantly. What about here? Did it rain inside the apartment too?'

'Um, no . . . What do you mean?'

'Nothing. Absolutely nothing.'

Daisy closed the door without another word.

Paul parked his car and went up to his apartment. He sat at his desk and was just about to start a new chapter, in which his mute opera singer ventures out on to the rooftop of the Opera, when the screen of his phone lit up.

```
My great-grandchildren would like

to join me in thanking you for giving

their future great-grandmother such

an unforgettable evening.

            Did you make it back in time???

Two minutes later, and I'd have been

a goner!

            I honked my horn to warn you.
```

I heard it.

Your roommate didn't suspect anything?

I think she may have seen my raincoat

sticking out of the duvet!

You sleep in a raincoat?

Didn't have time to take it off.

I'm really sorry about the police
station ...

We should split that fine.

Absolutely not - you were my guest.

Will you take me to see the Catacombs

next week?

Depends. Would that count or not?

Definitely wouldn't count.

Why not?

Because!

Can't argue with that.

So we're on?

Wouldn't you prefer an exhibition

at the Grand Palais? Not so many

dead people.

What exhibition?

Hang on, I'll check.

Okay.

The Tudors.

Oh no, I've had my fill of the

Tudors.

Musée d'Orsay?

Jardin du Luxembourg?

Sold. You're on.

Are you working?

Trying to.

In that case, I'll let you go. Day after

tomorrow, 3pm?

Done. Outside the entrance, on

Rue Guynemer.

The screen went black, and Paul returned to his novel. His singer was about to start her walk across the rooftop when his phone lit up again.

I'm starving.

Me too.

But I'm trapped in my bedroom.

Take off your raincoat and tiptoe over to the fridge.

Good idea. Okay, I'll really leave you to work now.

Thanks.

Paul put the phone on his desk. He kept checking the black screen, hoping it would light up again. Disappointed, he put it in a drawer, but kept the drawer half-open . . . just in case.

Mia undressed silently, pulled on a dressing gown and half-opened her bedroom door. Daisy was lying on the sofa, reading Paul's novel. Mia went back to bed and spent the next hour listening to her stomach growl.

# 11

He felt guilty at how little he had written in the last few days. And the previous night had only made matters worse. He wanted to revise the first few chapters so Kyong would like them. Even though she had yet to reply to his email, which worried him a lot.

He drew the curtains, plunging the room into darkness, turned on his desk lamp, and sat in front of the computer.


It had been a prolific day: ten pages, five coffees, two litres of water and three packets of crisps in seven hours.

Now he was hungry – starving, in fact – and he decided to stop working and go to the local café. It wasn't the best place to eat in the arrondissement, but at least he wouldn't have to dine alone. Whenever he sat at the counter, the café owner always stopped to chat. He could be relied on for all the neighbourhood gossip – who had died or got divorced, who'd moved away, which shop had opened or closed, what the weather was supposed to be like, and so on – as well as more serious news, like political scandals. All the murmurings of the city and the wider world reached Paul through the voice of Moustache, as he called him.

Back in his apartment, Paul opened the curtains to watch the evening fall. He checked his email: nothing from Kyong, but he did find one new message.

Dear Paul,

I hope all is well. Our time in the South was magical. Makes me wonder again why I spent four years in Paris when I could have gone to Provence instead. The people are so kind, the countryside so beautiful, and there are loads of street markets and endless sunshine... maybe you should consider it? Sometimes happiness can be found closer to home than we think.

We sure do miss you, man. We're spending a few days in Italy now, having just arrived. Portofino is one of the prettiest towns I've ever been to. In fact, all of Liguria is just gorgeous.

We've decided to go to Rome next, and to fly directly back to San Francisco from there.

I'll call you when we're home. In the meantime, let me know what's happening on your end.

Lauren sends her love...

Arthur

The email had been sent only a few minutes earlier. Assuming that Arthur was still online, he replied immediately:

Hey, old buddy,

I'm thrilled that your vacation is going so well. You should stay a bit longer... or should I say, you kind of have to! In a funny turn of events, I came across a short-term apartment rental website the other day. I'd heard great things about it and wanted to give it a whirl. You wouldn't believe how popular your apartment has been!

Don't worry, I've taken care of every-thing. Your tenants, whom I hand-picked personally - a nice couple with their *four* mild-mannered children - will stay there until the end of the month. The rent will be paid directly to the agency: you'll just have to show up to pick up your check. So hopefully that should help pay for your Italian adventures.

And now, old buddy, we're even!

Other than that, no real news in my life, except that I'm doing lots of writing and the Seoul trip looms.

```
Give Lauren my love...
```

```
Paul
```

Almost immediately, the following words appeared on the screen:

```
Please tell me you're kidding!
```

Savouring his vengeance, Paul thought about letting Arthur stew a bit longer. But he knew his friend would not stop pestering him until he had the truth, so he decided to reply before getting back to work.

```
Arthur,
```

```
Were it not for my fear that my godson
would end up spending more time with
his godmother than he should, I would
have done it. Fortunately for you, I'm
just too nice for that kind of thing.
I had you going, though, didn't I?
```

```
Don't worry, you'll still get what's
really coming to you.
```

```
Paul
```

And with that, he devoted his night to the creation of a new chapter.

'Tell me, just how did you meet him?'

'Meet who?'

'Him,' Daisy said, sliding the book down the counter of the bar.

'You wouldn't believe me if I told you.'

'And why not? I believed you when you turned up on my doorstep like a lost puppy, didn't I? When you asked me to let you stay, and when you cried all night in my arms over what David had done to you, and when you said it was all his fault. Right?'

'I met him through your dating site,' Mia admitted, lowering her eyes.

'I knew I'd seen his face somewhere!' Daisy railed. 'You've really got a lot of nerve, you know that?'

'It's not what you think, I swear.'

'Oh, now she's swearing! Spare me, please.'

Daisy walked past Mia and went to set the tables.

'Leave it,' said Mia, following her. 'I can take care of that. You've got enough work to do in the kitchen.'

'I'll do whatever I want in my own restaurant, thank you very much.'

'Am I fired?'

'Are you in love with him?'

'No, of course not!' Mia protested vehemently. 'He's just a friend.'

'What kind of friend?'

'Someone I can talk to, with no ambiguity at all.'

'On his end or on yours?'

'None at all, no grey zone. We agreed to that during our first dinner.'

'Ah, so you've dined together. When? The night you slept in your raincoat due to your debilitating retinal migraine?'

'No. We went to the Opera that night.'

'This just gets better and better!'

'Our dinner together was the night I told you I went to the cinema.'

'The Swede. I should have known. So you've been lying to me all this time?'

'You're the one who said he was Swedish.'

'What about his phone?'

'Oh, that was true. He really did forget it.'

'And your migraine?'

'It was real, it just didn't last that long . . .'

'The truth comes out!'

'He's just a friend, Daisy. I could even introduce you to him. I'm sure the two of you would hit it off.'

'I can't believe this.'

'He works nights, like you do. He's a bit gauche, but he's very funny, just like you. He's American, he lives in Paris, and he's single – another thing you have in common.'

'And you don't fancy him yourself?'

'Well . . . I guess I should say *nearly* single.'

'No way! Forget it. I've had it up to here with guys who are "nearly single". Why don't you start setting these tables instead of setting me up?'

Mia didn't wait to be asked twice. She grabbed a pile of plates and began placing them on tables. Daisy went into the kitchen and started peeling vegetables.

'You should at least meet him,' said Mia.

'No!'

'Why not?'

'Because first of all, it never works like that. Second, because he's only "nearly single". And most importantly, because you like him more than you're willing to admit.'

Mia turned towards Daisy, hands on her hips. 'I think I'd know how I feel about someone.'

'Is that so? Since when? You cross the city to give him his phone back, you lie like a teenager, you go with him to the Opera and—'

'No, not *to* the Opera – *on* the Opera!'

'What?'

145

'We didn't go to see a performance, he took me up on the roof – to see Paris at night.'

'Either you really are completely naive or you're lying to yourself. Either way, leave me out of it.'

Mia frowned.

'Get to work!' Daisy yelled. 'The customers will be here any minute.'

At 2 a.m., Paul was still struggling with the last line of a paragraph when he decided to call it a night. He checked his email again and, his pulse quickening, finally found a reply from Kyong, which he printed out. He liked to read her words on paper, as it somehow made her seem less virtual. He picked up the hard copy from his printer tray and waited until he was in bed before starting to read.

Soon afterwards, he turned off the light and hugged his pillow to him.

At 3 a.m., Mia was awoken by the vibrations of her phone. She grabbed it from the bedside table. The name *David* appeared on the screen.

Her heart began pounding wildly. She put the phone back on the table, lay down again, and hugged her pillow.

# 12

Mia turned up late at the gates of the Jardin du Luxembourg. She looked around for Paul, then sent him a text.

Where are you?

On a bench.

Which bench?

I'm wearing a yellow raincoat,
so you can spot me easily.

Seriously?

No!

Seeing her approach, Paul stood up and waved.

'Oh, so you're the one wearing a mac today,' she said, 'even though it's not raining.'

'That remains to be seen,' he replied, setting off along the path, his hands behind his back.

Mia followed.

'Did you have another bout of writer's block last night?'

'Nope. I even managed to finish a chapter. I'll start another one tonight.'

'Look at that. Do you fancy a game?' Mia asked, pointing to a group of men playing boules.

'Do you know how to play?'

'It doesn't seem all that complicated.'

'Well, it is. Like everything in life, I suppose . . .'

'Easy, now. Did you wake up on the wrong side of the bed?'

'How about . . . if I win, you have to make me dinner!'

'And if I win?'

'It would be dishonest of me to let you think you have a chance of winning. I've become seriously good at this stupid little game.'

'I'll try my luck anyway,' Mia replied, heading for the boules pitch.

She asked two players who were chatting if she could borrow their set of boules. They looked wary, so she leaned close to the older of the two and whispered something in his ear. The man smiled and gestured at the pitch, where the boules and the jack lay unused.

'Shall we?' she said to Paul.

Paul began the first round by throwing the jack. He waited for the little wooden ball to stop rolling, then bent forwards, arm pulled back, and threw his boule. It arced through the air before rolling along the ground and coming to rest next to the jack.

'Difficult to get any closer than that.' He whistled. 'Your turn.'

Mia got into position, watched by the two old men, who looked amused. Her boule did not go as high as Paul's and came to a halt an inch or two behind his.

'Not bad. Promising, but not a game-changer,' said Paul.

For his second throw, he twisted his wrist slightly. The boule slowly circled around the others before kissing the jack.

'Perfect!' Paul laughed triumphantly.

Mia got back into position, narrowed her eyes, and took aim.

Paul's two boules were knocked away from the jack, while Mia's appeared glued to its sides.

'*Putain!*' one of the old men shouted, while the other burst out laughing.

'Now *that* was perfect,' Mia declared.

Paul stared at her, speechless, then walked away.

Mia waved at the two men, who applauded. Then she ran after Paul.

'Come on. Don't be a sore loser!' she said, catching up with him.

'And you let me think that was the first time you've played . . .'

'I spent every summer of my childhood in Provence, as you might recall. Next time, try listening to women when they talk to you.'

'I was listening,' Paul protested. 'But my head was kind of spinning that night. Or must I do the unspeakable and remind you about the circumstances of our first encounter?'

'What's really the matter, Paul?'

He took out a sheet of paper and handed it to her.

'I got this last night,' he mumbled.

Mia stood still and began reading.

Dear Paul,

I'm very glad you are coming to Seoul, even if we won't have as much time to enjoy each other's company as I would have liked. I have professional obligations at the Book Fair from which I cannot escape. I think you will be pleasantly surprised by the welcome you'll receive from your readers, and I suspect you will be even busier than I am at the fair. You are famous here, and people are very excited about your arrival. Be prepared to devote a lot of your time and energy to your admirers for the duration of the visit. For my part, I will try to free myself as much

as I can so that I can show you around
my city... if your editor allows you
enough time.

I would have loved for you to stay with
me, but I'm afraid that is impossible.
My family lives in the same apartment
building, and my father is very strict.
For a man to spend the night in his
daughter's apartment would be against
all decorum, and it is something he
would never allow. I can imagine your
reaction to this news, and I share your
disappointment, but you must understand that morals and customs are not
the same here as they are in Paris.

I look forward to seeing you soon.

Have a good trip.

Your favourite translator,

Kyong

'Well, it is a little cold,' Mia admitted, handing back the sheet of
paper.
'Just a little.'
'Don't overreact. You have to be able to read between the lines. She
seems to be a very reserved person.'
'Believe me, she's not so reserved when she comes to Paris!'
'But Seoul is her home. It's different.'

'Listen, you're a woman. Work your magic and read between the lines for me. Tell me what I'm missing. Does she love me or not?'

'I'm sure she does.'

'Then why doesn't she write it? Is it really such a hard thing to admit?'

'For someone so reserved . . . it might be.'

'When you're in love with a man, don't you tell him?'

'Not necessarily.'

'What exactly would be stopping you?'

'Fear,' Mia replied.

'Fear of what?'

'Of scaring him off.'

'Oh, God, it's all so complicated! So what are you supposed to do, what should you say or not say when you're in love with somebody?'

'Maybe it's best to hold off, to wait awhile.'

'Wait for what? Until it's too late?'

'Until it's . . . not too early.'

'And just how do I figure that out? How do I know the time is right?'

'When you no longer feel any doubt, I suppose.'

'Has that ever happened to you? Being free of doubt?'

'Yes, on occasion.'

'And that's when you told him that you loved him?'

'Yes.'

'And he said that he loved you?'

'Yes.'

Mia's face darkened, and Paul noticed.

'I'm sorry! What a jackass. You're fresh out of a relationship, and here I am prying open old wounds. That was a selfish thing to do.'

'Not really. It was quite touching, actually. If more men would find the courage to show their sensitive side, things could be so different.'

'You think I should reply to her?'

'I think you're going to see her soon, and when she's with you, she'll fall under your spell once more.'

'If I'm being ridiculous, you can tell me.'

'Not at all. You're being sincere. Whatever you do, don't change that.'

Paul spotted a little refreshment stand just ahead of them.

'Hey. How would you like a waffle with Nutella?'

'Sure, why not,' Mia said with a sigh.

He led her over to the stand. He bought two waffles and handed the first one to Mia.

'If he came back hat in hand, begging your forgiveness, would you be willing to give him a second chance?' he asked with his mouth full of waffle.

'I really don't know.'

'So he hasn't called at all since—'

'No,' Mia cut in.

'Okay. What next? There's a pond over there where kids play with sail-boats, but that might be awkward without a kid. We have donkey rides over there . . . any of that sound appealing?'

'Not really, to be honest.'

'You know, I think I've seen enough donkeys as it is. Over there, we have some tennis-courts, but we're not playing tennis. And . . . that's pretty much all we got. Let's go – enough of this park and all these happy, smooching couples.'

Mia followed Paul out into Rue de Vaugirard. Together they walked down Rue Bonaparte, all the way down to the flea market at Place Saint-Sulpice.

They strolled up and down the aisles before stopping at one of the stalls.

'That's pretty,' Mia said, looking at an old watch.

'Yeah, but I'm too superstitious to wear anything that once belonged to somebody else. Unless I know that the wearer was a happy person.

'Don't laugh, but I actually believe objects have a kind of memory. They can give off good or bad vibrations.'

'You're going to have to elaborate.'

'A few years ago, I bought a glass paperweight at a market like this. The vendor told me it was nineteenth-century. I didn't believe him for a minute, but there was a picture of a woman's face engraved inside, and I thought she was pretty. As soon as I brought that thing home, my life turned to absolute shit.'

'Define "absolute shit".'

'You know something? I kind of like it when you swear.'

'What are you on about now?'

'I don't know. Maybe it's the accent. But it's kind of sexy. And now I've lost my train of thought.'

'Absolute shit.'

'You did it again! You should swear more often. It really suits you. Anyway, it started with a leak in my apartment. The next day, my computer breaks. The day after that, my car gets impounded. That weekend, I'm bedridden with the flu. Then on Monday, my downstairs neighbour has a heart attack, and then I put a mug on my desk near the paperweight and knock the thing over. A couple of days later, the handle on the mug breaks off and I nearly scald my thighs. That was when I began to suspect it had evil powers. You know. Cursed. Next thing I know: I'm *totally* blocked. Blank white pages, nothing but white in all directions, think Mount Everest, you get the idea. And then I trip on the edge of my rug, fall flat on my face, and break my nose. It's a sad sight, blood pouring out everywhere while I scream my head off in my apartment. Luckily, one of my writer friends is psychic. Every other week, I eat dinner with a bunch of writers in a bistro, and we tell each other about our lives. Anyway, this guy sees me with my nose all bandaged up, asks what happened. I tell him all the things that went wrong since I bought the paperweight. He closes his eyes . . . and asks me . . . if there was *a face engraved in the glass.*'

'Whoa! And you hadn't even told him?'

'Maybe I did. I can't remember. Anyway, he tells me to get rid of the cursed thing asap, but warns me not to break it at all, or else the evil spirits could escape.'

'So, what – did you throw it in the bin?' Mia asked, biting her lip.

'Better. I wasn't messing around. I wrapped it in a big scarf, tied it up nice and tight, hopped in my car, drove to the Alma bridge, and . . . adios, paperweight! Straight into the Seine.'

Mia couldn't contain herself any longer. She burst out laughing.

'You're too much!' she said, her eyes wet with tears of laughter. 'Just adorable.'

Paul stared at her, dumb-struck, and started walking again.

'You really get a kick out of teasing me, don't you?'

'Not at all, I swear. And so your problems stopped right after you drowned the paperweight?'

'Yep. Pretty incredible, huh? Everything went back to normal.'

Mia laughed even more, and hung on to Paul's arm as he quickened his pace.

They passed a bookshop specialising in antique manuscripts. In the window were a letter written by Victor Hugo and a Rimbaud poem scribbled on a piece of paper torn from a notepad.

Mia peered in at them, fascinated. 'A poem or a nice letter couldn't be an evil talisman, could it?'

'No, I'd say you're in the clear.'

She opened the door of the shop.

'It's really a beautiful thing,' she said, 'to hold a letter by an illustrious writer in your hands. It's a bit like entering a private world, becoming a confidante. A century from now, maybe people will marvel over the letters *you* wrote to your translator. She'll have become your wife, and those letters will mark the beginning of a precious and powerful correspondence.'

'There's no way I'll ever be considered an illustrious writer, Mia.'

'I must say I disagree.'

'Well, it's not like you've read any of my novels.'

'I've read two so far, for your information. The letters from the mother in the first one brought me to tears.'

'There you go, messing with me again.'

'I am not! Cross my heart. I would do a full re-enactment, but bawling in here seems a bit inappropriate.'

'Wow. I'm sorry I made you cry.'

'No, you're not. That's the first time I've seen you smile all day.'

'I guess in a way it does make me happy . . . not because you cried, but . . . okay, fine, yes, because you cried. To celebrate, let me take you to Ladurée for some pastries. It's not far and their macarons are absolutely life-changing. But there I go again, trying to tell a chef what's what about food.'

'Sounds good, but I will need to head back to the restaurant right after. My cooking won't be quite so delightful if I'm not there to supervise it.'

They sat at a table in the corner and ordered a hot chocolate for Mia and a coffee for Paul, along with an assortment of macarons. The waitress kept staring at them as she prepared their drinks. They could see her whispering to a co-worker, the two of them stealing peeks in Paul and Mia's direction.

*Shit, she's recognised me. Where are the toilets? No, I can't go to the loo – she might talk to him while I'm gone. If it gets out that I was seen here with a man, Creston will kill me! My only option is to convince her that she has mistaken me for someone else.*

The waitress came back a few minutes later and, putting the cups down, asked in a shy voice:

'Excuse me, but I couldn't help but notice. Aren't you—'

'Nope, I'm not who you think,' Paul replied sternly. 'Wrong guy, sorry!'

Deeply embarrassed, the young woman apologised and walked away.

Mia, whose face had gone bright red, put on her sunglasses and turned to Paul.

'I'm sorry,' he said to her. 'That does happen to me occasionally.'

'I understand,' said Mia, whose heart was still pounding. 'So it's not only in Seoul that you're famous?'

'Just this specific neighbourhood, but that's it. Believe me, I could spend two hours in the book section of a Fnac without any of the staff recognising me. Which is a good thing, of course. But she must have been one of my readers – I shouldn't have treated her like that.'

*Your ego just saved me!* 'Don't worry about it. Next time you come here, bring a signed copy of one of your books. I'm sure she'd love that.'

'Now that is an excellent idea.'

'So, tell me. What's happening with your opera singer?'

'The critic follows her home. He approaches her, but without revealing his suspicions. He introduces himself as a writer and says she looks like a character from one of his novels. Maybe, just maybe . . . he's starting to feel something for her.'

'And what about her?'

'I'm not quite sure yet, it's too early to tell. What she doesn't admit is that she noticed him a long time ago. She's scared, but at the same time she feels less lonely.'

'So what does she do?'

'She runs, I think. Takes off to keep her secret under wraps. She can't be sincere with him because she's lying all the while about who she really is. I'm thinking about introducing her old impresario to up the stakes. What do you think?'

'I don't know. I'd have to read it before I could give an opinion.'

'Would you be interested in reading the first few chapters?'

'I'd love to, if that's what you want.'

'I've never let anyone read one of my books before it's finished, apart from Kyong. But your opinion has come to mean a lot to me.'

'Right! Well, whenever you feel ready, I'd be honoured to be your first reader. And I promise to be honest with you.'

'And while we're on the subject, I'd love to come have dinner at your restaurant.'

'Oh . . . that's not such a great idea. Chefs are never at their best during a shift. Too much pressure, too much sweat . . . Don't take it the wrong way, but I'd really prefer if you didn't.'

'No, no, I understand,' said Paul.


They said goodbye outside the métro station at Saint-Germain-des-Prés. Paul walked past his editor's office and thought he caught a glimpse of him through the window. He continued on his way and arrived back at home.

He spent the evening working, trying to imagine what would happen to his tragic opera singer. The more he wrote, the more his character took on Mia's facial expressions, her way of walking, of answering a question with another question, her fragile smile when she was being thoughtful, her bursts of laughter, her absent gaze, her discreet elegance. The sun was rising when he finally made it to bed.


Later that day, Paul was awoken by a call from his editor. Cristoneli was expecting him at his office. On the way, he stopped to buy a croissant and ate it behind the wheel, arriving only half an hour late.

Cristoneli welcomed him with open arms and Paul began to suspect he was up to something.

'I have two pieces of news for you. Both good!' the editor exclaimed. 'Amazifying news!'

'Start with the bad news.'

Cristoneli frowned at him, baffled.

'I received a message from the Koreans: they want you to be a guest on the evening news, which will be followed by their flagship literature show.'

'And the good news?'

'What do you mean? That was the good news!'

'Any time I have to do a book signing with more than twenty people, I get so nervous I practically faint. How in the world do you expect me to appear on television? Unless you *want* me to fall flat on my face on live TV.'

'There'll only be the two of you writers there. No need to be nervous.'

'Two of us?'

'Murakami is the headliner. Do you realise how lucky you are?'

'On TV and side by side with Murakami to boot? Maybe before I faint I'll manage to throw up on the presenter's shoes. That'll give the viewers something to remember.'

'It's a great idea! You would probably sell many books the next day.'

'Are you listening to me? There's no way I can appear on television. I would suffocate. I'm suffocating right now just thinking about it! I would die in front of millions of viewers. In Korea. You'd be an accessory to murder.'

'Oh, give me a break! Just have a Cognac before you go on camera and everything will be fine.'

'Even better – drunk on live television! Amazifying idea.'

'Smoke something, then. Isn't it legal in your country now?'

'The only time in my life I ever "smoked something", I spent two days in bed staring at cows grazing on the ceiling.'

'Listen, my dear Paul, just pull yourself together and everything will go perfectly. I assure you.'

'I hope you're right. So what's your other bit of news?'

'Because your press schedule is getting fuller and fuller, we've had to advance the date of your departure.'

At those words Paul simply turned and left. Left without saying goodbye. On his way out, he picked up a copy of his latest novel from a coffee table in the lobby.

He walked down Rue Bonaparte, his mind spinning at the change of dates, and stopped in front of the antique bookshop. He went inside and emerged fifteen minutes later having negotiated the purchase of a little handwritten note by none other than Jane Austen, payable over three months.

Continuing on his way, he came to a halt at the patisserie, spotted the waitress, and approached her, asking her name.

'Isabelle,' she replied, looking a little bemused.

Paul opened the copy of his novel and wrote on the first page:

*To Isabelle, my faithful reader. Please accept my thanks*
*and my apologies for yesterday.*
*Best regards,*
*Paul Barton*

He handed her the book, and she read his inscription with a blank look on her face, clearly missing the significance.

But, being a polite young woman, she thanked him, then left the book on the counter and went back to work.

He felt like calling Arthur, but he didn't know if his friend was still in Rome or if he and Lauren had already caught the flight back to California.

On Rue Jacob, he thought about how much he would like to find a shop where he could purchase a sibling or a care-taker, or at least rent one for a few hours. He could already imagine himself alone in his apartment, succumbing to a fierce panic attack. He picked up his car, which he had left in front of the Hotel Bel Ami, gave a hollow laugh as he noticed the name, and drove off towards Montmartre.

*'Maybe my luck is finally turning around,'* he muttered to himself as he found a parking space on Rue Norvins.

He got out of the car and walked up the street.

*She told me I couldn't eat at her restaurant, but she didn't say I couldn't stop by. Would that be thoughtful or thoughtless? Let's say it does disturb her, it's not like I'll stay long. I'll just give her this little gift, along with the first chapters of my novel, and then go. No, not the novel with the gift – she might think it's a bribe to get her to read it. I'll go in, give her the letter, and walk straight out. That'll be fine. In fact, it'll be perfect.*

Paul retraced his steps, left the manuscript in the boot of the Saab, and returned with just the pretty little envelope, tied with a ribbon, containing Jane Austen's note.

A few moments later, he walked past La Clamada, glanced through the window, and stopped dead.

Mia, wearing a large violet apron, was setting tables.

The woman who had approached Mia's apartment the night of their misadventure stood in the kitchen at the back of the dining room. She appeared to be giving Mia orders.

Paul watched for a second and then hurried away, hiding his face behind his hand. Once he was past the restaurant, he began walking even faster, not stopping until he reached Place du Tertre.

*Why would she lie? Why should it even matter if she's the owner of the restaurant, or just a waitress? And they talk about men having fragile egos! Did she think I wouldn't want to be friends with a waitress? What kind of person does she think I am? 'Irresistible cuisine', my ass! Then again, it's not that big a deal, when you think about it. I've pretended to be other people before, under different circumstances. The way I see it, I could walk in there and call her bluff right now – which would be satisfying, but mean. Or I could say nothing at all, I could just dangle the carrot until she admits it herself. Maybe that's the best move.*

He sat on a bench, took out his phone, and sent a text to Mia.

Everything OK?

Mia felt her phone vibrate in the pocket of her apron. Last night, David had sent her three messages, begging her to call him back. She had held firm this long; she wasn't going to crack now. She straightened the napkins while squinting into the kangaroo pouch of her apron.

'Just making sure your belly button's still there?' Daisy asked.

'No!'

'Was it David again?'

'Probably.'

'Look, either turn off your phone or read his message before you start dropping plates.'

Mia took out her phone to read the message, and smiled as she typed her reply.

I'm fine. How about you?

Do you have a minute?

I'm in the kitchen.

It won't take long.

Fine. But if I call you, it doesn't count!
Because you asked me to.

Don't call. I'm on a bench at Place du Tertre.

No raincoat this time.

Are you OK?

Yeah. Can you come?

Give me five minutes.

Daisy, ladle in hand, was watching Mia.

'I'll be right back,' Mia said suddenly. 'I need to run out to the shop. Do you need anything?'

'Apart from a waitress, you mean?'

'The tables are all set and there are no customers,' Mia replied, taking off her apron. 'I'll be back in fifteen minutes.'

She looked at herself in the mirror above the bar, patted her hair into place, and grabbed her handbag and sunglasses.

'Pick up some Krisprolls,' said Daisy.

Mia winced. 'Um, I wasn't going to go to the supermarket. Sorry!'


She walked quickly, passing the caricaturist without saying hello, and finally located the bench where Paul sat waiting.

'What are you doing here?' she asked, sitting down next to him.

'I came to bring you the first chapters of my novel, but, like an idiot, I left them at home. It seemed a waste to leave without at least seeing you, though.'

'That's nice of you.'

'You look tired. Do you have a lot on your plate? No pun intended.'

'I didn't sleep much last night. I had a nightmare.'

'A nightmare is merely a dream that has outstayed its welcome . . .'

Mia stared at him in silence.

'Why are you staring at me like that?' Paul asked.

*Because I want to kiss you right now, the way you just said that . . .*

'No reason.'

'"An angel passed." That's what the French say about a comfortable silence.'

'Since you forgot to bring me the chapters to read, maybe you could at least tell me what's going on with your opera singer.'

'She's fine.' Paul rubbed his chin. 'Well, actually she's not. She has a problem.'

'A serious problem?'

'She wants to become friends with the critic. And he has proven to be very attentive towards her.'

'So what's stopping her?'

'Maybe the fact that she hasn't told him the truth about herself yet. Maybe she doesn't want to admit that she's just an usher.'

'Why would that matter?'

'That's exactly what I'm wondering.'

'That kind of prejudiced attitude is outdated.'

'One would think . . . But not for everybody . . .'

'Well, if anyone still thinks like that, they shouldn't. It's unfair.'

'I couldn't agree with you more.'

'You'll have to give her a different problem.'

'Meanwhile, the critic no longer has any doubt as to her real identity.'

'But she doesn't know that.'

'True, but how can she ever really be sincere with him, when everything she says is a lie?'

Mia looked into Paul's eyes and slid her sunglasses down to the tip of her nose.

'Where were you coming from when you called me?'

'Saint-Germain. Why?'

'So you took my advice and gave a copy of your book to that waitress.'

'Funny you should mention that. I did, yeah.'

Mia felt her heart start to race. 'And . . . what did she say?'

'I barely even got a thank you. She must still be bitter about it.'

'And that was it?'

'Yeah, she had lots of customers. She went back to work and I went on my way.'

Relieved, Mia pushed her glasses back up.

'I can't stay long,' she said. 'Is there anything special you wanted to talk about? You look a little run-down.'

'I went to Saint-Germain to meet with my editor. They've changed my departure for Korea to an earlier date.'

'That's great news! You'll see your girlfriend even sooner.'

'The bad news is the reason for the earlier timing. I have to appear on live television.'

'But that's wonderful!'

'Wonderful for someone else, maybe. But I feel like I've been having a heart attack ever since he told me. What the hell am I going to say? Live TV is terrifying!'

'When you're in front of a camera, it's not the words that count but the way they sound. It hardly matters what you say, as long as you say it with a smile. And if you're nervous, viewers might just find that charming.'

'What do you know about being in front of a camera? Like you've ever been on TV!'

'Right, of course I haven't,' Mia replied with a little cough. 'And if it ever happened to me, I'm sure I'd be just as scared as you. But I was speaking as a viewer.'

'Here,' Paul said, taking the ribbon-tied envelope from his pocket. 'This is for you.'

'What is it?'

'Open it up, you'll see. Careful, though – it's fragile.'

Mia drew out the little note from the envelope and read it.

'"Three pounds of carrots, one pound of flour, a packet of sugar, a dozen eggs, a pint of milk . . ."' Mia read out loud. 'It's very lovely . . . I guess . . . Does this mean I'm supposed to get your groceries for you?'

'Check out the signature at the bottom,' Paul said with a sigh.

'Jane Austen!' Mia exclaimed.

'Jane herself. I know it's not her most elegant prose, but you wanted something personal. Even illustrious writers have to eat, you know.'

Without thinking, Mia kissed Paul on the cheek.

'This is so sweet of you. I don't know what to say.'

'You don't have to say anything.'

Mia held the little note in her hands, caressing the ink with her fingertips.

'Who knows,' Paul said, 'maybe this note will inspire you to come up with a new recipe. I thought you might want to frame it and hang it in your kitchen. That way, Jane Austen would be with you while you cook.'

'No one has ever given me anything like this before.'

'Come on. It's only a little shopping list.'

'Written and signed by one of the greatest English writers of all time, thank you very much.'

'So you really like it?'

'*Like* doesn't cover it. I'll never let it go!'

'I'm glad. You'd better go — I wouldn't want the plat du jour to be overcooked because of me.'

'Thank you for a wonderful surprise.'

'But we're in agreement this visit of ours was totally impromptu? So it doesn't count.'

'Exactly, it doesn't count.'

Mia stood up and kissed Paul's cheek again before leaving.

The caricaturist had watched the whole scene unfold.

He and Paul both watched her walk down the street.

When she arrived outside La Clamada, her phone buzzed again.

Is your restaurant closed on Sundays?

Yes.

You know what I'd love?

What?

To taste your cooking.

Mia bit her lip.

Why don't we eat at your place?

No strings attached, of course.

Mia looked at Daisy through the window.

> My flat-mate will be there.
> Even better. The three of us!

She opened the door of the restaurant.

> All right, see you Sunday. You know
> the address. We're on the top floor.
> See you Sunday!

> Thank you. Signed, Mia Austen ☺

'Did you find what you were looking for?' Daisy asked, coming out of the kitchen.

'We need to talk.'

'Yes! Finally.'


Daisy categorically refused to take part in Mia's little scheme.

'Don't you dare leave me in the lurch. I can't possibly have him over here, just the two of us!'

'And why is that?'

'Because it might push us straight into one of those grey areas – into the danger-zone!'

'You ask me, you're already in the danger-zone.'

'No, we're not. He hasn't said or done anything ambiguous.'

'I wasn't talking about him. I meant you.'

'This is the beginning of a friendship, and that's all. I'm not over David yet.'

'You don't need to tell me that. I can see the look on your face whenever your phone starts vibrating. Still, you have to realise you're playing a dangerous game.'

'I'm not playing any games at all, I'm living my life. He's funny, and he's not trying to get me into bed. He has a long-distance girlfriend. We're just fighting off the loneliness.'

'Well, tomorrow, you continue your fight without me.'

'I don't even know how to make a proper omelette!'

'Just break some eggs and beat them with a bit of cream.'

'There's no need to be mean. I'm asking you for a favour, that's all.'

'I'm not being mean. I just refuse to take part in this charade.'

'Why do you always assume the worst?'

'I can't believe what you're saying! You are planning on telling your friend the truth at some point, aren't you? Have you immersed yourself so deeply in your role as a waitress that you've forgotten who you really are? What will you do when your film comes out – when you have to promote it with your husband?'

'Paul's leaving for Korea soon. Probably for good. When the time comes, I'll write to him and confess the truth. By then, he'll be back with his translator and he'll be happy.'

'Life isn't a movie script, Mia.'

'Fine, then I guess I'll have to cancel.'

'You're not going to cancel anything – that would be rude. No, I imagine you'll play your role to the end, no matter the consequences.'

'Why are you torturing me?'

'Because!' Daisy yelled before going out to meet some customers who had just entered the restaurant.

167

# 13

Mia had just thrown her third omelette in the rubbish. The first had burned, the second was too bland, and the third resembled a sorry attempt at scrambled eggs. How did the French do it?

At least the table looked good. It was set for three – Mia preferred pretending Daisy had stood them up at the last minute rather than having to explain her absence – with a bouquet of flowers in the centre, along with a basket of pastries. So at least there would be *something* edible. Her phone buzzed. She washed the egg-yolk from her hands and forearms, opened the refrigerator for the tenth time, and prayed that it was Paul telling her he couldn't make it.

`I'm downstairs.`

`Come on up!`

She cast a last look around the room and ran over to open a window. The Bakelite handle of a saucepan she was using to warm some premade apple compote had burned slightly and was giving off an acrid stench.

The doorbell rang.

Paul came in, holding a small parcel.

'You shouldn't have. What is it?' Mia asked.

'A scented candle.'

'Lovely. I'll get a lighter,' she said, thinking venomously of Daisy.

'Sounds good. *Wish I'd brought six more – smells like she's cooking tyres in here!*

'Did you say something?'

'No, I was just thinking how nice your place is. And what a wonderful view.' *She seems nervous. I shouldn't have invited myself. I should ask if she wants to head to a restaurant instead. Maybe we could sit outside, with the weather so nice and all. What am I saying? She's probably been slaving away cooking all morning – that would make it even worse.*

'Let's start with some croissants.' *Yes, excellent idea – I'll stuff him full of croissants and* pains au chocolat *until he explodes, and then I'll go round with the Hoover.*

'You know what, I'm sorry. It's your only day off all week, and I force you to cook and wait on me hand and foot. It was a selfish move, and I feel terrible about imposing. What would you say to a relaxed meal outside on a sunny terrace?'

'If that's what you'd prefer . . .' *Turns out there is a God! I'm sorry, Lord, for all the times I've doubted you. Tomorrow, I promise, I'll go to church and light a candle.*

'I know you've probably already gone to a lot of trouble, though, and I don't want to offend you. In fact, the only reason I suggested going out to eat was to avoid being impolite.'

*Ten candles! Twenty, if that's what it takes!*

'It's your call, whatever you prefer,' Paul continued.

'The weather certainly is lovely today. I should have put the table on the balcony . . .' *What is wrong with you? Why would you say something like that?*

'You want me to set up the table outside?'

'Just, um, which café did you have in mind?' Mia asked feverishly.

'Any. I'm starving.'

*Grab your bag before he changes his mind. Tell him it's a brilliant idea and run down the stairs now!*

Just then, the apartment door opened. Mia and Paul turned to see Daisy enter, carrying two large shopping bags.

Marc Levy

'You could have at least helped me carry them,' she said, placing the bags on the island.

She took out three large plates covered in tinfoil.

'I'm Daisy, Mia's business partner. You must be the Swedish writer?'

'Sort of. I'm actually American.'

'Of course. That's what I meant.'

'What's all that?' Paul asked, eyeing the food on the island.

'Brunch! Mia is a wonderful cook, but I'm the one who always gets stuck doing the serving. Even on Sundays. Disgraceful.'

'Oh, give me a break!' Mia protested. 'It hadn't finished cooking. And someone had to come up here and set the table.'

Daisy stepped on Mia's foot as she walked past.

'Let's see what you prepared for us, shall we?' Daisy said, removing the foil. 'Caramelised onion tart, chard pie and baked stuffed vegetables. If anyone's still hungry after all this, you should think of a new line of work!'

'Smells amazing,' Paul said to Mia.

Daisy started sniffing the air – once, twice. After the third sniff, she advanced towards the table, spotted the scented candle, made a face, blew it out, and threw it straight in the rubbish, smiling as she noticed what else was in there.

'Um . . . all right, then,' Paul stammered, somewhat taken aback.

Mia gave him a knowing look, suggesting that her business partner was sometimes a little odd. Daisy must have noted the exchange because she ordered them to eat immediately.


Paul wanted to know how the two had met and become friends. Mia started talking about Daisy's first trip to England. Daisy interrupted to tell him about Mia's first trip to Provence, and how she'd been terrified of cicadas. She recounted their nocturnal escapades and all the tricks they'd played on each other. Paul was only half-listening, thinking

170

constantly about his own adolescence with Arthur, the boarding school where they'd met, the house in Carmel . . .

As they sipped at coffee after the meal, it became Paul's turn to answer all of Daisy's questions. Why he had moved to Paris, what had made him want to write, which writers he admired most, what his working habits were. Paul played along, replying with good grace. Mia stayed nearly silent, simply watching the other two.

She stood up to clear the table and went behind the island. A little later, Paul tried to get her attention, but she stared fixedly at the soapy dishes.

Shortly after midday, he thanked them both for a lovely time and said goodbye, congratulating Mia on her amazing cooking - by far the best meal he'd had in ages. On his way out, he promised Daisy that he would devote one of his chapters to Provence. It was Daisy who saw him to the door. Mia just waved and carried on tidying up. He rolled his eyes and left.

Daisy closed the door and waited for a moment.

'He's much better-looking in real life than in the photo on his book,' she said with a yawn. 'I'm going to take a nap. I'm exhausted. It was fun, though, wasn't it? He certainly did seem to enjoy my cooking . . . I mean, *your* cooking.'

With these words, Daisy went into her bedroom, Mia into hers, and the two friends did not speak another word to each other all day.

Lying on her bed, Mia picked up her phone and re-read all David's messages.

In the early evening, she pulled on a pair of jeans and a light sweater and went out, slamming the door behind her.

The taxi dropped her off at Place de l'Alma. She sat outside at a café and ordered a glass of pink champagne, which she downed in one gulp while keeping an eye on her phone. She had just ordered a second glass when the screen lit up. This time it was a call, not a text. She hesitated before answering.

'What's going on? Why were you acting like that today?'

'Why were *you* acting like that?'

He sighed. 'Where are you?'

'Place de l'Alma.'

'What are you doing there?'

'Looking at the bridge.'

'Why?'

'Because I like it. Is that okay with you?'

'And where are you looking at it from?'

'From an outside table at Chez Francis.'

'I'm on my way.'

Paul turned up four glasses of champagne later. He double-parked his car and sat down next to Mia.

'Has your meal gone down yet?' she asked him.

'Listen, I couldn't care less if the truth is that you don't know how to cook, and I couldn't care less if you're actually a waitress and not the owner. But I will not accept you trying to set me up with your friend.'

Mia looked upset. 'So do you like her, or not?'

'Daisy is beautiful, lively and interesting, and she's a superb cook,' Paul admitted. Then, raising his voice: 'But it is up to me, and me alone, to decide who I meet and who I don't meet. I don't let my oldest friends meddle with my private life, and I'm sure as hell not going to let you do it.'

'Do you want to see her again?' Mia asked, speaking over Paul.

And, as they argued, their faces drew gradually closer together until their lips touched.

For a moment, the two of them were dumb-struck.

Then, in a calm voice, Paul told Mia: 'I hated that, back at your place today.'

'So did I.'

'There was this . . . distance between us.'

'Yes.'

'Tonight, I'm going to write a scene where my characters have a huge argument and then make up. I have enough material to fill a couple dozen pages.'

'So lunch wasn't a complete waste of time, then. If you want my opinion, he should apologise and admit he was wrong.'

Paul picked up Mia's glass and drained it.

'You've already had enough to drink, and I'm thirsty. Don't give me that butter-wouldn't-melt look. I can see it in your eyes. Let me give you a ride home.'

'No, I'll take a cab.'

Paul picked up the bill from the table.

'Six glasses? Well, there you go . . .'

'I'm not even drunk!'

'Stop disagreeing with everything I say. I'm taking you home, and that's all there is to it.'

He led Mia to his car. She staggered a little on the pavement. He put her in the Saab's passenger seat before climbing in behind the wheel.

They drove in silence to Rue Poulbot. Paul parked in front of the apartment building and got out.

'Are you going to be all right?' he asked, opening the door for her.

'The atmosphere's a bit tense, but we've had arguments before. It'll pass.'

'I meant, are you okay to climb the stairs?'

'I've had a few glasses of champagne. That doesn't make me drunk!'

'I'm leaving Paris at the end of the week,' he said, looking at the ground.

'So soon?'

'I told you already: the trip was moved up. Next time, try listening to men when they talk to you.'

Mia elbowed him in the ribs.

'We can't let that lunch be the last time we see each other.'

'When exactly are you leaving?'

'Friday morning.'

'What time?'

'The flight is at 11:30 a.m. We could have dinner the night before, but I'm sure you're working . . .'

'It would be a little sad, right before you leave. How about Wednesday?'

'Wednesday works for me. Any particular place you'd like to try?'

'Your place. Eight o'clock.'

Mia kissed Paul on the cheek, opened the front door, turned around, smiled, and disappeared inside the building.

The apartment lay in darkness. Mia swore as she bumped into a chair, narrowly avoided the coffee table, walked into and then straight back out of a cupboard, and finally made it to her room. She slid between the sheets and fell asleep.

Paul opened a cupboard when he got home too. He hesitated between two suitcases, chose the smaller, and put it at the foot of his bed. For most of the night, he sat in front of his computer, trying to find the right words. At about three in the morning, he sent an email to Kyong, reminding her of his flight number and his arrival time. Then he went to bed.

Daisy was sitting at the breakfast table. When Mia came out of her room, Daisy poured her a cup of tea and told her to sit down.

'What was the story with you yesterday?'

'I was going to ask you the same question.'

'You mean, why did I come to your rescue? Why did I spend all Sunday morning cooking so you could, once again, be the wonderful, extraordinary Mia, who is just perfect at everything?'

'Oh, spare me! You were going all out to lure him in. I've hardly ever seen you act like that.'

'Coming from an actress as talented as you, I'll take that as a compliment. Anyway, didn't you want the two of us to meet?'

'Yes, but not so you could flirt with him. I felt like the third wheel!'

'Oh, how tragic! The poor movie star realises the world doesn't always revolve around her.'

'Go on, be like that. You always have to be right.'

'Well, I was right about one thing, anyway. You are far from being as innocent as you claim to be in this little game of yours. And maybe you've started to like it.'

'You know, you're starting to be a real pain in my arse, Daisy.'

'You're already a real pain in my arse, Mia.'

'Fine, I can tell where I'm not wanted. I'll pack my bags and go to a hotel.'

'Jesus, when are you going to grow up?'

'When I get to be as old as you are?'

'David called me.'

'What?'

'I may be three months older than you, but apparently you're the one who's going deaf.'

'When did he call you?'

'Yesterday, while I was making chard pie for your Swede.'

'Stop calling him that! What did David want?'

'He wanted to use me to convince you to reply to his messages and give him another chance.'

'What did you say?'

'I said I wasn't your secretary. I told him that what he did wounded you deeply, and that he'd have to be extremely creative if he hopes to win you back.'

'Why should I give him another chance?'

'Because he's your husband. "I'm not over David yet." Your words, as you may recall, when you were pouring your heart out to me the other night. So. David had an affair, he had a fling, but you're the one he loves. Mia, you need to get your head straight. The day you turned up at my apartment, you said you wanted to live in the present and have some time alone. Now you've done that. But your new American friend will be leaving for Korea to join his girlfriend in just a few days, and what will you do then? Keep waitressing at a bistro in Montmartre? Is that how you plan to escape your life? For how long?'

'I don't want to go back to London. I can't, not now. I don't feel ready.'

'All right, but think about it. If you want to save your marriage, you'd better not wait until David finds a new girlfriend. And don't forget, you've never had a very high tolerance for solitude. Don't try to claim otherwise – I've known you too long for that. I can't help it if someone else makes you suffer, but I'm not going to sit by and watch while you suffer as a result of your own mistakes. I'm your friend, and if I don't say anything, I'll feel responsible.'

'So let's go in on the restaurant together. You can deal with the cooking and I'll take care of the dining room. We can plan our holidays. We could go to Greece for a few days, just the two of us, in September . . .'

'September is a long way off. In the meantime, let's just enjoy these last two days without fighting.'

'What do you mean, last two days?'

'I've hired a new waitress. She starts on Wednesday.'

'Why would you do that?'

'I did it for you.'

# 14

On Tuesday night, Paul set his alarm and went to bed around midnight. At nine the next morning, he left his apartment, stopped for some coffee, waved goodbye to Moustache, and went off to do his shopping. His first stop was the greengrocer, with its radiant display of colours. Next, he made stops at the butcher, the fishmonger, the cheesemonger and finally the patisserie. Back outside his apartment building, he did a U-turn in the direction of the wine-merchant. He chose two bottles of a *grand cru* Bordeaux, checked his shopping list, and finally went home again.

He spent the rest of the day in the kitchen, set the table at four o'clock, took a bath at five, got dressed at six, and sat on his sofa, skimming his latest chapters with one eye while checking his watch with the other.

Mia had allowed herself a lie-in. The night before, she had celebrated her last shift at Daisy's restaurant with a few drinks too many. Feeling very tipsy, the two friends had ventured outside to Place du Tertre, hoping the fresh air would sober them up. They had sat on a bench talking about life, and getting nowhere. Except Mia did manage to make Daisy promise she would close La Clamada at the end of September, so the two of them could spend a week together in Greece.

At noon, Mia went for a walk up to Place du Tertre and said hello to the caricaturist. She ate breakfast outside at a café, and then went to the hairdresser. Then she stopped at a boutique and emerged with a pretty spring dress. She went back to the apartment around five o'clock and ran herself a deep bath.

At seven thirty, Paul checked the temperature of the oven, browned the crayfish, chopped the fresh herbs and mixed them into the salad, coated the lamb-chops with a Parmesan-cheese crust, then went back to check that there was nothing missing on the table. Next, he opened one of the bottles of wine to let it breathe, went back to the living room to read, returned fifteen minutes later to the kitchen to put the rack of lamb in the oven, went back to the living room, looked out the window, examined his reflection in the mirror, tucked his shirt in and then immediately untucked it again, lowered the temperature of the oven, looked out the window again (leaning out this time for a better view of the street), decided to air the room, took the rack of lamb out of the oven, sat down on the sofa again, checked his watch, sent a text, started reading again, sent a second text at nine o'clock, blew out the candles in the candelabra at nine thirty, and sent one last text at ten.

'Why do you keep looking at your phone?'

'No reason. Just a habit.'

'Mia, look me in the eyes. I came all the way across the Channel to win you back.'

'I am looking you in the eyes, David.'

'So just where were you headed when I rang the doorbell at Daisy's?'

'Nowhere.'

'Right. Headed nowhere, all made-up with a new hairstyle. Why on earth would you cut your hair like that?'

'I just wanted a change.'

'You haven't answered my question. Did you have a date with somebody?'

'Yes, I was off to go screw my lover. Is that what you want me to say? At least then we'd be even.'

'God's sake, Mia! I came here to make up with you.'

'Have you seen her again?'

'No, I've already told you: I've been on my own in London since you left, and I haven't been thinking about anyone but you. I sent you so many messages, but you never replied to any of them. So here I am . . . to tell you I love you. That I made a stupid mistake. And I can't forgive myself.'

'Yet you want me to forgive you.'

'I want you to give our marriage another chance. What can I say to make you understand? It was nothing more than a lapse of judgement. It didn't mean anything.'

'To you, maybe.'

'I was in a bad place. That shoot was hard on both of us. You seemed inaccessible. I was weak. Mia, I would do anything for you to forgive me. I'll never hurt you again. I swear it. If you could agree to draw a line through this mistake, move past it, and forget the whole thing.'

'*Hit the delete key and make the past disappear like the pages of a manuscript . . . ,*' Mia muttered under her breath.

'What did you say?'

'Nothing.'

David grabbed Mia's hand and kissed it. She watched him, feeling a lump rise in her throat.

*Why do you have this effect on me? Why do I completely lose myself when I'm with you?*

'A penny for your thoughts.'

'I was thinking about us.'

'Will you give us another chance? Do you remember this hotel? We stayed here during our first trip to Paris, after we'd just started dating.'

Mia looked at the suite that David had reserved – the Louis XVI writing-desk, lyre-back chair and wing armchair in the sitting room, and the king-size bed with pointed crown canopy in the bedroom.

'We had a smaller room back in those days.'

'Yes, well, we've come a long way,' David said, taking her in his arms. 'Let's be young lovers on holiday again tomorrow. We can take a riverboat up the Seine. We can even go and have ice cream on Île de la Cité . . . I can't remember the name of that place, but you loved it.'

'It was on Île Saint-Louis.'

'Then let's go to Île Saint-Louis. Please, Mia, stay with me tonight.'

'I didn't bring anything with me.'

David led Mia to the wardrobe. Inside hung three dresses, two skirts, two blouses, two pairs of cotton trousers, and two V-neck sweaters. He pulled open the drawers to reveal four sets of lingerie. Then he took her into the gleaming marble bathroom. Next to the wash-basin lay a make-up bag and a toothbrush.

'I took the first plane here this morning and spent my day shopping for you.'

'I'm tired,' she said. 'Let's go to bed.'

'You didn't touch your food in the restaurant. Can't I order you something from room service?'

'No, I'm not hungry. I just want to sleep. And think.'

'What is there to think about?' David said, wrapping his arms around her. 'Let's stay together tonight, and tomorrow we'll start again from scratch.'

Mia gently pushed him out of the bathroom and locked the door.

She turned on the tap, picked up her phone, and scrolled through the texts she had received that evening.

```
It's all ready. Hurry up!

Where are you? It'll get cold.

Don't worry, I understand if you have to

work late at the restaurant. Just let me know

that everything's OK.
```

She was re-reading the last message from Paul for the third time when the phone vibrated in her hand.

```
I'm going to write now. Switching my phone
off.

We can talk tomorrow. Or not.
```

It was nearly midnight. Mia turned off her phone, undressed, and got into the shower.

Paul ran down the stairs, pushed open the front door, and took a deep breath of night air. Moustache was lowering the metal shutter outside his café. Hearing footsteps, he turned around.

'Monsieur Paul, what are you doing there, hanging around on the pavement like a lost soul?'

'Walking my dog.'

'You have a dog now? Where is he, then, out on the prowl?'

'Are you hungry, Moustache?'

'I always have room for a little something. But my kitchen is closed, I'm afraid.'

'Mine isn't. Come on up.'


Entering Paul's apartment, Moustache was amazed to see a table covered with a white tablecloth, elegantly set with a candelabra at the centre.

'Spring salad with crayfish, roast rack of lamb with a Parmesan crust, and a *gâteau Saint-Honoré* for dessert . . . oh, and I almost forgot, a very nice assortment of cheese and a bottle of Sarget de Gruaud Larose 2009. Will that do?' Paul asked.

'Just one thing first. This candle-lit meal . . . you didn't prepare it for me, did you, Monsieur Paul? Because, you know . . .'

'No, Moustache, don't worry. It wasn't for you. And the rack of lamb will undoubtedly be overcooked.'

'Understood,' Moustache replied, unfolding his napkin.

The two men sat there eating until late. Moustache talked about his native Auvergne, which he had left twenty years ago to become a butcher. He told the story of his marriage, his divorce, how he bought his first café in the Bastille area, before it became hip – he never should have sold it – and then how he bought his next café in Belleville, again before it became all the rage, and finally his move to a new up-and-coming neighbourhood.

Paul didn't say anything. He half-listened to his guest, lost in his thoughts.

At two in the morning, Moustache rose to leave, congratulating Paul on such an amazing meal.

On the doorstep, he patted him on the shoulder and sighed.

'You're a good guy, Monsieur Paul. I've never read your books – reading's not really my thing – but I've heard good things about them. When you come back from over there, I'll take you to a joint where the night workers hang out – it's way off the beaten path, but the boss is one hell of a cook – and you can give me the lowdown on your trip.'

Paul gave Moustache a copy of his keys, admitting to him that he didn't know when he'd be back. The café owner nodded, put the keys in his pocket, and left.

# 15

It was cool that Thursday. Out on the Seine, David reeled off a few anecdotes from their first trip to Paris. But standing on the shore was not enough to bring the tide in. They shared an ice cream on Île Saint-Louis and went back to the hotel. They made love and then lay in bed for a while. Mia wondered whether this would be a new beginning or a way to say goodbye.

In the middle of the afternoon, David called the concierge and asked him to book two theatre tickets for the best show in town, as well as two flights to London for the next day. When he hung up, he told Mia that it was time to go home. He offered to accompany her to Montmartre to pick up her things.

Mia replied that she would rather pack on her own. She wanted to say goodbye to Daisy and would meet up with David later on. She promised she would be on time, and left the hotel suite.

The limousine dropped her at Rue Poulbot. Mia asked the chauffeur to wait for her. She walked up the stairs to the apartment, trailing her hand slowly along the banister as she went.

Once she'd finished packing her suitcase, she took the portrait of Daisy out of the cupboard, set it on the worktop, and then left the apartment.

◆  ◆  ◆

Paul printed out his chapters, put the pages in a folder, and slipped it inside his suitcase.

He emptied the refrigerator, closed the shutters, and checked the taps. Finally, he walked around his apartment, took out the rubbish, and left to meet his editor.

◆ ◆ ◆

As they left Montmartre, Mia asked the chauffeur to take her to Rue de Bretagne.

'Could you stop here for a minute?' she asked as they approached number 38.

She lowered the window and stuck her head out. The fourth-floor shutters were closed.

When the car started up again, she took out her phone and re-read the message she'd received late that morning.

Mia,

I pushed my opera singer under a bus last night. She was crossing the road without paying attention. Oh, well.

When I called the restaurant, Daisy told me you were fine - of course, that's what matters.

I understand your lack of response. Maybe it's better this way. Goodbyes don't really make any sense.

Thank you for all the precious moments
we spent together.

Take care of yourself, even if that
phrase doesn't make any sense either.

Paul

When she reached the hotel, Mia pretended she had a migraine. David told the concierge to forget the theatre tickets and had their dinner brought up to the suite.

◆  ◆  ◆

At eleven o'clock, Daisy said goodnight to the last customers. Back at her apartment, she found a portrait of herself lying on the kitchen worktop, along with a short note.

*Daisy,*

*I'm going back to England. I couldn't muster the courage to stop by the restaurant. I am jealous of your new waitress. Joking aside, the truth is, if I'd seen you, I'd probably have changed my mind. These days I've spent with you in Paris have been like sketches of a new life for me, a life that I started to love from the bottom of my heart. But I took your advice. I am returning to my old life and leaving you to yours.*

*I'll call you from London in a few days, once I've got my bearings again. I don't know if you were aware that David was coming to fetch me, but if you were, you made the right choice in not warning me. I will never be able to thank you properly for being such a good friend, for always being there when I need you, for standing up to me, even at the risk I'd be angry with you, and for never lying to me. I lied to you — you know what about — and I'm still so sorry for that.*

*This drawing of you was done by a caricaturist on Place du Tertre. You won't have any trouble spotting him: he's a lovely guy, almost as lovely as this portrait of you.*

*I miss you already.*

*Your friend, who loves you like a sister,*

*Mia*

*P.S. Don't forget your promise. Last week of September. Greece. Just the two of us. I'll take care of everything.*

Daisy quickly grabbed her phone. She tried calling Mia but couldn't get through, so she sent her a text.

```
I hope you're going to miss me as much
as I'll miss you. My new waitress is an
imbecile. She's got hairy armpits and has
already broken two plates. You should call
me asap. Temporary insanity is fine, but not
to the point of taking my advice! I beg
you, never do that. Outside the kitchen,
your best friend is wrong about everything,
especially life.

I love you, too. Like a sister...
```

The next morning, the chauffeur took the slip road that led to the airport and pulled up to park right next to the departures level. David opened the door and held out his hand for Mia. She was about to exit the car when the doors of the terminal slid open. Mia had enough experience to quickly spot the paparazzi, and these vultures hadn't even bothered hiding. She could see two of them standing in front of the check-in desks now.

*You bastard! Who else could have tipped them off? Your whole visit to Paris, your entire charm offensive, was just to have the two of us seen together, wasn't it? The riverboat would have been too obvious, but the airport . . . ? Just a coincidence, of course! And I actually believed you, like a complete and utter fool . . .*

'Are you coming?' David asked impatiently.

'Sorry, wait for me inside. I need to call Daisy first.'

'Can I take your suitcases?'

'Don't worry, the chauffeur can handle that. I'll see you in five minutes.'

'Right, I'll go on ahead and buy newspapers. But don't take too long.'

As soon as David was out of sight, Mia closed the car door and leaned in towards the chauffeur.

'What's your name?'

'My name is Maurice, madame.'

'Maurice, how well do you know this airport?'

'I bring passengers here maybe four to six times a day, on average.'

'Do you know where the flights to Asia leave from?'

'Terminal 2E.'

'All right, Maurice, listen up,' she said, rummaging around in her handbag, 'the flight for Seoul takes off in forty-five minutes. If you can get me to Terminal 2E in five minutes, I will give you a huge tip.'

The chauffeur sped off.

'Uh-oh . . . do you take credit cards?' Mia asked, embarrassed. 'I don't have any cash on me.'

'Are you going to take this flight to Asia, while your husband goes to London?'

'I'm going to try.'

'Forget the tip, then,' he said, weaving between a taxi and a bus. 'That guy's unbearable.'

The car roared along full throttle and, three minutes later, came to a halt in front of Terminal 2F.

The chauffeur hurried out to open the boot, took out Mia's suitcase, and put it on the pavement.

'And what am I supposed to do with his?' He gestured to David's overstuffed bag.

'Maurice, you are now the proud owner of a pricey collection of cashmere sweaters and silk shirts. Thanks ever so much!'

Mia grabbed her luggage and hurried towards the check-in area.

There was only one agent left behind the desk.

'Hi, I have to go to Seoul. It's urgent.'

The woman frowned doubtfully.

'I was about to close the flight. I'm afraid it's fully booked.'

'I'm prepared to travel in the toilets if I have to.'

'For eleven hours?' the woman asked, looking up. 'I can put you on tomorrow's flight.'

'Please,' Mia begged, taking off her sunglasses.

The woman saw her face and her eyes lit up.

'I'm sorry. But are you . . . ?'

'Yes, I am! Could you please get me a seat?'

'You should have told me from the start! I have one first-class ticket left, but it's full fare.'

Mia put her credit card on the desk.

'What date would you like for the return flight?'

'I have no idea.'

'I need a return date.'

'In a week . . . no, ten days . . . or two weeks . . .'

'Which one?'

'Two weeks! Please hurry!'

The agent began typing furiously on her computer keyboard.

'Oh no, your suitcase! It's too late to check it . . .'

Mia knelt down to whip open her suitcase, took out her toiletry bag and a few other things, and jammed them into her purse.

'You can keep the rest!'

'I'm sorry, I really can't,' the woman said, leaning over the desk.

'Yes, you can!'

'Which hotel are you staying at?'

'I have no idea.'

The woman, who was now beyond being surprised by anything, handed Mia her boarding pass.

'Now run. I'll ask them to hold the doors for you.'

Mia grabbed her ticket, took off her heels, and ran towards security, shoes in hand.

She arrived at the walkway out of breath, spotted the gate, screamed at the staff to wait for her, and did not slow down until she was on the boarding bridge.

Before getting on the plane, she tried to regain some semblance of composure, then handed her boarding pass to the flight attendant, who welcomed her with a big smile.

'That was one close shave,' he said, pointing to an empty seat. 'You're in 2A.'

Mia walked straight past her seat and continued up the aisle.

The flight attendant called her back, but she pressed on until she found the row she was looking for, gave her boarding pass to the passenger, and told him he had been upgraded to first class. The man didn't need to be told twice, and gave up his seat.

Mia opened the overhead luggage compartment, squeezed her handbag between two cabin bags, and collapsed into her seat with a huge sigh.

Paul didn't even look up from the magazine he was leafing through.

The flight attendant announced over the intercom that the doors were closing. Passengers were asked to fasten their seatbelts and switch off all electronic devices.

Paul put his magazine in the seat-back pocket and closed his eyes.

'Can we talk or do you plan to sulk for eleven hours?' Mia asked.

'Right now, we keep our mouths shut and wait to die. A massive three-hundred-ton steel tube is about to attempt flight. And no matter what Bernoulli says, that is against the laws of nature. So, until we are up in the air, let's just breathe, stay calm, and that's it.'

'Right, then,' Mia replied.

'You wouldn't happen to have any anaesthetic, would you?'

'I thought we were strictly prohibited from conversing.'

'Valium?'

'Sorry.'

'A baseball bat? Any blunt object, really. If you'd be so kind as to knock me out cold, then not wake me until we've touched ground in Korea, that would be ideal.'

'Calm down. Everything will be fine.'

'So now you're a pilot.'

'Give me your hand.'

'I'd rather not. It's kind of clammy.'

Mia put her hand on Paul's wrist.

'What did you make for the dinner I missed?'

'Hmph. I guess you'll never know.'

'You're not even going to ask why I'm here?'

'Nope. I will take some satisfaction from the fact that your ticket must have cost you the moon. Is that normal, that noise?'

'It's the engines.'

191

'And so it's normal they're making so much noise?'

'If we intend to take off, then yes.'

'Okay. So are they making *enough* noise?'

'They're making exactly as much noise as they're supposed to.'

'What's that constant boom-boom-boom I'm hearing?'

'That . . . would be your heart.'

The aeroplane soared into the air. Shortly after take-off, it hit a patch of turbulence. Paul gritted his teeth. Sweat streamed down his forehead.

'Relax. There's no reason to be afraid,' Mia soothed him.

'Fear doesn't need a reason,' Paul replied.

He regretted not having tried the little gift that Cristoneli had offered him on the way to the airport: a homemade concoction that would, according to the editor, relieve him of all worries for several hours. Paul, who was such a hypochondriac that he was reluctant to take aspirin for headaches out of fear it would cause a brain haemorrhage, had decided not to give himself another reason to be anxious.

The plane reached cruising altitude and the cabin crew began moving through the aisles.

'Okay, now the flight attendants are up – that's a good sign. If they're moving around, everything must be fine, don't you think?'

'Everything has been fine since take-off and everything will be fine until we land. But Paul? If you keep gripping the armrest that tightly for the next eleven hours, we might have to use pliers to pry you free.'

Paul looked down at his white-knuckle grip and carefully relaxed his fingers.

A stewardess arrived with the drink cart. To Mia's surprise, Paul asked only for a glass of water.

'I've heard that alcohol and high altitude don't mix.'

Mia went for a double shot of gin.

'Maybe there's an exception for the English,' Paul remarked, watching her down her glass.

Mia closed her eyes and took a deep breath. Paul observed her in silence.

'I thought we had agreed not to talk,' she said, eyes still closed.

Paul began reading his magazine again. 'I've been working quite a bit for the last couple nights. My opera singer has been through some exciting adventures. Her ex resurfaced, for one thing. And naturally enough, she dove right back in. I have to figure out – does that count or does it not count?' he asked, casually turning the page. 'Not that I need to know – none of my business. I just thought I'd ask. In any event, it seems that's done now, so let's talk about something else.'

'What in the world could've inspired that plot twist?'

'I'm a novelist.' He shrugged. 'I dream stuff up. That's what I do.'

Paul closed his magazine.

'But what bothers me is seeing her unhappy. I don't know why, but that's just the way it is.'

A steward interrupted their conversation with meal service. Paul declined his meal and announced that Mia wasn't hungry. She was about to protest, but the attendant had already moved on to the next row.

'What the hell?' she exclaimed. 'Why would you do that? I'm starving!'

'So am I. But those little meals are not intended for consumption, just distraction. You end up spending half the flight trying to guess what's in them.'

Paul unbuckled his seatbelt and stood up to remove his bag from the overhead compartment. As soon as he was back in his seat, he took out ten small airtight containers and placed them on Mia's tray.

'And what might that be?' she asked.

'First she stands me up, now she gate-crashes my last meal.'

Mia took off the lids to find four smoked-salmon sandwiches, two slices of vegetable terrine, two small blocks of foie gras, two potato salads with black truffles, and, in the last two boxes, two coffee éclairs. She stared at Paul open-mouthed.

'As I was packing my suitcase, I decided if I was going to die on this flight, I may as well die happy.'

'By eating enough for two, you mean?'

'Give me some credit. I wasn't going to enjoy this feast all by my lonesome while the person next to me stared at their airplane food contemplating death by starvation. That would have ruined the whole thing for me.'

'You really do think of everything.'

'Only the essentials. Which still manages to take up most of my time.'

'Will your translator be waiting for you at the airport?'

'I sure hope so,' Paul replied. 'Why do you ask?'

'No reason, just thinking . . . I suppose we could say I was sent by your publishers to accompany you on the trip.'

'Alternatively, we could say we're just friends.'

'Your call.'

'And since we're just friends, maybe you could explain how the hell you ended up on this plane instead of at your restaurant?'

'Mm, this foie gras is delicious. Where did you get it?'

'Please answer the question.'

'I had to get away.'

'From what?'

'Myself.'

'So he did come back.'

'Let's just say that the opera singer dove back in, and quickly found herself in over her head.'

'Well, I'm glad you're here.'

'Really?'

'No. Not at all. I was just being polite.'
'I'm glad I'm here too. I've always dreamt of visiting Seoul.'
'Really?'
'No. Not at all. I was just being polite.'


At the end of the meal, Paul tidied away the containers in his bag and stood up.
'Where are you going?'
'To wash these.'
'Are you joking?'
'Absolutely not. I'm not going to throw away my Tupperware. I'll need it for the return trip.'
'So you're not planning on staying in Korea indefinitely?'
'Who knows? We'll see.'


They checked the inflight entertainment programme. Mia opted for a romantic comedy, and Paul for a thriller. Ten minutes later, Paul was watching Mia's movie and Mia was watching his. First they exchanged a look, then their earphones, and finally their seats.


Paul eventually went to sleep, and Mia made sure no one woke him up during the descent. He opened his eyes just as the plane's wheels touched the ground and stiffened as the pilot activated the reverse thrust. His nightmare was ending, Mia reassured him. In a few moments, they would be getting off the plane.


After going through passport control, Paul retrieved his suitcase from the baggage carousel and put it on a cart.

'Yours isn't out yet?' he asked.

'This is all I have,' she said, gesturing towards the satchel on her shoulder.

Paul said nothing, distracted by his growing anticipation. He looked at the sliding doors up ahead, trying to think how he would act as he walked through them.


A group of about thirty readers had unfurled a banner that proclaimed: *Welcome, Paul Barton.*

Mia put on her sunglasses.

'Wow, they really know how to make a guy feel welcome,' Paul hissed to Mia. 'I mean, hiring extras . . . just a little over the top . . .'

He scanned the row of faces in search of Kyong's, then glanced back over his shoulder. Mia had disappeared. He thought he caught a glimpse of her going past the arrivals barrier and melting into the crowd.

The group rushed towards him, notebooks and pens in hand, begging him to sign autographs. Embarrassed at first, Paul signed with good grace until a man he assumed must be his Korean editor arrived, scattering the crowd of fans and shaking his hand warmly.

'Welcome to Seoul, Mr Barton. It's an honour to have you here on Korean soil.'

'The honour is all mine,' Paul replied, continuing to scan the crowd. 'Really, you shouldn't have.'

'Shouldn't have what?' the editor asked.

'All these people, it's just a bit . . .'

'We tried to keep them away, but you are very popular here and they knew you were arriving. In fact, they've been waiting here for more than three hours.'

'But . . . why?'

'To see you, of course. Follow me, I have a car waiting to take you to your hotel. I imagine you're quite exhausted after the long voyage.'

Mia joined them outside the terminal.

'This lady is with you?' the editor inquired.

Mia introduced herself.

'Ms Grinberg. Assistant to Mr Barton.'

'Pleased to meet you, Ms Grinberg,' the editor replied. 'I am afraid Mr Cristoneli neglected to notify us of your presence.'

'Mr Barton's office handled my trip directly,' she explained.

Paul was speechless at the ease with which she donned a new identity. The editor opened the door to the car and ushered the two of them into the back seat. Paul cast one last look back at the empty pavement.

The car started up and moved off in the direction of the city centre.

Paul stared absently at the suburban landscape rolling past outside the window. Kyong had not come to the airport.

'There will be a small dinner party tonight,' the editor announced. 'We will be joined by a few employees from the publishing house, including our marketing director, your press officer, Ms Bak, as well as the manager of the bookshop where you will be signing books. Don't worry, we will do our best to keep it short. After all, you must get some rest. The next few days will be hectic. This is your schedule,' he said, passing an envelope to Mia. 'Ms Grinberg, are you staying in the same hotel as Mr Barton?'

'Absolutely,' Mia replied, looking at Paul.

Paul felt the conversation flow around him like water around a rock. Maybe Kyong's boss's presence had prevented her from coming.

Mia patted his knee to bring him back to earth.

'Paul,' she said, 'your editor is asking if you had a smooth trip.'

'You could say that. I'm still in one piece, thank goodness!'

His editor gave him a small smile in the rearview mirror. 'We have great hopes for the television show you will be appearing on tomorrow. There will also be another important event – the ambassador is organising a reception in your honour on Monday. There will be a few journalists there, as well as some senior lecturers from the university. I will inform the embassy secretary about the presence of your colleague.'

'Please, don't worry about that,' said Mia. 'Mr Barton can go without me.'

'Of course not. We would be delighted to have you with us. Isn't that so, Mr Barton?'

Paul, his face pressed to the window, did not respond. How would Kyong behave at the dinner party? Should he keep a certain restraint with her to avoid embarrassing her in front of her employer?

Mia elbowed him discreetly in the ribs.

'Sorry. Yes?' Paul asked.

Likely assuming that his author was overcome by fatigue, the editor kept silent until they reached the hotel.

The car pulled up under the awning. A young woman came out to meet them.

'Ms Bak will help you check in and will accompany you to the restaurant where I will meet you later this evening. In the meantime, I hope you can recharge your batteries. Goodbye, and I will see you later.'

The editor got back in the car and drove off.

Ms Bak asked Paul and Mia for their passports and invited them to follow her to the reception desk. A porter took Paul's suitcase.


The receptionist blushed when he saw Paul.

'This is a great honour, Mr Barton,' he whispered. 'I have read all your books.'

'Thank you, that's very kind of you,' Paul replied.

'Ms Grinberg, I cannot find your reservation,' he said apologetically. 'Do you have your confirmation number?'

'No, I'm afraid I don't,' said Mia.

The receptionist began to search on the computer, becoming even more flustered when Ms Bak reminded him that Mr Barton was coming off a long trip and that they were wasting valuable time.

Recovering his presence of mind, Paul leaned over the desk.

'You know, there's probably been a mix-up,' he said. 'Don't worry, it happens. Just give us a different room.'

'But Mr Barton, the hotel is completely full. I could try to find accommodation at a different hotel, but with the Book Fair, I am afraid they will all be full as well.'

Mia stared into space.

'Fine, not to worry,' said Paul jovially. 'Ms Grinberg and I have been working together for years. We can easily share a room. With twin beds.'

'But there aren't any left. We upgraded you to a suite, but it has only one bed. It is a very big bed, though – king-size!'

Ms Bak looked as if she were about to faint. Paul took her to one side.

'Have you ever flown on an airplane, Ms Bak?'

'Never, Mr Barton, never. Why?'

'Because I just did, and let me tell you: after eleven excruciating hours thirty thousand feet off the ground, with only a flimsy sheet of metal and a tiny little window between me and oblivion, it would take a hell of a lot more than this to faze me. The two of us can share the suite, just please don't say a word about this to your boss – in fact, don't tell anybody. All you have to do is make sure this young man forgets that Ms Grinberg was ever here today, and it can be our little secret.'

Ms Bak swallowed and her face seemed to recover its normal complexion.

'Two keys, please,' said Paul to the receptionist. Then, turning to Mia, he asked ironically: 'Shall we head up then, Ms Grinberg?'

Not a word was exchanged in the lift, or in the long hallway that led to the room, and still not a peep until the porter had deposited Paul's suitcase and taken his leave.

'I'm so sorry,' said Mia. 'It never even crossed my mind . . .'

Paul lay down on the sofa, his legs dangling over the armrest.

'Okay, that's not an option,' he sighed, standing up again.

He took a cushion, placed it on the carpet, and lay down.

'And that idea's out too,' he said, rubbing his lower back.

He opened the wardrobe door, stood on his tiptoes, grabbed two bolster pillows, and put them down the middle of the bed.

'Right side or left?' he asked.

'There must be a B&B with a vacant room somewhere. The entire city of Seoul can't really be booked, can it?' Mia exclaimed.

'Sure. We can just flip through the ads in Korean, should be a cinch. Look, this can work if we set a few ground rules. You can have the bathroom first in the morning, and I'll take it first at night. Remote control is all yours, carte blanche with the TV, as long as it's not sports. You should sleep with ear-plugs. I don't think I'm a snorer, but just in case, I'd like to maintain a shred of dignity. If I happen to talk in my sleep, anything I say may *not* be used against me in a court of law. We stick to that, and I think we should be able to make this work. I already have enough to worry about without piling on one more complication. And by the way, what in the world possessed you to say you were my *assistant*? Do I look like the kind of person who has an assistant?'

'I don't know. And just how is a person with an assistant supposed to look?'

'Let's take a poll. I've never had a personal assistant. Have you? Didn't think so. I hope you at least brought a toothbrush, because there's no way I'm sharing mine. I've got toothpaste,' Paul grumbled as he paced the room, 'but my toothbrush is where I draw the line.'

'Please calm down, Paul . . . I know you're nervous. You'll see Kyong at dinner.'

'Along with a dozen other people! This trip is off to one hell of a start. I have to call my friend "Ms Grinberg" and the woman I love "Ms Kyong". Just . . . marvelful, as my editor would say.'

'Thank you for that,' Mia said, lying on the bed.

'For what?'

'For calling me your friend . . . It's quite touching.'

She lay with her hands behind her head, staring at the ceiling. Paul watched her.

'So I take it that means you want the left side?'

Mia climbed over the bolsters, jumped up and down several times on the right-hand side, and then went back to the other side.

'Yes. Left it is,' she concluded.

'Did you have to break the bed to decide?'

'No, but it was fun. So, do we draw straws for the bathroom? Afternoon toilet privileges were left undefined.'

Paul shrugged to indicate that she could use it now. While she was gone, he unpacked his suitcase and hung his clothes in the wardrobe, hiding his underwear and socks under a pile of shirts.

Mia reappeared half an hour later wearing a bathrobe, with a towel wrapped around her head.

'What were you doing, counting shower tiles?' Paul asked sarcastically.

As he climbed into his bath, Mia spoke to him from the bedroom.

'Departure from hotel at eleven; Book Fair opening ceremony at noon; signing session at one; lunch-break from two fifteen to two thirty; signing session from two thirty to five; return to hotel; departure for television studios at six thirty; make-up at seven; on air at seven thirty; show ends at nine o'clock; dinner, and that's a wrap . . . *Wow. And I complain about my promotion schedules!*

'What was that?' Paul shouted.

'Like a good assistant, I was reading you tomorrow's schedule.'

Paul came bounding out of the bathroom, swaddled in towels.

Mia burst out laughing.

'What's so funny?'

'You look like some sort of fakir.'

'Did I hear you say I only get fifteen minutes for lunch?'

'Welcome to the world of celebrity. The crowd at the airport was impressive, and the hotel receptionist was positively beside himself. I must say I'm quite proud of you.'

'There were more people waiting for me to get off that plane than there usually are at my book signings; those people were hired to act like fans.'

'Don't be so modest. And hurry up and get dressed. A loin-cloth is not a good look on you.'

Paul opened the door of the wardrobe and looked at himself in the mirror.

'Are you kidding? I think it suits me just fine. Maybe I should go on TV dressed like this.' At the mere mention of TV, his voice had cracked.

Mia walked up to Paul, examined the contents of his wardrobe, and took out a pair of grey trousers, a black jacket and a white shirt.

'Here,' she said, handing them over. 'These will look just fine.'

'I was thinking of something blue.'

'No, that won't do, not in your present state. The shirt ought to be paler than your complexion; maybe after a night or two of rest, you can try the blue.'

Opening her bag, she found that the few items of clothing she had brought with her were badly wrinkled.

'Looks like I'm going to stay here and order room service,' she sighed, dropping her clothes on the floor.

'Precisely how much time do we have, Ms Grinberg, before this dinner party commences?' Paul asked in his best pretentious voice.

'Two hours, Mr Barton. And don't start getting a taste for this little arrangement, or I'll have my resignation letter in your hands so fast, it'll make your head spin.'

'Get dressed, Ms Grinberg. And please maintain a respectful tone with your employer.'

'Where are we going?'

'To go check out Seoul. It's the only thing I can think of to keep us conscious until that stupid dinner party.'

They went back down to the lobby. Seeing them emerge from the lift, Ms Bak leapt to her feet and stood at attention.

Paul whispered to her what he had in mind. She bowed and led the way.

Mia was surprised to find herself walking down a street with no tourist attractions in sight, and her confusion increased when Ms Bak led them into a shopping centre. Paul obediently followed her inside and on to an escalator.

'May I ask what we're doing here?' Mia said.

'No, you may not,' Paul replied.

On the third floor, Ms Bak gestured towards a shop window. She stood at the entrance to the shop and told Paul to call her over if he needed anything. Paul ventured inside and Mia followed suit.

'It's a nice idea to give Kyong a dress, but she probably would've preferred one from Paris!'

'I know. I didn't think of it.'

'Let's try to make up for it straightaway. Do you know her size or measurements?'

'I'd say same as yours, more or less.'

'Oh, really? *I pictured her shorter, and a bit chubbier, to be honest . . .*'

Mia looked around and then headed towards some shelves.

'This skirt is pretty. So are these trousers. A lovely top over here, and oh – there's another. Three perfect sweaters, easy as pie, and voilà – a wonderful evening dress.'

'You must have been a costume designer in another life,' Paul said, amazed at the speed with which Mia had picked out the items.

'Oh, come now,' she replied, 'I just have taste.'

Paul took all the clothes Mia had chosen and carried them over to one of the fitting-rooms.

'Now, if you don't mind . . . ,' he said, pulling back the curtain.

'Ah, the lengths a good assistant will go to for her boss,' Mia said, grabbing the clothes.

She went into the fitting-room, closed the curtain, and re-emerged a few minutes later wearing the first outfit. She twirled around like a model, a fake smile plastered on her face.

'Exquisite, perfect,' said Paul. 'Let's have a look at the next one.'

Mia tried it on reluctantly.

Paul looked on, undecided, as Mia went back into the fitting-room and came out again wearing another sweater. He went to get a black dress that he liked a lot and passed it over the curtain.

'You don't think it's a bit tight?' Mia asked.

'Try it on. We'll see.'

'Actually, it's . . . beautiful. You were right,' Mia admitted, coming out of the dressing-room.

'I know. See? You're not the only one with taste.'

After one more change of clothes, Paul found the perfect outfit. While Mia got dressed, he went to the counter to pay, then rejoined Ms Bak at the entrance to the shop. Mia came out of the fitting-room and watched them from a distance.

*My God, who does he think he is? A few fans waiting for him at the airport, and it's gone straight to his head. You want to play superstar, my friend? I'll give you a run for your money,'* she muttered as she walked up to them.

'Back to the hotel?' he asked.

'A little "thank you" wouldn't hurt.'

'Thank you,' said Paul, stepping on to the escalator.

'Are you hoping to charm your translator with two dresses?' Mia asked.

'Not to mention a skirt, three sweaters, two pairs of trousers and two tops.'

'A miniature Eiffel Tower would have done the trick. At least that would have shown you didn't forget about it until the last minute.'

They went back to their hotel room without exchanging another word. Paul lay down on the right side of the bed, hands behind his head

'With your shoes on? Really!' Mia cried.

'They're not even touching the duvet itself.'

'Take them off.'

'What time are they coming to get us?'

'Want to know? You can get up and check your junket schedule.'

'That's a funny term. What am I, a movie star?'

'Can a lowly waitress not employ such an advanced term?'

'Whoa! Calm down. I'm the one who's supposed to be nervous, not you.'

'Me, me, me -- that's all you've talked about since we got here! Go and be nervous by yourself. And you can accompany yourself to that dinner party too, while you're at it. I haven't got a single thing to wear, so I'll have to decline.'

'Actually, I'd say you've got a hell of a selection. I bought those clothes for you. Did you really think I was hoping to seduce Kyong by showering her with gifts? That would just be . . . vulgar. Does that sound anything like me?'

*No. It sounds like David* . . . 'Well, that's very kind of you, but I couldn't possibly accept. There's no reason for me to—'

'Yes, there is, and you just admitted it yourself. You're not going to wear the same clothes this whole trip, are you?'

'I'll go and buy some tomorrow.'

'Mia, come on. Wasn't buying the plane ticket crazy enough? I mean, look, you held my hand on the plane – my very clammy hand

– and bailed me out on the car ride by reining in my chatterbox editor. If it weren't for you, I'd be a total wreck right now, in the fetal position in a dreary suite in a dreary hotel in a foreign city on the other side of the world. There are no strings attached – hang those up on your side of the closet, pick something out to wear, but maybe keep the black dress for the embassy.'

'I'll have to insist on paying you back. These must have cost a fortune.'

'It wasn't me, it was Cristoneli – I squeezed an astronomical advance out of him before agreeing to take this trip.'

Mia took one of the bags into the bathroom. 'I'll let you put the rest away. Seems I have to get ready.'


When she came out, half an hour later, Paul thought she looked even more beautiful than she had back at the store, and still with barely any make-up on.

'So?' she asked.

*Stunning.*

'Not bad. It suits you.'

*What do you mean, 'not bad'?* 'You don't think the skirt is too short?'

*That skirt is making my head spin!* 'Nope. Just right.'

*Do you know how many men would throw their grandma under a bus to spend just one minute alone with me in a hotel suite? And all you've got is 'not bad'?* 'But the top . . . Is the cleavage too much?'

*Half an inch more and you'll cause an all-out riot . . .* 'I hadn't really noticed. Seriously, I think that outfit is just fine.'

*Ha! Wait till you see the look on your translator's face when she gets an eyeful of me, then we'll see who's 'not bad'!* 'If you say so, then I believe you.'

'What is up with you?'

'Did you say something?'

'Nope! Nothing at all.'

Paul gave her a thumbs up and went to the bathroom to get ready.

◆ ◆ ◆

As he entered the restaurant, Paul felt his pulse quicken. Before they had left the hotel, Mia had given him some advice on how to behave in this kind of situation. *Don't do anything that might embarrass Kyong in front of her employers, let her make the first move, and wait cautiously for the right time to express your feelings. If you're seated next to each other and brushing your hand against hers would be too obvious, a gentle knee-to-knee contact should be enough to reassure her.*

And in case he ended up unable to approach her without arousing suspicion, Paul had given Mia a little note that she could hand Kyong at the end of the meal.

When all the guests had taken their places around the table, Paul and Mia exchanged a look. Apparently, Kyong had not been invited.

A series of toasts in Paul's honour launched the evening. The marketing director of the Korean publisher said he'd been thinking of publishing all Paul's works in a single collection intended for students. He wanted to know if Paul would agree to write a preface explaining why he had dedicated his life's work to such a challenging cause. Paul wondered if the man was pulling his leg, but the marketing director's English was far from perfect, and in the end he decided simply to smile. The head of publicity showed him the cover of his latest novel, pointing proudly to the band with its red-letter announcement: *300,000 Copies Sold.* An extraordinary figure for a foreign author, the editor added. The book-shop manager confirmed that not a day went by without him selling several copies of the book. Ms Bak waited patiently before reeling off the list of interviews Paul would have to attend. The television news programme had negotiated exclusivity until the show was broadcast, but after that there would be an interview with the daily newspaper *The Chosun Ilbo*, as well as *Elle Korea*, a one-hour live broadcast with radio service KBS, a one-on-one with a journalist from *Movie Week*, and a more delicate meeting with the radical daily *Hankyoreh*, the only newspaper to support the government's policy of political dialogue with North Korea. When Paul asked why *Hankyoreh* wanted to interview him, everyone at the table laughed. Paul was not in the mood for jokes, and his dazed state contrasted with the liveliness of his companions. Mia came to his rescue, asking a whole series of questions about Seoul – the weather throughout the year, the best places to visit, and so on. She began a conversation about Korean cinema with Paul's editor, who was impressed by her knowledge of the subject. She took advantage of this new-found bond to quietly suggest that he bring the evening to a close, as Mr Barton was exhausted.

Back at the hotel, Paul hopped straight into bed. He adjusted the bolster that separated him from Mia and turned off his bedside lamp before she had even come out of the bathroom.

Mia got under the sheets and waited a few moments.

'Are you asleep?'

'No. I was waiting for you to ask me that question before I could fall asleep.'

'She'll call tomorrow, I'm sure she will.'

'How can you be so sure? She hasn't even left a message for me at the hotel.'

'She did warn you in her email that she would be very busy. Sometimes work just takes over to the point where you can't do anything else.'

Paul propped himself up and peered over the bolster.

'Just a short message – I mean, is that too much to ask? It's like she's been named minister of culture. Why are you making excuses for her?'

'Because . . . it bothers me to see you unhappy,' Mia replied, sitting up in turn. 'I don't know why, that's just the way it is.'

'There you go again, stealing my lines.'

'You know what? Why don't you just shut up.'

In the silence that followed, their faces drew closer and closer . . . until at last they came together, in what can only be described as a moment of infinite tenderness.

'Tell me that wasn't just a pity kiss,' Paul said.

'Have you ever been slapped just after a kiss?'

'No. At least, not yet.'

Mia pressed her lips to his and wished him goodnight. Then she adjusted the bolster and turned off her bedside lamp.

'One question . . . did that count?' Paul asked in the darkness.

'Oh, just go to sleep!' Mia replied.

# 16

Mia had great fun playing the perfect assistant and grew positively giddy about calling Paul 'Mr Barton' every time she spoke to him. Paul was not so amused.

She stood back during the opening of the Book Fair as flash-bulbs popped. It felt good not to be the one in the spotlight for once.

Three hundred people formed a line that stretched out of the bookshop and right down the street. The scale of the reception reminded Mia of her own career – and of Creston, just one more reminder that she should have called him a long time ago. He must be worried sick. She tried to invent a lie that would conceal her whereabouts, but it would have to wait. She hadn't turned her phone back on since the flight – and she wasn't ready to.

Sitting behind a desk, Paul smiled and greeted the seemingly endless stream of readers, all the while struggling to spell or even understand the names of those who introduced themselves. The bookseller bent down and whispered his apologies. It was regrettable that his translator was indisposed and could not come.

'Really. What's the matter with Kyong?' Paul whispered.

'No, I said it's your translator who is sick.'

'Isn't that what I said?'

'No, no. Your translator's name is Eun-Jeong.'

A sudden surge in the crowd put an end to their conversation. Paul remained frozen in shock while the security guards ushered a few fans out of the building and ordered the public into an orderly line once more.

The lunch-break was extended on Mia's orders. Mr Barton needed a rest. Paul was escorted to the bookshop café, which had been closed just for him. His eyes darted back and forth in search of the bookseller, but with no success.

'You look worried,' Mia said.

'I'm not used to there being this many people at a signing. So yes, I'm nervous. And exhausted.'

'That's hardly surprising. You haven't even touched your food. Eat something – you'll need all the energy you can get for the second round. Have you realised how wonderful all this is for your career? Your readers are positively beaming about meeting you. Even I'm touched. Do try to smile a little more – though I know it's tiring. The greatest reward we can ever receive is the love of our fans. It gives meaning to our work . . . to everything we give others. What could be more satisfying than sharing that joy?'

'Have a lot of experience with this type of thing, do you?'

'Of course not, that's not what I meant.'

'I'm just saying I've never experienced anything like this in my life.'

'Well, you may have to get used to it.'

'I don't think so. I'm not really sure it's my thing. I didn't leave California just to go through the same thing abroad. I mean, it's a pleasant experience, and I'm touched, but . . . I'm definitely not star material.'

'Anyone can be star material. Believe me, you'll get a taste for it pretty quickly.'

'I'm not so sure about that,' Paul replied in a sullen voice.

'Still nothing from her?' Mia asked casually.

'Not a word.'

'It'll happen. And soon.'

Paul looked up at her.

'Mia, about last night—'

'Sorry, it's time to see your devoted, adoring public once more,' Mia interrupted, rising to her feet.

The security guards accompanied Paul back to the signing desk, and Mia stayed at the café. Moments later, a young female fan rushed up and stole the glass that Paul had been drinking from.

*You seem so helpless in the face of your own success,* Mia thought. *And so utterly sincere when you say you don't want fame. And yet you had to meet me, of all people . . . Makes me wonder if two people like us could ever really be compatible . . .*

Little by little, the bookshop emptied out. The last reader took yet another selfie with Paul, who smiled his last smile of the day. He heard his bones creak as he stood up slowly from his chair.

'It's the price of fame,' the bookshop manager said when he came over to thank Paul.

Mia was waiting for him near the exit with Ms Bak.

'Who exactly was this Ms Jung you mentioned earlier?' Paul asked.

'Eun-Jeong,' the bookseller corrected him. 'I told you: she translates your books. Your success is partly thanks to her, you know. I've never met her, but I can tell you she certainly has a remarkable way with words.'

'Kyong. My translator's name is Kyong!' Paul protested. 'I think I would know that.'

'Her name must have been spelled wrong in English – our language is full of subtle nuances – but I can assure you that her name is Eun-Jeong. It is written on the cover of all your books. In Korean, of course. I'm sorry she couldn't be here today. She would have been so proud.'

'What's wrong with her?'

'A bad case of flu, I think. But it's time to go now: your day is far from over, and your editor will be cross with me if I keep you any longer.'

A limousine took them back to the hotel. Ms Bak was sitting in the front passenger seat. Paul didn't say a word, and Mia began to worry.

'Tell me what's wrong,' she whispered to him.

Paul pressed a button and the glass partition that separated them from the chauffeur and Ms Bak slid up.

'Huh. Look at that! Maybe I could get used to this . . .'

'Paul!'

'She's sick. Bad case of the flu, apparently.'

'Well, that's good news. Not for her, obviously, but at least it could explain the absence and lack of contact. Now, just think, how long does a bad case of flu last? A week? More? When did she fall ill?'

'How should I know?'

'I thought you might have asked. You must have inquired about her, if you learned she was ill.'

'No. Not at all. It was the bookshop guy who told me. She was supposed to be there today.'

'And what else did he tell you?'

'Nothing – he probably didn't know more than that.'

'So let's be optimistic and hope she gets back on her feet in a few days . . . *Back on her big, ugly feet . . . Horrid and huge, in fact . . .*'

'You're muttering.'

'I never mutter. Muttering is completely foreign to me.'

Mia turned to the window and stared out at the landscape passing by.

'Forget Kyong, at least for tonight . . . *Or go ahead and forget her, full stop!* What you need to do is focus on your very first television appearance.'

'I don't want to do it. I'm sick of all this. I just want to go back to the hotel, order room service, and go to bed.'

*Tell me about it . . .* 'Paul, don't be childish. This is your career we're talking about. Pull yourself together and act professional. The show must go on.'

'You're supposed to be playing assistant, not taskmaster.'

'Oh, all I've been doing is playing, then?' Mia said crossly, turning to face him.

'Sorry, I'm nervous. I'm talking out of my ass. I should just keep my mouth shut.'

'Once, after hearing a young actress boast that she never got stage-fright, Sarah Bernhardt said: "Don't worry, it comes with talent."'

'Am I supposed to take that as a compliment?'

'Take it however you want. There's the hotel. You should have a bath – it would do you a world of good. After that, get changed, and don't think about anything but your characters, your friends . . . the things that reassure you. You can't ignore your nerves, but you can fight to overcome them. As soon as you get out on that set, they'll disappear.'

'I don't get how you know all this,' Paul said in a lost voice.

'I just do. Trust me.'


Paul lay for a long time luxuriating in the hot, foaming water. He put on the jacket, trousers and white shirt Mia had picked out for him. Cameras hated blue, he was learning, and men who wore blue had less presence on television. Mia claimed everyone knew that. Around six o'clock, she ordered a snack and Paul forced himself to put something in his stomach. She then made him learn a short introduction by heart, being sure to thank his Korean readers, telling them how touched he was by their warm welcome, what an amazing city Seoul was, even if he hadn't had time to see all of it yet, and, of course, that he was delighted to be visiting the country. Paul reeled the phrases off in parrot-like fashion, eyes fixed on the television clock as it counted down the minutes. And as time ticked by, his anxiety grew, tying his stomach in knots.

At six thirty sharp, they were ready and waiting in the limousine, per the schedule.

Halfway through the ride, Paul suddenly knocked on the glass partition and begged the chauffeur to stop the car.

He rushed outside and threw up his snack. Mia held him by the shoulders. When the spasms had calmed down, she gave him a tissue and some chewing-gum.

'Marvelful,' said Paul, straightening up. 'Clammy hands on the plane and now I vomit all over the pavement. You really hit the jackpot, coming to Korea with me.'

'All that matters is that your jacket isn't stained. How do you feel?'

'Like a million bucks. How do you think I feel?'

'Well, at least you didn't vomit up your sense of humour. Shall we?'

'Let's. Can't be late for the slaughter-house.'

Back in the car, Mia turned to Paul abruptly and said, 'Look me in the eyes . . . I said in the eyes! Does your mother watch Korean television?'

'She's dead.'

'I'm sorry to hear that. What about your sister?'

'I'm an only child.'

'Do you have any other Korean friends?'

'Not that I know of.'

'Perfect! Kyong is bedridden with flu, and when you have flu, even the glow from a night light can make your headache unbearable. So there's no risk that she'll be watching telly tonight, and nor will anyone else you know or love. In other words, this programme *does not matter*. So it doesn't mean a thing if you're brilliant or pathetic. Besides, anything you say will be translated anyway.'

215

'So why bother going?'

'For the show, for your readers. So you can describe the experience in full detail in one of your future books. When you go out on that set, try telling yourself that you're one of your characters. Try to act the way he would, and you'll be perfect.'

Paul looked at Mia for a long moment.

'What about you? I assume you'll be watching.'

'Not a chance.'

'Liar.'

'Now spit out that chewing-gum, will you? We're here.'


Mia stayed with Paul during make-up, intervening twice to prevent the make-up artist from concealing the crow's feet around his eyes.

When the floor manager came seeking Paul, Mia followed them through the backstage area and dispensed her final piece of advice just before he went on set.

'Don't forget – the most important thing is not what you say, but how you say it. On TV, the sheer musicality of words is more important than their meaning. I know what I'm talking about. I am a . . . die-hard talk show fan, after all.'

The banks of spotlights snapped on, the floor manager pushed Paul forwards, and he walked out on to the set, eyes dazzled.

The presenter invited Paul to take a seat in the chair across from him, and a technician approached to fit him with an earpiece. It tickled Paul's ear, causing him to wriggle. The sound mixer had to try three times before he got it right.

'See? He's going to be fine.' Mia sighed backstage as she watched the colour return to Paul's face.

Paul heard the voice of his interpreter introducing himself in his ear. The translation would be simultaneous, so he asked Paul to speak in short sentences, with pauses in between. Paul nodded, which the presenter took as a hello and felt obliged to return.

'We're going to begin soon,' the interpreter whispered from the control room. 'You can't see me, but I can see you on my control panel.'

'Okay,' Paul said, heart pounding.

'Don't address me or reply to what I say, of course, Mr Barton. Please only respond to Mr Tae Hoon. Watch his lips and listen to my voice. The viewers won't hear yours.'

'Who is this Mr Tae-Hoon?'

'The host of the show.'

'Ah. Right.'

'Is this your first time on TV?'

Another nod, immediately returned by Tae-Hoon.

'We're on the air now.'

Paul focused on Tae-Hoon's face.

'Good evening, we are pleased tonight to welcome the American writer Paul Barton. To our great regret, Mr Murakami has the flu and cannot be with us tonight. We wish him a speedy recovery.'

'The flu, of course,' said Paul. 'First, it hits the only woman in the world I care about, now Murakami. Oh, shit. Don't translate that, please!'

Hearing this, Mia removed her earpiece and stormed out of the backstage area. She asked the floor manager to accompany her to Mr Barton's dressing-room.

'Mr Barton,' said the presenter after a brief hesitation, 'your books have been a huge success in our country. Could you explain to us what led you to embrace the cause of the North Korean people?'

'North Korean . . . I beg your pardon?'

'Was my translation unclear?' asked the voice in his ear.

'The translation wasn't the problem; it was the question.'

The presenter coughed and went on.

'Your latest novel is very powerful. It describes the life of a family under the yoke of dictatorship, trying to survive the repression of

Kim Jong-un's regime, and it does so with an accuracy that might seem surprising from a foreign writer. How did you manage such in-depth research on the subject?'

'Houston, we have a problem,' Paul muttered to his interpreter.

'What's the problem?'

'I haven't read the latest Murakami yet, but I have a feeling Mr Tae-Hoon has mixed the two of us up. Please don't translate that either!'

'I had no intention of translating it, but I don't understand what you're saying.'

'I have never written a single word about the North Korean dictatorship in my life, not one goddamn word!' Paul hissed, forcing himself to keep smiling.

The presenter, receiving no reply in his earpiece, mopped his brow, apologised, and announced that they were experiencing a small technical problem that would soon be resolved.

'This is not the time or place for jokes, Mr Barton,' the interpreter said. 'This show is being broadcast live. Please answer the questions seriously – my job is on the line here. If you keep acting like this, you'll get me fired. I must say something to Mr Tae-Hoon now.'

'Well, you can start by saying hello from me, and warning him that he's made a mistake. I don't know what else to tell you.'

'I have personally read all your books. I cannot understand your attitude.'

'You have got to be kidding – is this a hidden-camera thing, or what?'

'The camera is in plain sight, directly in front of you. Have you been drinking?'

Paul stared at the lens and the red light blinking above it. Mr Tae-Hoon seemed to be losing his patience.

'I would like to take a moment to thank all my Korean readers, from the bottom of my heart,' Paul said. 'I'm very touched by the warmth of their welcome. Seoul is an amazing city, even if I haven't had time to see all of it yet. I am overjoyed to be here visiting your wonderful country.'

Paul heard his interpreter sigh with relief before translating his words into Korean.

'Excellent,' said Tae-Hoon, 'I think we have resolved our technical difficulty. So I will now put the same two questions to our author, and this time, he will be able to provide his answers.'

While the presenter was speaking, Paul muttered to his interpreter: 'As I have no idea what he's talking about, and as you've personally read all my books, I'm just going to recite my Parisian butcher's recipe for beef stew over and over again, and you, my friend, can reply directly to Mr Tae-Hoon's questions on my behalf.'

'That's impossible! I could never do such a thing,' the interpreter whispered.

'You're going to have to. Your job is on the line here, remember? On TV, the musicality of words is more important than their actual meaning, I'll have you know. So don't worry, you do the talking and I will try to keep smiling.'

And so the programme went on. The interpreter translated the interviewer's questions into Paul's ear, while the interviewer persisted in questioning the author about books that he hadn't written, all of which seemed to revolve obsessively around the condition of the North Korean people, and Paul, with a smile glued on to his face, said anything that came into his head, keeping his sentences short, with pauses in between each of them. The interpreter, unable to translate this into anything intelligible, became the author for the night, responding brilliantly in Paul's place.

The nightmare lasted a full sixty minutes, but no one suspected a thing.

Walking off the set, Paul looked around for Mia. The floor manager guided him to the dressing-room.

'You were wonderful,' Mia assured him.

'Yeah, I killed it. Thank you for keeping your promise.'

'What promise was that?'

219

'Not to watch the show.'

'I watched enough. What a pity . . . you were so looking forward to meeting Murakami. First, the "only woman you care about" comes down with flu, then him.'

'Look, I didn't mean that.'

'Let's go. You're not the only one who is exhausted by the day's events,' she said as she left the dressing-room. 'By the way, I'm afraid I have to tender my resignation, effective immediately.'

Paul rushed after her and caught her arm.

'Mia! I didn't mean a word of it.'

'But you said it.'

'Well, it was crap. And believe me, it wasn't the only crap I spouted tonight!'

'I'm sure you were excellent.'

'The only reason I survived at all tonight was because of you. So . . . thank you, from the bottom of my heart. And I really do mean that.'

'Fine. You're welcome.'

Mia broke free from his grip and walked resolutely towards the exit.


Back at the hotel, Mia fell straight asleep. On the other side of the bolster, Paul lay with his eyes wide open, trying to make sense of the day's bizarre developments. Failing to do so, he began worrying about what the next day would hold.

# 17

Mia was awoken by the creak of a door. She opened her eyes. Paul was pushing a room service cart into the room. He went to her side, saying good morning.

'Coffee, freshly squeezed orange juice, pastries, hard-boiled eggs and cereal. Would the lady care for anything else?'

He poured her a cup of coffee.

Mia sat up and arranged the pillows behind her back.

'To what do I owe all this special treatment?'

'Nothing special about it. Now that I've fired my assistant, I'm going to have to do everything around here myself,' Paul replied.

'That's strange, I heard she resigned.'

'Well, she had the right idea. I would much rather lose an employee and keep a friend. Sugar?'

'Yes, please.'

'And as I am now my own assistant, I took a few liberties this morning. All today's appointments have been cancelled. Our only obligation is the reception at the embassy. The rest of the day is free. Seoul is ours to explore until this evening, so let's make the most of it. Every last moment.'

'You cancelled *all* your appointments?'

'Postponed them until tomorrow. I said I was coming down with something. After all, I can't let Murakami monopolise the flu. It's a question of status.'

Mia caught sight of the newspaper lying folded on the breakfast-table and quickly made a grab for it.

'Your photo's on the front page!'

'I know. They didn't get my good side. Awful. Looks like there's about ten pounds more of me than there should be.'

'Come on, you look good. Have you called your press officer to ask her to translate the article for you? A front-page photo – that's a big deal!'

'For now, I have no way of knowing if the coverage is positive or negative, but I do have a creeping suspicion the whole thing might actually be about Murakami's latest novel and not mine.'

'Where did this obsession with Murakami come from? That's the second time you've mentioned him in the past five minutes.'

'There's no obsession. Although, after last night, I'd have good reason to be obsessed.'

'What do you mean?'

'I half-wish you *had* watched the thing. It was so surreal. Getting interviewed by a journalist who hasn't read my books is one thing, but nothing could have prepared me for an interview with someone who was mixing up my book with somebody else's!'

'What in the world are you talking about?'

'Last night! The moron kept asking me questions that were obvi-ously intended for . . . I'm not going to say his name, or you'll accuse me of being obsessed again. There I am, alone on the set, sitting across from the host. "So, what led to your interest in the fate of the North Korean people? How did you find out so much information about the lives of those oppressed by Kim Jong-un's regime? Why are you so committed to this cause in particular? Do you think the days are num-bered for the dictator's reign? In your opinion, is Kim Jong-un a puppet leader appointed by an oligarchy or is he really, truly in control? Are your characters inspired by reality or did you invent them?" Et cetera, et cetera . . .'

'You can't be serious!' said Mia, unsure whether to laugh or show sympathy.

'That's exactly what I said to the interpreter talking to me through that stupid earpiece. Those things really do itch, you know. I thought it might be some kind of prank. That seemed like the most logical explanation. At first, I told myself I wasn't going to let them put one over on me, not that easily, but after twenty minutes, the joke was getting pretty stale. Except it wasn't a joke. Those jackasses somehow got their authors mixed up, and the interpreter was too scared to tell them.'

'That is absolutely crazy,' Mia replied, covering her mouth with her hand to suppress the laughter she could feel welling up inside her.

'Go ahead, laugh it up, I haven't stopped laughing since we got back last night. I mean – this is the type of thing that could only happen to me. Only me.'

'But how could they have made such an outrageous mistake?'

'Stupidity has no bounds. Let's not waste our day on that,' Paul said, grabbing the newspaper from Mia's hands and tossing it to the other end of the room. 'Finish your breakfast and let's head out for a walk.'

'Are you sure you're okay?'

'Oh, I'm fine. I only made a complete fool of myself in front of hundreds of thousands of viewers. Somebody must have told the TV channel about their screw-up, which is presumably what that article is all about. So if anyone on the street bursts into laughter when they see me, let's try to pretend we can't hear them.'

'I'm so sorry, Paul.'

'Don't be. Let's move on. You said it yourself: no one cares about that TV show. And look what a beautiful day it is outside!'

Paul persuaded Mia to leave the hotel through the back car park, in case Ms Bak was waiting for him in the lobby. He planned to spend the day alone with Mia, and the last thing he wanted was the added encumbrance of a guide.

They spent the morning visiting Changgyeonggung Palace. Walking through Honghwa Gate, Paul attempted to pronounce all the names he saw, and his guttural exaggerations had Mia in stitches. Standing on Okcheongyo Bridge, she admired the ornamental pond and the beauty of the historical surroundings.

'That's Myeongjeongjeon, the throne hall,' said Paul, pointing to a small single-storey building. 'It was opened in 1484. All the houses you see are facing south, because the ancestral shrines of the royal family are located in the south, but Myeongjeongjeon faces east, going against Confucian tradition.'

'Did Kyong teach you all that?'

'What? Who's this Kyong? No, I picked up a brochure when I was buying the tickets. It was my attempt at impressing you. Would you like to see the botanical garden?'


They left the palace and visited the Insa-dong district. They wandered into art galleries, stopped to sample traditional pancakes, and spent the rest of the afternoon rummaging through antique stores. Mia wanted to get a present for Daisy. She was hesitating between an old spice-box and a beautiful necklace. Paul advised Mia to go for the necklace, while he discreetly signalled the antique dealer to wrap up the spice-box. He presented it to Mia and said: 'Give this to Daisy from me.'


They got back to the hotel just in time to prepare for the evening. Catching sight of Ms Bak standing vigil in the lobby, Mia pushed Paul behind a pillar. They crept from one pillar to the next, finally taking advantage of a passing bell-boy and his luggage cart to reach the lifts without being spotted.

At seven o'clock, Mia put on her dress.

'If you say I look "not bad" one more time, we'll see how good you look showing up stag to the ambassador's!' Mia announced, admiring herself in the mirror.

'All right, I'll keep my mouth shut, then.' Paul allowed himself a smile of pride at having bought the dress for her.

'Paul!'

'What can I say? You look—'

'Don't you dare!' Mia interrupted.

'Beautiful. You look beautiful.'

'Well, in that case, thank you for the compliment.'

Half an hour later, the limousine dropped them in front of the American ambassador's residence.

The ambassador was waiting for his guests in the entrance-hall. Paul and Mia were the first to arrive.

'Mr Barton. It's an honour and a pleasure to welcome you to my home,' the ambassador began.

'The honour is all mine,' Paul replied, introducing Mia.

The ambassador bent to kiss her hand.

'Tell me a little about yourself, Ms Grinberg,' he said.

'Mia has a restaurant in Paris,' Paul replied on her behalf.

The ambassador led them into a large drawing-room.

'I haven't had time to read your latest novel yet,' he whispered to Paul. 'I speak a little Korean, but unfortunately not enough for a whole book. On the other hand, I can tell you that you made my partner cry his eyes out. You're all he's talked about for the past week. He was deeply moved by your novel. Part of his family lives in North Korea and he told me that your story was incredibly accurate and detailed. How I envy the freedom you have as a writer. Giving voice to viewpoints that people in my position are forced to keep under wraps, due to diplomatic obligations. But allow me to say that with this novel, with this story, you are speaking for all of America.'

Paul frowned at the ambassador for several moments.

'Um . . . Would you mind elaborating on that a bit?' he asked warily.

'My partner is Korean, as I said, and . . . Oh, there he is! I assure you he's far more eloquent than I am. I'll let you go ahead and introduce yourself. He's dying to meet you. In the meantime, I should probably go and welcome our other guests. And, if you don't mind, I'm going to kidnap your charming friend here to come along as back-up. Don't you worry, I'm harmless,' the ambassador added with a smile.

Mia shot a pleading look at Paul, but their host was already leading her away.

Paul barely had time to come to his senses before a slender and extremely elegant man flung his arms around his neck and pressed his head against Paul's shoulder.

'Thank you, thank you, thank you,' he said. 'I'm so honoured to meet you.'

'Um . . . Me too,' said Paul, attempting to free himself from the man's grip. 'But for what exactly am I being thanked?'

'For everything! For being who you are, for your words, your deep concern for the fate of my people. Who else cares these days? What your work means to me . . . you can't even imagine.'

'You're right, actually, I can't. Is this some sort of mass prank or what?'

'I don't understand.'

'Neither do I,' said Paul, exasperated. 'I don't understand anything any more.'

The two men looked each other up and down.

'I hope you are not shocked by my relationship with Henry, Mr Barton. We've been deeply in love for ten years. We even have a child together, a little boy we adopted, whom we love very dearly.'

'No, no – that's not it. I grew up in San Francisco and I'm a Democrat. Love whoever you want. What I don't understand is what you were saying about my book.'

'Did I say something offensive? If that is the case, please excuse me. Your novel is so very important to me.'

'My novel? *My* novel? The one I wrote?'

'Yes, yours, of course,' the man replied, holding up the book he gripped in his hand.

While Paul was incapable of deciphering the hangul characters, he had no trouble recognising his photo on the back cover, the same his editor had shown him the day before yesterday. The deep well of confusion filled Paul with doubt. And this doubt grew and grew, until finally he felt as though the ground were giving way beneath his feet.

'Would you agree to sign it for me?' the man pleaded. 'My name is Shin.'

Paul took him by the arm.

'Is there someplace nearby where we could talk for a moment in private?'


Shin led Paul down a corridor and into an office.

'We won't be disturbed here,' he assured Paul, gesturing to a chair.

Paul took a deep breath and tried to find the right words.

'You speak perfect English. And I assume you're fluent in Korean?'

'Yes, of course. I am Korean,' Shin replied, sitting down opposite Paul.

'Good. And so you've read my book?'

'Twice! It had such a powerful effect on me. And every night before I go to sleep, I re-read a passage.'

'Fantastic. Shin, I just have a small favour to ask.'

'Anything.'

'Don't worry, it really is small.'

'What can I do for you, Mr Barton?'

'Tell me . . . what happens in my book.'

'Excuse me?'

'You heard me right. If you don't know where to start, just give me a summary of the first few chapters, and we'll take it from there.'

'Are you sure? But why?'

'It's impossible for a writer to assess the fidelity of a translation in a language he doesn't speak. But you . . . are bilingual. So go ahead. It'll be easy.'


Shin seemed to take Paul's request at face value. He told him what happened in his novel, starting at the beginning.

In the first chapter, Paul was introduced to a child who had grown up in North Korea. Her family lived in unimaginable poverty, as did all the inhabitants of the village. The dictatorial regime, imposed by a cruel dynasty, kept the entire population in slavery. Their free time was devoted to worshipping the leaders. The school – which most children were not allowed to attend, being forced instead to work in the fields – was merely a propaganda tool designed to mould impressionable minds into thinking of their torturers as supreme deities.

In the second chapter, Paul met the narrator's father, a university lecturer. In the evenings, he secretly taught English literature to his brightest students, undertaking the perilous task of teaching them to think for themselves and attempting to instil in them the wonderful virtues of liberty.

In chapter three, the narrator's father was denounced to the authorities by the mother of one of his students. After being tortured, he was executed in front of his family. His students suffered the same fate, and their bodies were all dragged by horses through the streets. The only student spared was the one whose parents had betrayed the lecturer. Instead of being killed, that girl was imprisoned in a labour camp for the rest of her life.

In the next chapter, the heroine of the novel recounted how her brother, who had stolen a few grains of corn, was beaten and locked in a cage too small to stand up or lie down in. His torturers burned his skin. One year later, the narrator's aunt, after accidentally damaging a sewing-machine, had her thumbs chopped off by her employer.

In chapter six, the heroine was seventeen years old. The night of her birthday, she left her family and ran away. Crossing valleys and rivers on foot, hiding by day and travelling by night, eating only roots and wild grass, she managed to sneak past the police officers patrolling the border and at last entered South Korea, the land of resilience.

Shin paused, seeing that the author of the story was just as overwhelmed at hearing the saga unfold as Shin himself had been upon reading it, if not more so. It suddenly hit Paul how insignificant his own prose was.

'What happens next?' Paul asked. 'Tell me what happens next!'

'But you already know what happens!' Shin replied.

'Please, just go on,' Paul begged him.

'In Seoul, your heroine is welcomed by an old friend of her father's, another defector from the regime. He looks after her as if she were his own daughter and provides for her education. After university, she gets a job and devotes all her free time to informing the world about the plight of her compatriots.'

'What sort of job?'

'She starts out as an assistant in a publishing house, then she is promoted to copy editor, and finally she becomes editorial director.'

'Go on,' said Paul, through gritted teeth.

229

'The money she earns is used to pay people smugglers, and to fund foreign opposition movements, all with the intent of making Western politicians aware of the situation and pushing them into finally taking action against Kim Jong-un's regime. Twice a year, she travels abroad to secretly meet with these groups. Her family members are still at the mercy of a ruthless regime; if anyone were to make the connection, her mother, her brother and especially the man she loves would pay a heavy price.'

'I think I've heard enough,' Paul interrupted, looking at the floor.

'Mr Barton, are you all right?'

'You know, I'm really not sure.'

'Can I help you?' Shin asked, handing him a tissue.

'One last question. The main character in my story, my heroine,' Paul asked, wiping his eyes. 'Her name . . . is it, by any chance . . . Kyong?'

'Why yes, of course,' said the ambassador's partner.

Paul found Mia in the drawing-room. Upon seeing how pale and haggard he looked, she put down her glass of champagne, apologised to the person she'd been talking to, and came over to him.

'What's the matter?' she asked, concerned.

'Do you think there's an emergency exit in this building?' he said numbly. 'Or in life in general, preferably . . .'

'You're white as a sheet.'

'I need a drink. A stiff one.'

Mia grabbed a martini from a tray held by a passing waiter and handed it to Paul. He downed it in one gulp.

'Let's go somewhere quiet and you can tell me everything.'

'Not now,' Paul replied, his jaw clenched. 'I can't just keel over and faint right before the ambassador gives his speech.'

During the meal, Paul couldn't shake the vision: a family could be starving to death only a hundred miles from this room where waiters proffered lavish trays of petits fours and foie gras canapés. Two worlds, separated by a border. His own world had ceased to exist one hour earlier. Had Kyong planned this all along? Mia kept trying to catch his eye, but Paul couldn't see it. When he left the table, Mia followed him. He thanked the ambassador and apologised for the fatigue that forced him to leave.

Shin accompanied them to the door. He shook hands with Paul for a long time on the steps of the mansion. Seeing his gentle, sad smile, Paul felt certain Shin had pieced together some of the truth of the situation.


'What in the world could have put you in this state? Did something happen to Kyong?' Mia asked as the limousine drove away.

'Yes, sort of. It happened to both of us, apparently. My success in Korea was never real. My novels never really existed here, and Kyong was a hell of a lot more than just a translator.'

Mia listened in shock as Paul went on.

'She kept my name on the covers of the books, but that was all. Under that front, she published her own novels – her story, her battles. That TV host yesterday wasn't a moron at all, and neither was the interpreter. I'll have to be sure to apologise to them. And, you know, all this would be like one gigantic farce, if the real subject of my Korean novels were not so tragic. To think . . . for years I've been living off royalties from books I didn't even write. You were right to tender your resignation – you were working for an impostor. My only excuse is that I didn't know a thing about any of this.'

Mia asked the chauffeur to stop the car.

'Come on,' she said to Paul. 'You need some fresh air.'

They walked side by side in silence until Paul started speaking again.

'I have every right to hate her for what she did. But behind all the betrayal and deception is something noble. If she had published those books under her own name, it would have been a death sentence for her family.'

'What are you planning to do?'

'I don't know. I need to think. All throughout dinner, I was trying to wrap my head around it. I guess I'll have to play along, at least while I'm here. Otherwise, I risk putting her in danger. When I get back to Paris, I'll send her the money she's owed and cancel that contract. Cristoneli's going to be just thrilled: I can see it now, him having a conniption right at the Deux Magots. And when the dust settles, I'll have to figure out a way to make a living.'

'Nothing is forcing you to do any of that. That money came from Korean publishers, and they must have made a fortune off your books.'

'Not my books. Kyong's.'

'If you really decide to go through with this, you're going to have to give some kind of explanation.'

'We'll see. Anyway, at least now I understand why she's been MIA. I have to find her so we can talk about this. I can't leave without seeing her.'

'You do love her, don't you?'

Paul stopped and shrugged. 'Let's go home. I'm freezing. God, what a weird night!'

In the lift that took them up to their suite, Mia stood in front of Paul. She gently stroked his face and then abruptly slapped him. Paul snapped out of his stupor. Mia pressed him against the wall and kissed him.

They were still kissing when the doors opened and they continued kissing out in the corridor, his back pressed against the wall, sliding from door to door until they reached their room.

They were still kissing as they got undressed, and didn't stop even as they fell on to the bed together.

Mia whispered: 'This doesn't count. None of it counts, nothing but the present moment . . .'

And they kissed mouths and necks, stomachs and hips, legs and thighs, their limbs entangled. Their breath came faster as they locked each other in a furious embrace until, weak with exhaustion, they fell asleep on the damp sheets.

# 18

Paul and Mia were yanked out of bed by the ringing of the telephone.

'Fuck!' he yelled as he saw the clock on the TV, flashing *10.00 a.m.*

Ms Bak was on the line, apologising profusely but reminding him that the first interview of the day was supposed to start thirty minutes ago . . .

Paul located his boxer shorts underneath the curtains.

. . . the journalist from *The Chosun Ilbo* was waiting for him . . .

He grabbed his trousers from the armchair and pulled them on, hopping over to the dresser.

. . . in one of the rooms . . . and he was getting quite impatient . . .

Paul's shirt was torn. Mia rushed over to the wardrobe and threw him a clean one.

. . . an interviewer from *Elle Korea* had just arrived as well . . .

*'It's blue!'* Paul whispered.

. . . and soon enough there'd be no way to get to the KBS radio studios on time . . .

*'That's fine for the press!'* Mia whispered back.

. . . Ms Bak had managed to postpone the one-on-one discussion with a columnist from *Movie Week* until after the interview with *Han-kyoreh* . . .

Paul buttoned his shirt.

. . . the one that was known for supporting the government's policy of political dialogue with North Korea . . .

Mia unbuttoned the shirt and redid the buttons, this time in the right button-holes.

. . . and then there would be a public event . . .

'*Where the hell are my shoes?*'

'*One's under the dresser, the other's in the doorway!*'

. . . with students, on the main stage of the Book Fair.

Ms Bak had managed to recite the whole schedule for the day in one single breath.

'Don't worry, I'm already on my way down!'

'*Liar! Go on, I'll catch up with you later.*'

'When?'

'*Just before you leave for the radio station.*'


The door of the suite closed. There was a crash in the corridor outside and the sound of Paul yelling obscenities.

Mia looked out and saw a room service cart knocked on to its side in the corridor, its contents scattered in all directions across the carpet.

'Seriously?' she asked, watching Paul get to his feet.

'I'm fine. No stains, and I barely got hurt.'

'Just go!' she ordered him.

Back in the room, she walked over to the window and looked down at the city all stretched out under a grey sky. She picked up her phone and turned it on. Thirteen messages appeared on the screen. Eight from Creston, four from David and one from Daisy. Mia threw the phone on to the bed and ordered breakfast, warning the room service staff of a clean-up needed out in the hallway.

◆ ◆ ◆

From the lobby, Ms Bak led Paul in a mad sprint to an adjoining room.

'Could I get a coffee?' he begged.

'It's waiting for you on the table, Mr Barton. Don't blame me if it's cold, though.'

'A little something to munch on?'

'You can't give an interview with your mouth full. That would be impolite!'

She ushered Paul into the room. He apologised to the journalist, and the interview began.

It felt strange to appropriate Kyong's story. Stranger still, stepping into her shoes seemed somehow natural, like he'd already walked a thousand miles in them. He was surprised at the ease with which he answered each question, embellishing his account with deep and sincere thoughts, so much so that, by the end, the interviewer was almost in tears. And the very same thing happened with the journalist from *Elle Korea*. Afterwards, Paul agreed to a photo shoot, giving free rein to the photographer who had already been snapping away throughout the interview. He dutifully sat on a table, crossed his arms, uncrossed them, placed a hand under his chin, smiled, looked serious, stared into space, looked left, looked right. Ms Bak finally rescued him by announcing that he had other obligations to fulfil.

She was hurrying him towards the limousine when Paul managed to escape and make a run for the reception desk.

'Call my room, please,' he told the concierge.

'Ah, Mr Barton, the young lady left a message for you. She fell back asleep after you left and— '

Paul leaned over the desk and pointed at the switchboard.

'Now! Call her now!'

Ms Bak was going from tense to frantic, and Mia still wasn't picking up.

'The young lady is in the bath,' said the concierge. 'She said she'll meet you later at the Book Fair. She asked what time your speech was.'

The press officer promised to do what was necessary. She would send a car to pick up his colleague, she said, clearing her throat as she uttered the word *colleague*.

Paul hung up and followed Ms Bak, his heart heavy. Suddenly he turned on his heel, plunged his hand into the bowl of sweets sitting on the desk, and filled his pockets.

The hour he spent at the KBS studios seemed to last an eternity, but he felt more confident as the interview went on. By the end, even Ms Bak had to wipe away a tear.

'You were perfect,' she said as they left the building, before ushering him into the limousine.

He was escorted from the entrance of the exhibition centre on to the stage, in front of two hundred students eagerly awaiting the chance to hear him speak.

When he was introduced, the standing ovation he received left him with a helpless, crushing feeling. He began to scan the audience for Mia, his eyes flitting from row to row, when the first questions from the floor brought him back to the role he was supposed to be playing.

Paul played his part with a fervour that was almost militant. He denounced, incriminated and hurled accusations at the monsters of the totalitarian regime, adding a full-throated condemnation of the inertia of Western democracies. Several times, the crowd broke into spontaneous applause.

Just as he was starting to get even more carried away with his own eloquence, a sight stopped Paul mid-sentence. He had just seen Eun-Jeong, alias Kyong, in the audience. From the last row, her smile was enough to make him lose his train of thought.

◆ ◆ ◆

Half-hidden behind a pillar, Mia smiled too, a serene and tender smile.

She hadn't taken her eyes off Paul, feeling a tug at her heartstrings each time the audience applauded. Then, as the students pressed towards the stage to get his autograph, she lost sight of him.

Having been through similar experiences many times herself, she could imagine the sense of euphoria he must be feeling at that moment, surrounded by his admirers.

Kyong was the last person to approach the stage.

'Still no sign of Mia, right?' Paul asked Ms Bak, who was waiting outside the small room where he had taken refuge.

'Your colleague was in attendance for the speech,' she replied, pointing to the place where Mia had stood, 'but she asked to be taken back to the hotel.'

'When was this?'

'Just over an hour ago, I would say. She left while you were talking to Ms Eun-Jeong.'

This time, it was Paul who hurried his press officer towards the limousine.

He rushed across the hotel lobby towards the lifts, then sprinted down the corridor to their suite, stopping short to straighten his clothes and run his fingers through his hair before opening the door.

'Mia?'

He went into the bathroom. Her toothbrush was no longer in the glass, and her toiletry bag was gone from the rim of the sink.

Paul walked back into the bedroom and found a note lying on the bolster.

*Paul,*

*Thank you for being there for me, thank you for your joyful nature, your lapses of sanity, and for this unexpected journey that began with a walk over the rooftops of Paris. Thank you for managing, against all odds, to bring laughter back into my life. Laughter, and new memories. Our paths must part tonight. These past few days have been a dream.*

*I understand the dilemma you are facing and how you must be feeling. You've been living a life that wasn't truly yours, in love with the idea of happiness rather than happiness itself. In some ways, you don't even know who you are any more. But you are not responsible for this duplicity, and there's no way I can help guide you through the coming choices.*

*Because you love her, because her treachery was so sublime, not to mention heroic, you should forgive her. Perhaps that's what it means, in the end, to truly love someone. Forgiveness, without reservations and above all without regrets. Hitting the delete key and erasing the grey pages so that you can rewrite them in full colour. Better still, maybe love is fighting tooth and nail to make sure the story has a happy ending. Take care of yourself, even if that phrase doesn't mean very much. I will truly miss your company and all the intimate moments we have shared. I can't wait to find out what happens to our opera singer. Please hurry up and write her story so I can read it.*

*May your life be full of beauty – you deserve nothing less.*

*Your friend,*

*Mia*

*P.S. Don't worry about yesterday – it doesn't count.*

'No, you got it all wrong – she's the one who doesn't count,' Paul muttered as he folded up the letter.

He rushed out of the room and back down to reception.

'Tell me what time she left,' he begged the concierge, gasping for breath.

'I'm not sure exactly what time,' the concierge replied. 'The young lady requested a car.'

'To go where?'

'The airport.'

'Which flight?'

'I'm afraid I can't tell you, sir. We didn't make the reservation.'

Paul turned towards the glass double doors. Under the awning, he could see Ms Bak about to get in the limousine. He rushed outside, pushed her out of the way, and climbed in behind the chauffeur.

'The airport, international departures. Get me there fast and you'll have the biggest tip of your life.'

Ms Bak rapped on the window, but the chauffeur set off at top speed, and she was forced to watch as the limousine vanished in the distance.

*I'll be the one to make a surprise entrance on the plane this time, and if the person sitting next to you won't give up his seat, I'll yank him up by the lapels and shove him in the overhead compartment. No fear this time, not even during take-off, and we can make do with airline meals. I'll even give you mine if you're still hungry. We'll watch the same film this time. Because this counts, Mia. It counts far more than all those novels I didn't write . . .*

The chauffeur weaved in and out of traffic, but the farther into the suburbs they advanced, the busier the roads became.

'It's rush hour, sir,' he said. 'I could try a different way, but it might take even longer.'

Paul begged him to do his best.

Tossed back and forth in the back seat of the limousine, he rehearsed what he would say to Mia when he saw her again: the resolutions he had made, what he'd told Kyong, whose name was actually Eun-Jeong, and who wasn't even Paul's translator at all. She had actually been his Korean editor all along.

An hour and a half later, Paul paid the chauffeur.

He ran into the terminal and looked up at the departures board. There were no flights for Paris displayed.

At the Air France desk, the agent informed him that the plane had taken off thirty minutes earlier. There was still one free seat on the next day's flight.

# 19

As soon as the wheels of his plane touched ground, Paul switched on his phone and tried calling Mia. After getting her voicemail three times in a row, he hung up. The things he had to say to her could not be left in a message.

A taxi dropped him off at Rue de Bretagne. He picked up the keys to his apartment at the Café du Marché, went home, and dumped his suitcase in the hall, without bothering to read his mail or call Cristoneli to return his messages.

Showered and dressed in clean clothes, he drove to Montmartre, parked on Rue Norvins, and walked to La Clamada.

Catching sight of him from the kitchen, Daisy came out into the main room.

'Tell me where she is,' Paul said.

'Sit down. We need to talk,' Daisy replied, slipping behind the bar.

'Is she up at your place?'

'Can I get you a coffee? Or a glass of wine?'

'I need to see Mia. Right away.'

'She's not at my place. I couldn't really say where she is. Back in England would be my best guess. She left over a week ago, and I haven't heard a word from her since.'

Paul peered past Daisy's shoulder. She followed his gaze to the old spice-box, on the counter beside the percolator.

'All right,' she conceded. 'She was here yesterday morning, but only very briefly. Was that present really from you?'

Paul nodded.

'It's beautiful. I'm very touched, thank you. Could I ask what's going on between you two?'

'No, you can't,' Paul replied.

Daisy didn't insist. She poured him a coffee.

'Her life is more complicated than it seems, and she is a more complicated woman than she'd like to admit. But I love her just the way she is. She's my best friend. She's finally decided to make a rational choice, and she has to stick to it. Let her. If you're truly her friend, let her do what's best for herself.'

'You're telling me she's back in London? Or back with her ex?'

'Listen, I have lots of customers and lunch isn't going to cook itself. Come see me tonight after ten. It'll be quieter then. I'll make you dinner, and we can talk. I read one of your novels, you know – I loved it.'

'Which one?'

'The first one, I think. I got it from Mia.'

Paul said goodbye to Daisy and left the restaurant, noticing a missed call from Cristoneli. He drove to Saint-Germain-des-Prés.


Cristoneli came out of his office and welcomed Paul with open arms.

'There's my favourite superstar!' he exclaimed, throwing his arms around him. 'So? I bet you're glad I twisted your arm and made you go to Korea, yes?'

'Easy . . . you're smothering me, Gaetano!'

Cristoneli stepped back and adjusted Paul's jacket.

'My Korean colleague sent me an email with all the press cuttings – and, my God, what a lot of them there are! They haven't been translated yet, but apparently the reviews have been staggering. Seems you are a total smash in Korea!'

'We need to talk,' Paul muttered.

'Of course we need to talk . . . as long as you're not looking for another advance. You sly fox!' Cristoneli said jovially, slapping him on the shoulder.

'You've got it all wrong. This whole thing is so complicated.'

'It's never simple with women. And by women, I mean the normal ones, the type you meet every day. But you? You play for the keeping!'

'It's "You play for keeps".'

'Same thing. But you can have it your way today, my friend. Come on, let's have a drink to celebrate . . .'

'From the sound of it, maybe you've had enough already. You're even harder to decipher than usual.'

'Me? Maybe it's you, all messed up in the head . . . but who could blame you! Oh, Paul! You sly fox, you!'

'This whole "sly fox" thing is really starting to get on my nerves. What exactly did Eun-Jeong say to you?'

'Eun-Je-*who*?'

'My Korean editor. Who else are we talking about?'

'Listen, my dear Paul, my lips are moving, but I don't think you're hearing the words coming from my mouth. Maybe the aeroplane make your eardrums go pop? Pressure in the cabin, something like that. I cannot stand the aeroplanes; I refuse to fly unless I have no other choice. When I go to Milan, I take the train – a little long, admittedly, but at least I don't have to go through an X-ray before getting on board. Anyway, how about that drink? You *sly fox*, you!'

They sat at an inside table at the Deux Magots. Paul gestured at a folder Cristoneli had placed on the seat beside him.

'If that's the contract for my next novel, we seriously need to talk first.'

'I thought we already had you under contract? Hmmm, maybe you're right. I sometimes wonder what my assistant is really up to. Anyway, I hope you are not going to take advantage of the situation, considering all the years I have supported you, through good and bad! But you can walk me through your next masterpiece another time. Right now, I want you to spill the details – all the details – just between you and me. I won't tell a soul. These lips are peeled!' Cristoneli whispered, putting a finger to his lips.

'Gaetano! What are you on?' Paul asked, taken aback.

'What kind of a question is this?'

'Help me understand: what did Eun-Jeong tell you?'

'Nothing I haven't already said: she sent me an email and I was so very happy to hear about this warm welcome for you in Seoul. What did I tell you, eh? The numbers are gorgeous. I'm going to call the Chinese publishers and inform your American editor, and we can follow my plan to the letter.'

'Um . . . So if we're still following your plan to the letter, then what exactly has gotten into you today?'

Cristoneli stared deep into Paul's eyes. 'I thought I was your friend, someone you can trust. So I have to tell you, I was a little bit let down that I have to learn the truth like this, like everybody else.'

'I have absolutely no idea what you're talking about. And I'm getting pretty sick of your cryptic double-talk,' grumbled Paul.

Cristoneli began humming a familiar aria, before sliding the folder up on to the table. He half-opened it, still humming his tune, flipped it closed, then back open again, until Paul finally snapped and yanked the folder from him.

The tabloid magazine covers inside were enough to make him gasp, and his eyes grew wide as saucers.

'I told you I'd seen her somewhere before, when I came to pick you up from the police station,' Cristoneli muttered. 'But her? Melissa Barlow? I thought my jaw was going to hit the pavement!'

Photos of Mia and Paul were plastered all over every cover and on the first few pages of each tabloid. Images of them walking side by side, entering the hotel, standing in the lobby, waiting for the lift . . . Paul leaning over a gutter while Mia held him upright, him holding open the door of a limousine as Mia climbed inside. And under each picture, there were captions describing Melissa Barlow's crazy whirlwind romance. In the second magazine that Paul flicked through, his hands trembling, a picture of Mia at the Book Fair was accompanied by the description:

*Mere days before the release of a film in which she appears on-screen with her real-life husband, Melissa Barlow is seen playing in her own romantic comedy with American writer Paul Barton.*

'It's a little intrusive, I must admit. But for sales, this is more than marvellous! You sly fox, you! Hey, friend. You don't look so good.'

Paul retched and ran outside.

A few moments later, doubled over a dust-bin, he became aware of a handkerchief being waved in front of his eyes. Cristoneli stood behind him, arm outstretched.

'This is not a pretty picture. And you accused *me* of drinking!'

Paul wiped his mouth and Cristoneli helped him over to a bench.

'Feeling a little sick?'

'How'd you guess?'

'Is it because of the photographs? You must have realised this would happen sooner or later. What do you expect, dating a movie star?'

'Have you ever had the feeling that the world was slipping away right beneath your feet?'

'Oh, yes,' replied his editor. 'When my mother died, for starters. And then when my first wife left me. Come to think of it, when I separated from my second wife also. With the third, it was different – it was mutual.'

'That's exactly what I'm talking about – when you think you've hit rock bottom, you have to be careful, because there's another abyss just below it, even deeper. And I'm beginning to wonder where it will all end.'

◆ ◆ ◆

Paul went home and slept until evening. Around eight o'clock, he sat at his desk. He checked his email, reading only the subject lines, and then turned off his computer. No word from her. A little later, he called a taxi and got out at Montmartre.

It was nearly eleven when he entered La Clamada. Daisy was clearing the last tables.

'I thought you weren't going to show up. Are you hungry?'

'You know what? I have no idea.'

'Let's find out.'

She let him choose a table while she went back to the kitchen, returning a few minutes later, plate in hand. She sat across from Paul and ordered him to try her plat du jour. They would talk when he had a full stomach. She poured him a glass of wine and watched him eat.

'You knew, I assume?' he asked her.

'That she wasn't a waitress? I told you her life was more complicated than it seemed.'

'And what about you? You're about to tell me you're not really a chef but a secret agent for the French government? Give me your best shot. Nothing could surprise me now.'

'You writers! You really are something,' Daisy laughed.

As the evening went on, she told him the story of her life, and once more Paul enjoyed listening to memories of Daisy and Mia growing up side by side, though he longed for Mia to be sharing them with him.

At midnight, he accompanied Daisy to the front door of her apartment building. Paul looked up at the windows.

'If you hear from her, promise you'll tell her to call me.'

'I can't make any promises.'

'I swear I'm not a bad guy.'

'That's exactly why. Believe me, the two of you were not right for each other.'

'And what if I told you I miss her as a friend?'

'Then I'd tell you you're as bad a liar as she is. The first days are the hardest; after that, it gets easier. There will always be a table for you at my restaurant, Paul, anytime. Goodnight.'

Daisy opened the door and disappeared.

Three weeks passed. Paul wrote constantly. He barely left his desk, except to eat lunch at Moustache's café and Sunday brunch at Daisy's apartment. Though Daisy was pleasant company, she maintained her silence on all things Mia. The tabloids had quieted as well.

One evening, at eight o'clock exactly, he received a call from Cristoneli.

'Are you writing?'

'No.'

'Watching television?'

'No.'

'Perfect. Whatever you're doing . . . you keep doing it.'

'You're calling just to find out about my schedule?'

'No, I wanted to check how you are, and how your novel is going.'

'I threw out the one I was writing and I've started a whole new one.'

'Excellent.'

'Completely different.'

'Oh, really? You'll have to tell me what it's about.'

'I'm not so sure you're going to like it.'

'Oh, nonsense! You're just saying that to pique my curiosity.'

'No, I really don't think so.'

'What is it, a thriller?'

'Check back in with me a few weeks from now . . .'

'A detective story? Procedural?'

'Right now I'm just going to focus on getting that first draft out.'

'Erotica, you little devil?'

'Gaetano, is there something in particular you wanted to talk about?'

'No . . . as long as you tell me you are okay.'

'I'm fine, thanks. Scratch that. I'm great. And since you've taken such an intense interest in my life, I should tell you I did some tidying up this morning, then I had lunch at the café down the road, after which I spent most of the afternoon reading, and tonight I've warmed up some lentils for dinner. Which are currently going from lukewarm to cold. After I'm off the phone with you, I'm going to write, and then go to bed. Does that satisfy your new-found curiosity?'

'Lentils? A little tough to digest at night, if you ask me.'

'Goodnight, Gaetano.'

Paul hung up, shaking his head, and turned back to his computer. As he began a new paragraph, he re-ran the bizarre conversation with his editor in his head.

Suddenly seized with doubt, he grabbed the remote control and turned on the TV. The news was on TF1 and France 2. He kept flicking through channels, frowned, then went back to France 2, which was showing the trailer for a new film.

In it, Paul saw a man kissing a woman in an evening dress. The man took the woman in his arms and laid her on a bed before undressing her. He kissed her breasts as she moaned with pleasure.

There was a close-up of the actors, which became a freeze-frame and then cut to a television studio where the same two actors were live on camera.

'*Alice's Strange Journey* opens in cinemas tomorrow,' the host declared. 'And while we have high hopes for the film, the greatest anticipation and liveliest buzz is all centred on watching you as a couple, as real-life sparks ignite between the two of you on the big screen. Melissa Barlow, David Babkins – welcome, and thank you for joining us tonight.'

The camera showed the two of them side by side.

'Thank you for having us, Monsieur Delahousse,' they chorused.

'First, I have to know – as do all of our viewers – does starring alongside your real-life spouse make the performance easier or more challenging?'

Mia let David speak. He explained that it depended on the scene in question.

'Of course, whenever Melissa performs a stunt, I'm terrified. And vice versa, naturally. People automatically think that the love scenes are easier, though that's not necessarily the case. Obviously, we know each other better than anyone else, but it's not like having a whole crew full of technicians there really helps set the mood. They're not generally invited into our bedroom,' he added, chuckling at his own joke.

'Mr Babkins, your comment on the subject of love brings me to my next question. Melissa Barlow, about the many photographs recently released . . . Should we interpret your appearance together here tonight as a sign that the stories are nothing but gossip? To put it another way, who exactly is this Paul Barton to you, Melissa?'

'He's a friend,' Mia replied tersely. 'A very dear friend. Who writes lovely books.'

'So you admire him? As a writer.'

'A writer and a friend. The rest doesn't count.'


Paul switched off the television. His hands were trembling so much he could barely keep his grip on the remote control.

Over the next hour, he struggled to write a single word. Around midnight, he picked up the phone.

The limousine with tinted windows drove into the hotel car park. David put his hand on the door handle and turned to face Mia.

'You need to be absolutely sure this is what you want, Mia.'

'It is. Goodbye, David.'

'Why don't we give it one more shot? You've had your revenge. Plastered it all over the tabloids, even.'

'I didn't have anything to hide. But now that we can leave this pretence of conjugal bliss behind, hiding is exactly what I need. From everyone, from myself. I feel dirty, and that's worse than feeling alone. One last thing: you'd best sign the papers that Creston sent you, otherwise I'll ditch the phoney cover story and let everyone know the truth about what you did.'

David stared at her with contempt, then got out of the car, slamming the door behind him.

The chauffeur asked Mia where she wanted to go. She told him to take the southbound expressway. Then she took out her phone to call Creston.

'I'm sorry, Mia, I wanted so much to be there for your last promotional appearance, but I can hardly walk with this damn sciatica. So, tell me. Do you feel free now?'

'Free of him, yes. And of you. But the rest is still there.'

'I did my best to protect you, you know. You made it impossible.'

'I know that. I don't blame you, Creston. What's done is done.'

'Any idea where you're heading?'

'Sweden. Daisy keeps going on about it.'

'Pack lots of layers. It's positively frigid there. Be sure to drop a line now and again.'

'I will. But not for a while.'

'In a few weeks, all of this will be behind you, with nothing but your glorious future lying ahead. So savour this time away, recharge your batteries.'

'Sounds beautiful. Like hitting the delete key, to wipe away all your mistakes and start again. Sadly, it only works that way in books. Goodbye, Creston. Get well soon.'

Mia hung up. Then she opened the window and threw her phone out of it.

# 20

'Tell me what happened after you watched the two of them on TV.'

'I paced around my apartment for a while. Then, at midnight, just when I thought I was going to snap, I picked up the phone and called you. I had no idea you'd be ringing my doorbell the next day, but I can't tell you how glad I am to see you.'

'I came as fast as I could. You might recall doing the same for me, way back when.'

'Way back when, I only had to cross town.'

'You look awful, man.'

'Are you on your own, or have you got Lauren stashed away in your bag?'

'Why don't you make me some coffee instead of just standing there blabbering?'


Arthur stayed with Paul for ten days, during which their friendship rekindled something like happiness in Paul's heart.

In the mornings, they ate breakfast at Moustache's café and chatted. In the afternoons, they strolled around Paris. Paul bought all sorts of useless objects – kitchen utensils, knick-knacks, clothes he would never wear, books he would never read, and gifts for his godson. Arthur tried to curb his sudden shopaholic tendencies, but to no avail.

They had dinner at La Clamada two nights in a row.

Arthur found the food delicious and Daisy charming.

During one of these meals, Paul explained the bizarre, crazy plan that was occupying his mind. Arthur warned him of the dangers he would face. Paul could easily imagine the consequences, but he had no choice. It was the only way for him to reconcile the past, for both his job and his conscience.

'The day I saw Eun-Jeong at the Book Fair,' he said, 'it was a long time before either of us could even get a word out. And then she started trying to justify her actions, which of course hadn't done me any real harm, nor would they in the future. Thanks to her, I experienced fame and earned quite a bit of money, while she got to use my name to tell her story. A story that would never have been read beyond the borders of South Korea, because no one else cared about the fate of her people. In the end, everyone was a winner. All the same, I couldn't just accept that I'd been living off her work. And even aside from the money, I was truly fascinated by her courage and her determination. She told me everything. How she would use her stays in Paris as a front in order to visit her networks. She swore her feelings for me were sincere, even though deep down she does love another man, a prisoner of the regime she's struggling against. You probably think I should have put her in her place, but let me tell you, she was magnificent. And most of all, for the first time in months, I felt free. I wasn't in love with her any more. It wasn't seeing her again that made me realise that, and it wasn't discovering the truth about her, either. It was Mia . . . all Mia. When we said goodbye, I swore to myself that I would rewrite Kyong's story, partly to reveal it to the world. And, I admit, perhaps partly to prove to myself that I could write it better than she could. My editor doesn't know anything about this yet, and I can only imagine the look on his

face when he cracks open that manuscript. But I'll do everything I can
to make him publish it.'

'Are you planning on telling him the truth?'

'No, I won't tell a soul. You're the only one who can know. Don't
even mention it to Lauren.'

At the end of the meal, Daisy joined them. They drank to life, friendship and the promise of all the happiness yet to come.

Arthur went back to San Francisco. Paul took him to the airport and
solemnly swore that he would come and visit his godson, now that he was
barely afraid of flying any more – just as soon as he'd finished his book.

Arthur left feeling reassured. Paul was on top form, and the only
thing that mattered to him at that moment was his novel.

Paul worked relentlessly. He only stopped to visit Moustache's café, and
occasionally La Clamada.

One evening, while he and Daisy were sitting on a bench chatting, a
caricaturist came by with a drawing.

Paul looked at it for a long time. It was a picture of a couple,
seen from behind, sitting on the very bench he and Daisy were on
at present.

'It's from the summer,' the caricaturist told him. 'That's you, on the
right. It's nearly Christmas, so consider it my gift to you.'

As he was leaving, the caricaturist brushed Daisy's hand, and she
smiled at him with an air of mischief.

◆ ◆ ◆

Two months later, as he was writing out the final lines of his novel, Paul got a call from Daisy. It was late at night, but she urged him to come as quickly as he could.

Paul detected a thrill in her voice that convinced him she'd heard from Mia.

In order to avoid getting stuck in traffic, he took the métro and then ran up Rue Lepic. He passed the Moulin de la Galette, panting and sweating despite the bitter cold. He burst into La Clamada, his lungs on fire, exultant, sure she would be there.

But the place was empty except for Daisy, who was standing behind the bar.

'What's going on?' he asked, sitting down on a stool.

Daisy continued wiping glasses.

'I won't tell you I talked to her recently, because that wouldn't be true.'

'I don't understand.'

'If you keep quiet, I'll be able to tell you what I know. But first, let me make you a little cocktail. You look like you need it.'

Daisy took her time. She waited until he'd drunk it. The drink was so strong that Paul felt a sort of instant intoxication.

'Damn, that's powerful!' he coughed.

'They used to give this drink to people who'd been lost in the Alps at night. Something to tear them from the jaws of death.'

'Tell me what you know, Daisy.'

'It isn't much, but it's something . . .'

She walked over to the cash register and took out a manila envelope, which she placed on the bar. Paul was about to pick it up when she grabbed his hand.

'Wait, I have something else to bring up first. Do you know who Creston is?'

Paul remembered Mia mentioning the name in Seoul, talking about him as if he were a close friend – without, of course, ever revealing his true role in her life. He had even felt a little jealous.

'He's her agent. Or rather, he was,' Daisy went on. 'We have something in common, he and I, but it has to remain a secret, in case things work out one day.'

'What does that mean, "things work out"?'

'Shut up and let me finish. Creston and I have both taken her absence pretty hard. Initially I thought he was just hurting financially, but that's not the case.'

'How do you know all this?'

'He was here last night. It's always kind of strange, putting a face to a name. I thought he would look like one of those old English farts with a bowler-hat and an umbrella . . . but he was nothing like the cliché. He's in his fifties, very handsome, with a bone-crushing handshake. I like that. A firm handshake like that says a lot about a man. Your grip is like that too. Anyway, he dined here alone last night. He waited until he'd paid the bill and the room was empty before he spoke to me. That was a classy move; if I had known who he was, I would never have allowed him to pay. In fact, I was the one who approached him. It's possible he wouldn't have even introduced himself if I hadn't. As he was my last customer, I went to ask him if he'd enjoyed his meal. He hesitated for a moment, and then simply said: "Your scallops are outstanding. Now I understand why she was so in love with this place." He handed me this envelope, and when I opened it I understood what it was. He hasn't heard from Mia in months himself. She only called once, to tell him she wanted to sell her flat and everything in it, but she refused to say a word about where she was. When Creston saw the moving vans taking away her things, he went to the auction-house to buy them back. He got everything. She was his protégée, you see. He couldn't stand the idea of a stranger sitting at her desk or sleeping in her bed. All Mia's furniture and belongings are currently in a storage unit on the outskirts of London.'

'So what's in the envelope?' Paul demanded, nerves on edge.

'Be patient, just listen. He came to spend a night in a place she loved. I can't blame him for that; if you only knew how long I've spent staring at the table where we used to eat together, or at her bench on Place du Tertre. I'll let you in on a secret. I only give our table to customers when the restaurant is completely packed. Sometimes I even turn people away and leave it empty, because every night since she left, I've dreamt that she'll walk through that door, asking if I have scallops on the menu.'

Paul couldn't wait any longer. Without asking Daisy's permission, he tore open the envelope. Inside were three photographs.

They had been taken from a distance, probably from the seating area of the restaurant that ran the length of the Carrousel du Louvre. People were lined up in front of the pyramid. Daisy pointed out one of the faces.

'She knows how to alter her appearance until she's almost unrecognisable – I don't need to tell you that – but Creston has no doubt: the woman in the middle of the crowd is her.'

Paul peered at the photograph, his heart racing. Daisy was right: no one would have recognised her, but they both knew it was Mia.

He felt a huge sense of relief when he saw the dimples on her cheeks. When they were in Seoul, he'd noticed that her dimples always appeared whenever she was truly happy. He asked Daisy how Creston had obtained the pictures.

'Creston has contacts in the paparazzi circuit. Sometimes, he pays an even higher price than the newspapers to keep her photos *out* of print. For Seoul, he was too late to make a difference. Anyway, he told all the photographers he knew – and he knows quite a few – that he would pay top dollar for a photograph of Mia, wherever it was taken, as long as it was dated. And yet, these were sent to him free of charge.'

Paul was about to ask Daisy if he could have one, when she gave them to him.

'She must have started a whole new life,' Paul said.

'She's alone, isn't she? Why do you seem so hurt, if she's all alone?'

'Because . . . it hurts to have even a shred of hope.'

'You dummy! *Not* having hope is what makes people miserable. She was in Paris and she didn't even come to see me. That means she was on her own. Rebuilding her life. Creston received these photos a week ago. That's why he decided to go looking for her. Before turning up here, he spent two days wandering around Paris, with the crazy idea that he might just bump into her on a street corner. The English really are mad! But you and I are here every day, so who knows . . . maybe with a little luck . . .'

'How do we know she's still here?'

'Trust your instincts. If you really love her, you'll be able to hear her heart beating . . . somewhere out there.'

Daisy was right. Paul didn't know if it was just his imagination, or the powerful sense of hope he was trying in vain to ignore, but in the following weeks, he sometimes caught the scent of Mia's perfume on street corners, as if she were walking ahead of him and he'd just missed her. Whenever it happened, he would quicken his pace, sure that he would see her around the next corner. He even found himself calling out to strangers and walking around at night, looking up at illuminated windows and half-expecting to see her.

His novel was published. Or rather, Kyong's story, which he had entirely rewritten, was published. It was the first time he had moved beyond the realm of fiction. Each night, he asked himself the same questions: had he turned truth into fiction? Had he over-embellished or dramatised her story? He was aware of having given flesh and blood to Eun-Jeong's characters. Where she had been content to list their trials and tribulations, tragic as they were, Paul had described their actual lives, portraying their suffering and their deepest emotions. He had done what any writer must do when he takes hold of a story he did not invent.

The press, too, took hold of the story. As soon as it was published, it provoked a whirlwind of interest that Paul couldn't comprehend. Maybe it was just a passing trend, but at a time when everyone still wanted to believe in the virtues of individual freedom, turning a blind eye to the tightening noose beyond the borders of the East, ignoring the growing influence of dictators seeking shelter behind the power of national economies they had simply pocketed, a story denouncing what was undeniably a dictatorship hit a nerve and helped raise awareness. Paul was happy to accept this idea, especially as he did not take any personal credit for the book. In his eyes, it was all due to Eun-Jeong and her incredible courage.

The reviews were glowing, and Cristoneli's desk piled up with interview requests. Paul refused them all.

For the first time, Paul saw his name on the cover of a book in the bestseller pile. He even found it in the self-declared temples of fashionable thinking.

And then rumours of a literary-prize nomination began to buzz in the corridors of his publishers' offices.

Cristoneli took him out to lunch more and more often. He spoke of society events in Paris, opening his Moleskine diary and taking on a serious expression as he listed the cocktail parties and soirées where it was crucial Paul make an appearance. Paul avoided them all, and after a while stopped listening to the messages on his answering machine.

All the noises around him seemed to echo as if bouncing off the walls of an empty apartment.

It was six weeks before he saw Cristoneli again, this time at Café de Flore.

People stared at him, smiles of admiration or envy on their faces. But that evening, Cristoneli ordered champagne before announcing that about thirty foreign publishers had acquired the rights to his novel.

How ironic: his translator's story would now be translated into thirty languages. As Cristoneli toasted this triumph, Paul could not help but wonder what Eun-Jeong would think. He had not been in touch with her at all since the book fair in Seoul.

Paul's mind remained elsewhere, despite the celebration. He was going to have to brace himself, however, because it was only the beginning.

# 21

One day in autumn, Paul was disturbed around noon by the incessant ringing of his phone. He finally picked it up, only to find Cristoneli stammering on the line:

'M . . . M . . . M . . .'

'What?'

'La Me . . . Med . . .'

'Medication? That's it, you've finally cracked.'

'No, for God's sake! La Méditerranée! You call me crazy, but you're late for your own party. Hurry up! Everyone's waiting for you!'

'Well, that's very nice of you, Gaetano, but what am I supposed to do in the Mediterranean?'

'Paul, shut up and listen to me very carefully, I beg you. You have won the Prix Médicis. The press are lined up waiting for you at the restaurant La Méditerranée at Place de l'Odéon. There's a taxi for you outside right now. Is that clear enough for you?' Cristoneli yelled.

From that moment on, nothing was clear to Paul any more. His mind spun.

'Shit,' he mumbled.

'What do you mean, shit?'

'Shit, shit, shit.'

'Stop, please. Why on earth are you repeating "shit" again and again?'

'I'm talking to myself.'

'Well, you shouldn't talk like that, even to yourself.'

'This can't be happening,' Paul said. 'You have to stop this.'

'Stop what?'

'The prize. I can't accept it.'

'Paul, can I just say that you are beginning to drive me up the hall? No one refuses the Médicis, so get in that taxi and hurry up or I'll be the one telling you shit. In fact, let me start now: shit, shit, shit! They're going to announce the prize winners' names in fifteen minutes. I'm here, whether you make it or not. This is a great triumph, my friend!'

Paul hung up and immediately felt as if he were going to have a heart attack. He lay down on the floor, arms crossed, and began a series of breathing exercises.

The telephone rang again and again. And it continued ringing until the taxi dropped him at Place de l'Odéon.

Cristoneli was waiting for him outside the restaurant. Flash-bulbs popped and Paul had a feeling of déjà vu that froze his blood.

All he could manage by way of communication was a stammering *thank you* and a nervous smile at the banks of photographers every time his editor elbowed him in the ribs. He barely answered a single question, at least not intelligibly.

At three o'clock, while Cristoneli was rushing over to his office to order reprints and sign off on a new book band for the cover, Paul went home and locked himself inside the apartment.

Daisy called late that afternoon to congratulate him. She'd heard the news on the radio while she was cutting radishes and had almost chopped her finger off in shock. She told him he'd better drop by La

Clamada to celebrate his success, and soon, or else he would end up on her blacklist.

At eight o'clock, he was still pacing his apartment in a blind panic, waiting for Arthur to call him back.

Yet it was Lauren who called. Arthur was with clients in New Mexico. They had a long conversation, and, before an emergency forced her to hang up, she helped him find a way of calming down.

Paul sat down in front of his screen and opened the file of a project he had abandoned a long time ago. Lauren had been right when she suggested he revive his opera singer. His familiar character quickly provided him with the comfort he needed.

A few pages later, Paul felt the vice around his chest loosen, and the words flowed freely for the rest of the night.

Early in the morning, Paul made a decision and vowed to stick to it, no matter the cost. His best friend would be happy. The time had come to return home.

The next day, Paul went to see Cristoneli. He was only half-listening to his editor, opening his mouth only to turn down one interview request after another.

Paul had said no twenty times in a row, so when he did finally say yes, Cristoneli didn't even notice and continued running through the names of journalists seeking interviews.

'Um . . . I just said yes.' Paul sighed.

'Oh, did you? To which one?'

'*La Grande Bibliothèque.* That's the only show I'll appear on.'

'Okay, whatever you want,' said Cristoneli, on the verge of depression. 'I'll tell them straightaway. The show will air live tomorrow night.'

Paul spent his last day in Paris putting his affairs in order. At noon, he went to Daisy's to eat lunch. When the time came to say goodbye, she hugged him and fought back her tears.

Late in the afternoon, he bid farewell to Moustache and gave him his keys. The café owner promised he would treat the removal of his belongings as though he were removing his very own.

At eight o'clock, Cristoneli came to pick him up. Paul put his suitcase in the boot of the taxi and the two headed to the studios of France Télévisions.

Paul didn't say a word during make-up, except to ask them not to conceal the crow's feet around his eyes, on the off-chance that Mia would be watching. When the floor manager came to get him, Paul asked Cristoneli to hang back in his dressing-room. He could follow the programme on the TV screen there.

François Truelle, the host, shook Paul's hand backstage and showed him to his seat beside four other novelists.

Paul greeted his colleagues and took a deep breath. A few moments later, the show began.

'Good evening, everyone, and welcome to *La Grande Bibliothèque*. Tonight we will be discussing literary prizes and foreign fiction, featuring an exclusive interview with an author largely unknown to the general public, at least until two days ago, when he won the Prix Médicis for a foreign novel. Paul Barton, thank you for joining us tonight.'

An image of Paul appeared on-screen, while off-screen a voice outlined his career – his past life as an architect, his decision to move to

France, and his six previous novels. At the end of the brief report, François Truelle turned to Paul himself.

'Paul Barton, the novel that won you the Médicis is very different from those that preceded it: a poignant, surprising, deeply moving and enlightening novel. I would go as far as to call it an *essential* novel.'

Truelle continued to sing the book's praises, before asking Paul what had inspired the story he had written.

Paul looked straight into the camera.

'I didn't write it. I only translated it.'

François Truelle gaped at Paul wide-eyed and held his breath.

'Did I hear you correctly? You did *not* write this novel?'

'No. This is a true story, from beginning to end, and one that does not belong to me. It was absolutely impossible for the woman behind the story to publish it under her own name. Her parents, her family and the love of her life all live in North Korea and would have faced certain death if the writer's name were made public. For this reason, I will never reveal her identity, but I refuse to take credit for her work.'

'I don't understand,' Truelle exclaimed. 'Then why publish it under your name in the first place?'

'I acted as a figure-head, by mutual agreement. The real Kyong had only one dream: that the story of her loved ones be known as widely as possible, that people around the world could finally know of their fate. There is no oil in North Korea, so our Western democracies turn a blind eye to one of the most horrific dictatorships in the world. I spent months immersing myself in her story, giving life to her characters, but I repeat: this story belongs entirely to her. She alone deserves the prize that I was awarded two days ago. I came on this programme tonight to tell the truth. If and when the regime that oppresses her people at last comes tumbling down, I will reveal her name as soon as she allows me to. As for the royalties I've earned, they will be transferred directly to Amnesty International and similar organisations that work to help the victims of this abominable regime. I would like to apologise sincerely to my editor, who knew nothing of this until tonight, and apologise to the members of the Médicis jury as well. But let us not forget that this prize is awarded first and foremost based on the quality of the novel, not which author's name is on the cover. To everyone watching this programme, I would beg you to read it, in the name of liberty and hope. Thank you for your time.'

Paul stood up, shook hands with Truelle and the dumbfounded guests, and walked straight off the set.

Cristoneli awaited him backstage. They walked side by side in silence until they reached the lobby.

When they were alone, Cristoneli looked Paul in the eye and held out his hand.

'I am very proud to be your editor, even if I have the overwhelming desire to strangle you. It's a fine book, and no great book can be published abroad without the work of a great translator. Now I can understand why you are going back to San Francisco for a while. I am very much looking forward to reading the further adventures of your opera singer. I loved the first chapters you allowed me to read, and I can't wait to publish it.'

'Thank you, Gaetano, but you are by no means obligated. I'm afraid I may have lost any possible readers tonight.'

'I think quite the opposite is true. But only time will tell.'

# 22

Paul and his editor walked down the steps together. As they reached the empty pavement, a young man emerged from the shadows and approached them with a piece of paper.

'There. See? You still have at least one admirer,' said Cristoneli.

'Or else it's one of Kim Jong-un's agents sent to kill me.' Paul chuckled.

His editor refused to even crack a smile.

'For you,' the young man said, handing a small envelope to Paul. He opened it and found a strange little handwritten note inside:

> *Three pounds of carrots, one pound of flour, a packet of sugar, a dozen eggs, a pint of milk . . .*

'Where did you get this?' Paul asked the young man, who pointed to a figure on the pavement across the street, then walked away.

A woman crossed the street towards him.

'Sorry to say I broke my promise after all,' said Mia. 'I watched the show tonight.'

'It wasn't a promise for forever,' Paul replied.

'Do you know why I fell in love with you so quickly?'

'I have no idea.'

'Because you're so utterly incapable of pretending.'

'And . . . that's a good thing?'

'No. It's a wonderful thing.'

'I missed you, Mia. More than you could know. I missed you . . . *ferociously.*'

'Really? That much?'

'Take my word for it. After all, I am totally incapable of pretending.'

'Why don't you stop all that talking and just kiss me?'


The two stood looking at each other in silence, holding their breath.

Cristoneli waited a few moments, glanced at his watch, and cleared his throat.

'As you two don't seem in much of a rush, I'm going to take your taxi now and leave you to it. Mine should arrive shortly – take that one instead.'

He handed Paul the suitcase he'd been carrying for him.

Then he bowed to Mia, closed the cab door, lowered the window, and yelled out one last message as the car drove away.

'You sly fox, you!'


'Where is this taxi supposed to take you?' Mia asked.

'To my hotel, next to Roissy. I leave for San Francisco tomorrow morning.'

'But you'll be back soon.'

'I don't think so.'

'Can I call you, then?'

'I have a better idea. How about we get rid of the person sitting next to me on this flight, and you take their place? 'Cause I have a suitcase here full of culinary wonders just waiting for you.'

Paul put down his bag. The two met in a long kiss, right there in the street.

They kissed until they were startled by the sound of a taxi honking its horn.

Paul ushered Mia in first and sat down next to her.

Before telling the driver their destination, he turned to her and asked:

'One question. This here, right now. Does this count?'

'Yes. This time . . . it really counts.'

# ACKNOWLEDGEMENTS

My thanks to . . .

Pauline, Louis and Georges.

Raymond, Danièle and Lorraine.

Susanna Lea.

Emmanuelle Hardouin.

Cécile Boyer-Runge, Antoine Caro.

Elisabeth Villeneuve, Caroline Babulle, Arié Sberro, Sylvie Bardeau, Lydie Leroy, Joel Renaudat, Céline Chiflet, Anne-Marie Lenfant.

All the teams at Editions Robert Laffont.

Pauline Normand, Marie-Eve Provost.

Léonard Anthony, Sébastien Canot, Danielle Melconian, Naja Baldwin, Mark Kessler, Stéphanie Charrier, Julien Saltet de Sablet d'Estières, Aline Grond.

Katrin Hodapp, Laura Mamelok, Kerry Glencorse, Julia Wagner.

Brigitte and Sarah Forissier.

# ABOUT THE AUTHOR

With more than forty million books sold, Marc Levy is the most-read French author alive today. He's written eighteen novels to date, including *All Those Things We Never Said, Children of Freedom,* and *Replay.*

Originally written for his son, his first novel, *If Only It Were True,* was later adapted for the big screen as *Just Like Heaven,* starring Reese Witherspoon and Mark Ruffalo. Since then, Levy has not only won the hearts of European readers; he's won over audiences from around the globe. More than one and a half million copies of his books have been sold in China alone, and his novels have been published in forty-nine languages. He lives in New York City. Readers can learn more about him and follow his work at www.marclevy.info.

# ABOUT THE TRANSLATOR

A novelist and translator, Sam Taylor is the author of *The Republic of Trees*, *The Amnesiac*, *The Island at the End of the World* and *The Ground Is Burning*. He has translated more than a dozen novels from the French, including Laurent Binet's acclaimed *HHhH* and the bestselling *The Truth About the Harry Quebert Affair* by Joël Dicker. Born in Nottinghamshire, England, and a former journalist for *The Observer*, Taylor lived with his family in France before moving to the United States.

Printed in Great Britain
by Amazon